Encore Performance

Encore Performance

Kim Pritekel

SAPPHIRE BOOKS

SALINAS, CALIFORNIA

Encore Performance
Copyright © 2022 by *Kim Pritekel* All rights reserved.

ISBN - 978-1-952270-52-9

This is a work of fiction - names, characters, places, and incidents are the product of the author's imagination or are used fictitiously. Any resemblance to actual persons living or dead, business, events or locales is entirely coincidental.

All rights reserved. No part of this publication may be reproduced, distributed, or transmitted in any form or by any means, including photocopying, recording, or other electronic or mechanical methods, without written permission of the publisher.

Editor - Heather Flournoy
Book Design - LJ Reynolds
Cover Design - Fineline Cover Design

Sapphire Books Publishing, LLC
P.O. Box 8142
Salinas, CA 93912
www.sapphirebooks.com

Printed in the United States of America
First Edition – February 2022

This and other Sapphire Books titles can be found at
www.sapphirebooks.com

Dedication

To what will be.

Prologue —

Present Day—New York

The rain was falling so hard it was difficult for Gray to see much of anything. She quickly climbed out of the Uber, the driver paid and tipped, lugging her large backpack and roller bag behind her.

"Thanks!" She called to the driver over the sound of the storm before slamming the car door shut.

Shrugging into the straps of the heavy bag, which at the moment carried her worldly possessions, she ran through the deluge to the steps that led up to the lavish front door of the brownstone. Her hand shot out to grab the wrought iron railing as her booted foot slipped in her haste to get to the door.

Steadying herself, she hurried up the last couple stairs to the door, using her fist to knock firmly on the hard wood. Within a few moments, she heard locks disengage, and then the door was pulled open. Kevin stood on the other side, concern marking his handsome face.

"Come on in, sweetheart," he said, reaching out and taking her hand, pulling her into the warmth of the home and out of the rain. "So glad you called. Michael is still at his meeting but will be home soon."

"Thanks," she said, allowing herself to be taken in a quick hug before she was ushered upstairs.

"I've got you all set up in here," he said, taking

her to one of the spare bedrooms on the third floor of the luxurious home. "With Michael and me on the second floor, I figured you could have privacy up here."

Looking around, Gray felt lost, sad, and deeply hurt. How on earth had her life become a backpack and a guest room in her best friend's house? She turned to look at him, and clearly he saw something in her eyes because he gently removed the backpack straps from her shoulder, setting the bag aside before he took her into a long, warm hug.

"It'll be okay, Gray," he murmured into the hug. "We'll get you through this. Stay as long as you need to, okay?"

She nodded, unable to speak.

Chapter One

Nine Months Ago

*G*ray Rickman slowly brought the glass of champagne to her lips, unable to take her eyes off the blonde standing at the table where the wedding cake was set up. She was assigned to cutting the pieces and placing them on the provided small plates.

The dress she wore was form-fitting, yet totally appropriate for the occasion of Gray's best friend Michael's wedding to his beloved Kevin, and the station she held within the event. A summer wedding, the halter-top style maroon sundress left the creamy flesh of beautiful shoulders and her upper back revealed. Gray's gaze in that moment, however, was drawn to the hint of cleavage. Tasteful, yet sexy.

Her makeup was light, this beauty not remotely needing it. Her blond hair was cut into a jaw-length bob, one side tucked behind an ear which glinted with small, dangling diamond earrings.

She. Was. Gorgeous.

She'd looked long enough. It was time to talk to her. Gray finished her champagne and set the empty flute on a nearby table before casually making her way over to the beauty.

The blonde glanced up at her. "Well, hello there. Care for some cake?"

Gray glanced down at the small, square pieces,

alternating in black and white. The vanilla-and-chocolate cake was quite appropriate as Kevin Hardy, a Black man, was marrying the whitest white boy on the planet. "Chocolate, please."

Without taking her eyes off Gray, the server offered a plate, which held the last piece she had cut. "Enjoy."

Gray took the plate with the smirk on her lips that she knew broke through barriers—and panties. "Thank you." Gray gabbed a fork from those laid out on the linen-covered table. "Besides a piece of cake, I came over here to tell you you're the most beautiful woman I've ever seen."

The blonde cocked her head slightly to the side and raised a perfectly arched eyebrow. "Oh?"

"Absolutely. And," Gray added, stepping a bit closer to the table which separated them. "The only thing that would be sweeter than this cake would be for me to see what's beneath that beautiful dress."

The other eyebrow shot up to join the first. The woman cleared her throat, looking down at her task as she cut another piece of cake to plate. "I must say," she said at length. "I'm used to women being more...what's the word? Eloquent, perhaps, in their compliments?"

Gray grinned. "Oh, I can be eloquent. I'm a writer."

"Really?" the blonde asked, her tone less than impressed.

Unhindered, Gray said, "I am."

"So," the woman said, her eyes hooded a bit in an expression that could be read as seduction or revulsion, depending on the perspective. "What makes you think I'd be interested in offering you a second piece of cake, let alone anything under this dress?"

Gray glanced around to make sure they were alone—or at least nobody else within earshot—then leaned in, murmuring into the woman's ear. "The fact that you fucked my brains out in the shower this morning." She smiled when a visible shudder flowed through the woman.

The blonde cleared her throat softly. "Well, I guess there is that."

Gray chuckled, leaving a small kiss on the neck of the woman she'd been in love with her entire adult life and had lived with for four years.

"You. Are. Bad," she murmured back, making Gray grin. "But I love you anyway."

"Despite or because of?" Gray asked, bringing her fork up to her piece of cake.

The blonde, otherwise known as Christian Scott, grinned. "Yes."

Amused, Gray took a small bite.

"I'm almost done here," Christian remarked. "Still going to dance with me?"

"Of course." Gray cut another small bite. "That's why I came over here all ninja, predator-like."

"Oh, honey," Christian said, eyeing her love. "If that's what you've got for moves, be glad you're no longer single."

"Oh! Ow!" She glared playfully. "You pain me." She placed a hand over her heart.

Christian leaned forward and said against Gray's lips, "I'll make it all better later, baby."

Gray accepted the short yet possessive kiss, which took her breath away just like the woman who initiated it. And, twenty minutes later, once Christian's cake-cutting duties were finished, the two found themselves a place on the dance floor, a slow song playing.

Gray loved how Christian felt in her arms, like they were made to fit together. As they made their graceful way in their small area of the dance floor—graceful simply by virtue of Christian's excellent leadership as one of the greatest dancers on the planet—Gray met the dark green gaze of the woman she held. Christian looked up at her with that adoring expression that never got old, nor did the feel of her fingers absently playing with Gray's short, dark hair.

"I have a confession to make," Christian murmured, just loud enough to be heard over the music.

"Oh?" Gray asked, an eyebrow raised. "Don't tell me, you stuck your finger in the cake's icing?"

Christian grinned. "As tempting as that may have been, no." She trailed her fingernails through the short hair at the nape of Gray's neck, sending a shiver through the younger woman. "Being here today, watching just how amazingly happy Michael and Kevin are, I'm thinking that maybe, *maybe*, I want to talk about this," she said, indicating the room filled with guests around them. "For us."

"Really?" Gray asked, shocked.

Growing up with two parents deeply in love and committed to each other, Gray had always wanted that for herself, even once she realized that would be with a woman. Christian, however, had a very different view of marriage. Though she'd been estranged from her parents for half of her thirty-four years on the planet, she'd seen enough of her father's controlling ownership of her mother to have a very leery view of marriage.

It had come up several times, and though they'd

had productive discussions about it, had made no progress on changing Christian's mind. Gray had no choice but to respect Christian's fear and discomfort, accepting that they had a wonderful relationship as it was. It had been hard at times to not take it personally, especially after all they'd been through to be together, but love was about understanding. It was all a learning experience.

"So," Gray drawled. "Third time might be a charm?"

Christian smiled softly. "Let's not put the cart before the horse. Just wanted you to know that my perceptions are being tickled."

Gray grinned at her choice in wording. She leaned down to say in her ear, "I can definitely think of something to tickle later."

Christian, as always, beat her at her own game of seduction as her hand slid down to cup Gray's jaw. "You better," she murmured against Gray's lips. "I expect the kind of tickles that end in orgasms."

Gray cleared her throat. "Duly noted."

As the evening and event wound down, Gray and Christian said their goodbyes. Michael, whom she'd known since middle school, had never looked more handsome and proud. With his red hair slicked back and Eric Stoltz good looks, he beamed. His husband, Kevin, was a gorgeous, soft-spoken Black man with a great smile. The two were the yin to the other's yang. Gray thought it was beautiful.

"You have fun, sweetheart," Christian said, giving Kevin a tight hug.

"Thanks, sunshine," he responded.

"You," Gray said, poking Michael in the chest. "You guys be safe. We need you back in one piece."

He grinned, pulling her into a painfully tight hug. "Always." He gave her a lingering squeeze. "Thanks for everything, Gray," he murmured into the hug, emotion in his voice. "If it weren't for your encouragement, I never would have given him a chance."

She smiled, squeezing him just as hard. "The important thing is you did."

Michael gave her a kiss on the cheek before releasing her, his gaze set on Christian. "Maybe we can return the favor someday, huh?" he said playfully to her, indicating the brand-new, shiny gold bands both men sported on their left ring fingers now.

She gave him a Mona Lisa smile. "Perhaps."

Michael shook his head as he took Christian into a hug.

Ten minutes later, Gray stood behind Christian with her arm wrapped around her waist from behind. They, along with the rest of the wedding party, Gray's parents, and guests, stood outside the event space and watched the two men climb into the limo to head out for their honeymoon.

It was a bit surreal for her to watch Michael and his *husband*. How could he possibly have a husband? Her mind went back to when they met, Michael chased up a tree by school bullies. They were so young, so naïve. Michael had understood himself early, coming out to her in middle school. Gray, however, had taken a bit longer. Though she'd known she liked women as far back as she could remember, she hadn't been ready to label herself *lesbian* until after high school.

The woman leaning back into her was the magic elixir to bring her to her senses—and her knees. Christian had affected her from the moment she met her at age seventeen. Now, aged twenty-nine, she still was smacked upside the head like a lovesick teenager every time she looked at her.

～～～～

After getting back home to their apartment in the Hudson Heights neighborhood located in upper Manhattan, they had spent a couple hours making love, cuddling and talking, then making love again. Christian was currently asleep and Gray was sitting on the couch with her laptop.

Christian had bought the apartment six or so years before. It was a great place, though it was getting a bit tight for the two of them, their giant fawn-colored bullmastiff Brutus, and Caesar, the black-and-white feline with intense green eyes who had followed Gray home one day and wouldn't step yelling at her until she brought him in. Now, he always lay nearby when she was writing, as she was at the moment.

Unable to sleep as her latest book idea had been nagging at her, Gray had left the bed as quietly as she could and had grabbed her T-shirt and shorts off the floor, carrying them with her in the dark until she could close the bedroom door behind her before padding to the living room where she logged onto her computer as she got dressed.

Brutus, who was lying on his back on the rug in front of the cold fireplace, glanced over at her, groaning deep in his throat. Caesar trotted out from wherever he'd been hiding in the shadows to take his place on the back of the cushion near Gray's head as she sat down.

Gray used to write off and on as a kid, but she began to seriously work on her craft—outside of her job as a journalist with *The New York Times*—a few years back. Most of her stories lay unfinished or simply saved in a file and tucked away in her *Wishful Thinking* folder. Over the last year, she'd had more of a potent need to write, and when she wasn't at work or spending time with Christian, she was writing.

Pulling up the current manuscript she was working on, she absently reached back and rubbed Caesar's ears. His soft, low purring in her ear made her smile. Writing had always been an outlet for her to vent her feelings, thoughts, or emotions, but creative writing had never felt like a compulsion for her. Until now.

More than once she'd been woken up by her characters, urging her to get up and tell their stories. Now, she even worked storylines out on the subway heading to or from work. Sometimes she felt like it was an addiction, a monster that had to be fed.

Somewhere in the back of her mind she fantasized about getting published. A few of her colleagues at the paper had, and it was a little knife in her heart every time one of them waltzed in with a copy of their own book. She was genuinely happy for them, she just wished she had the courage to try it herself.

Maybe one day.

Tired and irritated with herself for staying up way too late writing, Gray was in the kitchen making coffee. Lord, she needed it. While the brew brewed, she washed out Caesar's wet food bowl to give him his breakfast.

As she popped open a can of the disgusting-smelling fillets that the *gato* loved, Christian entered the room, freshly showered. She was dressed for rehearsal, her trunks and midriff sports bra hidden beneath mesh shorts and a tank top. Her wet hair was slicked back from her face. It was in a similar short style now as it had been when they'd met. Christian was one of those women that could wear it long, short, or anywhere in between and still be stunning.

"Good morning, baby," she said, walking over to Gray and giving her a quick kiss before she grabbed herself a yogurt cup from the fridge. "What time did you finally come to bed?"

"Way too late," Gray admitted sheepishly. She opened the cabinet door that housed their mugs. "Coffee?"

"No, I have to get going." She set the unopened yogurt cup and a spoon down on the cooking island and walked over to Gray. "Sweetheart," she said softly, reaching up to brush dark bangs out of Gray's eyes. "I love your eyes," she said softly. "So beautifully blue. Electric."

Gray smiled. "Thanks, baby."

"I can tell by the way you're leaning on the counter that your back is killing you," Christian continued. She studied Gray for a long moment before speaking again. "What do you think about maybe looking outside the City, looking for something bigger?" She cupped Gray's jaw. "Get you a home office with a thing called a desk and chair so you don't cripple yourself trying to work from the couch."

Stunned, Gray met her gaze. "Seriously?" She placed her hands on Christian's narrow hips. "But you love this place."

"I do," Christian admitted. "But I love you more. Besides," Christian added with a shrug. "Bethany wants to continue with lessons from me and she said she has some friends that are interested, so maybe we can find a place that we can renovate or add a dance studio." She placed her hands on Gray's shoulders. "What do you think?"

Gray's grin was broad. "I think it's a fabulous idea."

"Okay," Christian said. "Well, then let's start researching what makes sense." She leaned in and left a lingering kiss on Gray's lips. "Love you, baby," she murmured against those lips. "Be safe and have a wonderful day."

"I love you too, my sweet." Gray reached out and grabbed Christian's yogurt and spoon, which the dancer had walked off without. "Baby?"

Grabbing her large dance bag, Christian glanced back at Gray as she shouldered the heavy duffel. "Ah hell," she muttered, walking back to retrieve the yogurt. She gave Gray another kiss as she grabbed it before hurrying to the door. "Bye, babies!" She called out to Brutus and Caesar, then was gone, only for the door to open up again. "What night were your parents coming to see the show?"

"Thursday," Gray responded.

"Oh, opening night, huh?" Christian said with a grin. "All right."

"Why?"

"Got something special planned for them. Bye, love."

Gray's eyebrows rose. Usually when Christian said she had something planned, it involved chocolate syrup or whipped cream and privacy.

Turning to Brutus, who stared up at her, she reached down and lovingly grabbed him by his snout. "Guess we'll see, huh, big boy?"

Chapter Two

"What's up, Doc?" Gray said, plopping down in Amir's office. "You're interrupting me from finishing up the story you just bugged me about an hour ago, so you best have a good reason."

Amir, her editor of six years, glanced over at her, heavy dark eyebrows raised. "Oh?"

Gray gave him a sheepish grin. "Mint?" she asked, pulling out the tin of little white round breath mints. "They're curiously strong."

She waited for a snippy response, but instead she got a bark of laughter as he shook his head and held out his hand. She placed a couple of mints in his palm before popping one into her own mouth.

"Rickman," he said, drawing his mint-laden hand back and dumping all of them into his mouth in one go. "You are strange."

"Which is precisely why you haven't fired me yet," she retorted.

"Yet," he added, removing his glasses and pointing at her with one of the arms of the eyewear. "Is the operative word at play, here." He tossed the glasses to the cluttered desktop before rubbing his eyes with his fingers. "Now, we have an issue."

"Okay," Gray said, shifting into serious mode. "What's up?"

"As you know, Jacobs managed to land the Cox interview." Gray was indeed familiar with Sir Richard

Cox, an actor who was Britain's answer to Robert DeNiro. "Incredibly tough to get as he rarely talks to anybody, let alone an American reporter."

"Right," Gray said with a nod.

"Well," he continued with a heavy sigh, grabbing his glasses again. He spritzed the lenses with cleaner before rubbing them down with a microfiber cloth. "The interview was planned to happen this Friday, but Jacobs's mother-in-law decided this was the perfect time to crawl into her deathbed in Brazil."

"Oh, boy," Gray murmured.

"Indeed. Cox claims he's old school and won't do interviews by phone or Zoom, et cetera."

"So, he canceled?" Gray asked, trying to get to the crux of the situation.

"Not quite," Amir said. "He still wants to do it, and has handpicked Jacobs's replacement."

Gray nodded, understanding. She flipped open her assignment notebook. "Okay, whose story am I taking over?" she asked, glancing up at him. "I'm guessing Xander or Fatima, with them being in the entertainment beat—"

"He chose you," Amir said.

"Who?"

"Cox. He chose you."

"Me? I'm not on the entertainment beat," Gray said, confused.

"Agreed. But," Amir said, replacing his glasses on his face as he read from a printed page. "'Miss Rickman has a feisty spirit, flowing way in written speech, and I'm a great fan of her parents and life partner.'" He tossed the printed-out email to her side of the desk.

Gray grinned. "He's a fan of Christian?" she

murmured, feeling schoolgirl shy. She'd accepted long ago that, between the two of them, Christian was the one endowed with massive talent, and she never grew tired of hearing accolades for her love's abilities.

"Would appear so." He turned back to his computer and tapped away on his keyboard before hitting a final key with flourish. "I just forwarded you Jacobs's notes and his list of possible interview topics, so you've basically got four days, including today, to read up on Cox, watch as many of his films as you can, previous interviews, whatever." He turned back to her. "This is the only American interview he'll give this year and perhaps even this decade, so don't screw it up, Rickman."

"No pressure," Gray blew out, running a hand through her hair. "I'll get on it."

≈≈≈≈

"Baby," Gray whispered, running her hands through blond hair. "Wake up."

Grass-green eyes blinked open, disoriented for a moment before a few more blinks brought clarity. Christian sat up from where she'd been leaning against Gray, head on her shoulder.

Christian looked at the television, where credits were rolling for the movie they'd been watching cuddled together on the couch. "Oh, baby, I'm sorry," she said, just barely managing to stifle a yawn. "I fell asleep."

"It's okay." Gray left a kiss on the side of her head. "You only run, skip, prance, and jump for thirteen hours a day," she said dryly. "Burning off calories I haven't even consumed yet for your job."

Christian grinned. "Yes, well." The yawn that came forth popped her jaw. "'Scuse me," she murmured. "Was the movie good? The last thing I remember was the scene on the train."

"Great movie," Gray said, stopping the movie with the remote and turning off the TV. "Only about four hundred eighty-two to go."

Christian grinned, more awake now. "Well, I got through one-third of one with you, so what's next?"

Gray chuckled. "Next is bed. It's after ten and we both have an early day tomorrow."

"Mm," Christian hummed, snuggling back into Gray. "Don't wanna."

Gray smiled, holding the dancer close. "Well," she prodded softly. "You can go back to rehearsal tomorrow and brag that Sir Richard Cox is a fan of yours."

Christian smiled, eyes still closed. "Okay, okay." With a groan, she pushed away from Gray again. "Let's go to bed."

Ten minutes later they were lying in bed, Christian already asleep and resting against Gray, who lay on her back holding the dancer and staring up at the ceiling. She was tired, but her mind was running wild and free with the assignment ahead of her. She knew that Amir never would have given it to her had he not thought she could do it, regardless of what the actor wanted.

Even still, she felt this was a huge opportunity for her, and she wasn't entirely certain why. She'd interviewed huge names in business, politics, local and DC players, and even a star athlete or two. Every so-called "big name" had its own effect on the stomach and nerves, but overall they were just people.

This one, however, felt different. Perhaps it was just a strange feeling knowing that a famous actor of Cox's acclaim, in the business for more than forty years, knew who she was, knew who her parents were, and admired their work and that of her girlfriend. She felt the pressure, and though she knew she was capable of doing the work, she was scared to death that she'd fail. Or worse, *he* would think she failed and could possibly sink her career.

As she held Christian closer, she decided worrying about it now would do her no good. Closing her eyes, she let out a long, contented sigh and drifted off into the peaceful arms of sleep.

※※※※

Christian did between two and four shows per year, depending on the contract, commonly a three-month or six-month run with a show. In their years together, Gray had seen all of them. Some were better than others, but no matter the specifics of the dance, Christian was by far the outstanding talent. Whether she wanted to be or not, she was the star.

Now, she stood next to her parents, a single red rose in her hand. Since that very first show when Gray had garnered the courage to wait for Christian after the show, that time with a white rose, it was such a moment of pride for her, watching as the fans waited for the cast to leave the theater. This opening night of her newest production was no different.

"She's so beautiful," her mother Bernadette said softly, almost to herself, as they watched Christian sign autographs and take selfies with fans.

"She is," Gray agreed.

"Who's the brunette gal with the large…uh… earrings?" Dennis asked, seated in his new wheelchair.

Gray glanced over at her father to see her mother was glaring down at him. She smirked. Turning back, she saw the blonde in question, her large bosom—and earrings—leading the way as she bulldozed her way into the crowd of fans and fellow castmates.

"That would be Leandra Faulkner," she explained. "New to the Broadway set from California, I think. Christian is not a fan."

"Good dancer," Bernadette noted. "But it looks like she can be a real bitch."

"That's my feeling, too," Gray murmured.

"Gray. Rickman."

Turning at the male voice that came from her right, she was stunned to see Richard Cox standing there. He was a handsome man in his seventies with grey hair and brown eyes. Despite his tough-guy portrayals on British television and film, his quiet manner and way of speaking reminded Gray more of Christopher Plummer.

He strolled over to them, snow-white goatee neatly trimmed and brown eyes twinkling. He wore casual trousers and a neatly ironed button up tucked into them. "Good evening to you." He stepped up to the small group of three, hands tucked into his pants pockets.

Gray shook herself out of her shock and cleared her throat. "Good evening, Mr. Cox," she managed.

He glanced at her, that ever-present little half smile in place. "You'll be getting inside my head on the morrow," he said. "I think you can call me Richard, young Gray."

Gray glanced over at her parents to see if they

were seeing what she was seeing. From the awestruck look on her father's face, she guessed they were. "Well, Richard," she said, turning back to the actor. "I'd like to introduce you to my parents. This is Bernadette and Dennis Rickman." She turned to her parents. "Mom, Dad, this is Sir Richard Cox."

Dennis wheeled his chair closer to the actor, who Gray knew was a favorite. "Sir," he said, extending his hand. "A great pleasure."

"Oh, no, sir," Richard said, taking his hand in a firm grip. "The pleasure is all mine." He gave the seated man a small bow of reverence then turned to Bernadette, taking her hand and lightly brushing her knuckles with his lips. "I saw the two of you in 1985, my first experience of a Broadway production." He smiled at Bernadette. "Nobody will ever be Odette but you, my dear, and you, sir," he said, looking back to Dennis. "Will forever be the Swan."

Gray smiled, enjoying the interaction. Richard turned to her.

"Gray?" he said, looking at her but indicating her parents. "I've seen productions of *Swan Lake* all over the world, but your parents managed to ruin it for me."

"Gray?"

Turning, Gray saw Christian standing behind her, looking at the actor with confusion in her eyes. "Hello, love," Gray said, presenting Christian with the rose she held. "You were absolutely breathtaking." She leaned forward and left a soft kiss on Christian's lips, careful not to get too PDA considering their unexpected company.

"Thank you," Christian said, taking the rose and then pulling Gray to her in a tight hug. "So glad you're here," she murmured. "I love you."

Gray smiled, hugging her back. "I love you too, baby." Stepping out of the hug, she took Christian's hand and pulled her toward Richard, who still stood by her parents. "Sweetheart, this is Richard Cox, who I'll be interviewing tomorrow."

The charm was instantly turned on as Christian smiled and held out her hand. "Mr. Cox," she said. "It's an honor. We've been watching your movies all week."

He returned the smile, and much like he had done with Bernadette, he took her hand and brushed her knuckles with his lips. "I hope you've enjoyed them as much as I've enjoyed following your career, Miss Scott."

"Thank you, sir," she said, looking at Gray, shock in her eyes. "I'm so deeply pleased."

"Mr. Cox?" Dennis said, the group turning to look over at him. "My wife and I were going to take these two to dinner," he said, indicating Gray and Christian. "It would be an honor if you'd join us."

The actor looked at each one in turn before returning his gaze to Dennis. "Let me collect my wife."

≈≈≈≈

She was nervous. Her stomach was in knots, and she'd yet to be able to trust herself to drink the cup of coffee that Christian had brought her. She was worried her stomach would rebel worse than it already was.

"You look so amazing in this suit," Christian said softly, standing in front of Gray and smoothing the women's-cut suit jacket out over her chest. "This color brings out your eyes," she continued, looking into those very eyes.

Gray met her gaze, able to see so much pride in their green depths, so much love. "Thank you." She leaned forward for a kiss, which was given. "So," she said. "What was it that you had planned for my parents last night?"

Christian snaked her arms up around Gray's shoulders, her hand going to where it always did in Gray's hair. "Well, I wanted to ask them a question, but the appearance of Richard and Eva left me a little too shocked to follow through with my plan."

"Yes, that was a little shocking, indeed." Gray grinned. "Sorry 'bout that."

"No apologies needed," Christian murmured. "I still can't believe we all had dinner with them."

"I know. I always thought it would be you who introduced us to all the fancy-schmancy famous people. Which," she added, resting her hands on Christian's hips and pulling her in against her. "You have. Can you say Michael Ball? Sarah Brightman?"

Christian's grin was downright devilish. "Yes, well..." She lazily ran her fingers through Gray's hair as she gazed into her eyes for a long moment before speaking again, her energy markedly different from the playful woman a few moments before. "I wanted to ask your parents a question."

"Okay," Gray said, almost feeling as though she were being hypnotized by the gentle fingers in her hair and depths of Christian's eyes. "What was that?" she asked. "Your question."

"I wanted to know if they would mind having a second daughter-in-law."

It took Gray a moment, but finally her brain kicked in. "Wait," she said, eyebrows falling. "What are you saying?"

"I'm saying that I love you more than I ever thought would be possible, Gray. For so long, I didn't think I was capable of love, at least not romantic love. I thought," she continued softly. "I thought Brandon had robbed me of that dream. My parents had robbed me of that dream." The softest smile curved her beautiful lips. "They'd robbed that ability in me to trust someone enough to give them all of me."

Gray remained silent, listening, even as her heart began to beat faster. She did her best to slow it down and just listen, to be there for a woman who had had such a difficult first nineteen years of her life.

"It's been you, Gray. It's been you, your parents, even Ivan to a small degree," she added, speaking of Gray's brother. "Who have shown me a very different kind of family. A very different kind of love. What I used to dream about as a kid, seeing my friends and others in the Olympics world. Support, love, honor." She shook her head slowly. "Nothing I ever knew." The soft smile on her lips grew as she brought her hand from Gray's hair to cup her face. "Until you," she whispered.

Gray swallowed, feeling emotion threatening behind her eyes at such amazing words.

"I don't know why I was holding back," Christian said. "What I was trying to prove to myself. Gray?"

"Yes?"

"Will you marry me?" Christian asked softly, no fanfare, no bended knee, just a woman asking to be loved.

Gray nodded, unable to speak for a moment. She swallowed again. "Yes," she whispered, emotion stealing her voice. "With all my heart, yes."

Relief painted Christian's face, then her eyes closed as she pulled Gray into a bone-crushing hug, holding them together. "I love you."

"I love you," Gray said, pulling out of the hug and cupping Christian's face as she took her in a deeply passionate kiss.

Gray lamented the fact that they didn't have time for more, but the clock kept marching forward. She ended the kiss and pulled Christian to her again. Nothing had ever felt better to her than to hold Christian, feel her against her. In that moment, knowing that Christian truly wanted to make it final, make it official, and share it with those they loved, made it all the more incredible.

A love like theirs, so strong, so deeply passionate...nothing could tear it apart.

Chapter Three

"Okay," Gray said, looking down at the notepad resting on her thigh. "All right, Richard," she said, looking back up at the man sitting in an identical wingback chair in his hotel suite in downtown Manhattan. "Final question. When you look back over your career, spanning sixty-two years, with the first twelve on stage in the West End, London's famed Theatreland, are you satisfied?"

The actor stroked his goatee as he stared off into space for a long moment, which he'd done often during the interview, considering his responses carefully. "I am not," he finally said. "I love what I do, proud of many of the projects I have done and will leave behind when I leave this world. But, satisfied? No."

"And, why is that?" Gray asked, intrigued.

He met her gaze, the little half smile in place. "Because I'll always have more to say, more stories to tell." His smile grew. "A born storyteller is never done, never satisfied."

His words hit her in a deep place that she didn't fully understand in that moment, but which touched her soul. She nodded, unable to speak. She was just glad the entire interview was being both recorded and filmed so stills could be taken from it for the profile she was doing on the actor.

"Well," she said at length, clearing her throat, gathering her professionalism, and pushing to her feet. "I can't thank you enough for—"

"Wait now," he said, waving for her to retake her seat. "My turn."

She reclaimed her seat, confused. "I'm sorry?"

"My turn," he said again, that cryptic smile in place. He remained seated in his relaxed position in the chair, head slightly cocked to the side and curiosity in his eyes. "I did some research on you, Gray," he began. "Before I agreed to do this with you. Your written career, carefully reading between the lines to understand you as a person."

"Okay," Gray drawled, uncertain where this was going.

"I read a paper you wrote in college. *Dance With Me*, it was called."

Gray considered how to react for a moment. College was a long time ago—what could he be getting at? Finally, she nodded. "Yes. Freshman year."

"Indeed. You wrote of the beginnings of your relationship with Miss Scott." He rubbed his chin. "Why?"

"My professor at the time wanted us to write a biographical moment in our life, something that was significant to us," Gray explained.

"Yet you wrote it like a story." Gray nodded. "The facts were true?" Richard asked.

"Yes. Everything in that story was true."

He smiled. "Just written with the narrative of a story, a real-life event made to read like fiction."

Gray nodded. "Yes. For me, it was easier to tell, to be honest. When I think of a biography, or a nonfiction story, I think dry, boring." She wrinkled her nose. "Not my cup of tea."

He nodded. "Interesting," he murmured. "Very

interesting."

※ ※ ※ ※

"As you can see," Karen said, opening some of the cabinet doors. "Plenty of storage space. The counter space is a bit lacking, but plenty of room to add an island or peninsula."

Gray looked around the space, which looked like it hadn't been updated since at least the year she was born. She and Christian met gazes several times, and the silent communication of truly connected people made it clear: it was a pass on this one.

"You know, Karen," Gray said, turning to the older woman who'd been leading them to properties for sale all afternoon. "I think we need to talk about what we've seen today."

"Are you sure?" the Realtor asked, looking from one woman to the other. "This was the home with the layout I thought might make for a good combined home office and dance space."

"Not quite what we're looking for," Christian said, giving the older woman a bright smile. "But you've given us a lot to think about today."

"All right," Karen said with nod. "Well," she handed them the printouts for all four houses they'd seen as well as her business card. "Give me a call if you make a decision or want to see more properties."

The two parties left the single-family home and went their separate ways. Christian and Gray held hands as they made their way to the subway, walking along the street. The houses were small, the yards smaller, but it was what they could afford in Queens.

As they walked, Gray noticed the slight limp in

Christian's gait. She'd wrapped her knee that morning before they'd left the apartment again, something she'd noticed her doing more and more.

"Want me to call an Uber, baby?" she asked.

Christian glanced over at her and, a look of irritation at herself appearing on her beautiful face, Christian nodded. "Yeah. I don't want to push it."

"'Kay."

After getting home, they'd enjoyed a quiet evening with their fur babies, catching up on some of the shows they recorded while eating dinner, and now lay in the calming darkness of night, Christian snuggled into Gray.

"How did you feel about the second one?" Christian asked, referring to the properties they'd been shown that day.

"Honestly," Gray said, fingers absently running through blond hair, Christian's head resting on her shoulder. "I wasn't moved by any of them. I think the third would have been the closest, but I really didn't like the area. And, the schools nearby are some of the worst in the district."

Christian was quiet for a moment, then said, "Schools?"

Gray winced, as her thoughts and impressions had just fallen out of her mouth. "Well," she muttered. "I know that we want the house we pick to be, if not a forever home, at least a longtime-because-it's-too-expensive-to-do-this-very-often home."

Christian lifted her head and moved to her side next to Gray. She planted her elbow into her pillow, head resting in the upturned palm. She looked down at Gray with bemused skepticism. "I see," she said, a small smirk on her lips. "Something we haven't talked about in a long time, kids."

Gray felt a little panic as she knew what a sensitive topic this was for Christian, especially after everything she'd been forced to endure while living with her figure skating coach as a young teenager.

"Well," she finally said, hoping to ease any tension her Freudian slip may cause. "Between the two of us, we've been so busy we haven't even figured out when we want to get married." Which was true.

Christian studied her for a long moment, her expression serious. "Do you want kids, Gray?" she asked softly. Clearly Gray's attempt at redirection had not worked.

In that moment, looking up into the face of the woman she loved more than anything, Gray knew she had to be honest. She nodded. "Yes. With you, yes." When Christian said nothing, she asked, "But, the question is, do you?"

Christian studied Gray for a long moment, so long Gray almost began to feel a bit antsy. "If we never had kids, would it be a void for you?" she asked at length, her tone gentle, seeking information.

Gray considered and shook her head. "Not exactly. Would I be sad, as I think we'd make amazing parents, especially you? Yes. But is it a dealbreaker for me? No. I know your history, Christian. For you, this goes beyond a simple yes or no, black or white."

Christian didn't say anything, simply brought up a hand and cupped Gray's jaw. She leaned down and initiated a slow kiss, her lips so soft as Gray responded. As Christian began to make love to her, Gray wasn't surprised. She'd learned over the years that, where Gray's currency was words, Christian's was expression with her body.

If she was angry, that little body would nearly rumble like a volcano about to explode. If she was grateful or happy, her smile and affection was a balm to the soul. If she was emotionally overwhelmed, she would find a place to dance, her body speaking the words she wasn't ready to say. In a case such as the current one, Gray knew the love Christian was feeling in that moment was beyond her words, so she opted to show Gray how she was feeling rather than use what, to Christian, was her secondary instrument of communication.

Gray's eyes were closed and her back slightly arched as Christian paid homage to her right breast, her tongue slowly licking the very tip of a hard nipple. Gray's hand found Christian's hair, burying her fingers in the soft strands and cupping the back of her head. A small groan escaped her throat as one of Christian's hands slipped between her legs, two fingers stroking her clit, which was quickly growing in size and sensitivity. She spread her thighs, welcoming those fingers as they moved from her clit to ease their way inside of her.

Christian sighed as her fingers slid fully inside, the slow, hot breath over Gray's flesh causing goosebumps. The dancer kissed and licked her way down Gray's body, her mouth joining her fingers, which slowly thrust into her, Christian's tongue finding Gray's clit.

Gray had not been with many women in her life, only two, her virginity lost to Christian when she'd been eighteen. The dancer had opened Gray's eyes and world to sensuality, sexuality, and the pleasures of the body long before she'd laid a hand on her in that little apartment she and Michael had been renting in

Denver.

Now, as Gray was nearing her climax, Christian's touch was still the only one that could affect her as it did, could pull her emotion and orgasm from the depths of her very soul. As so often happened, Gray felt tears pressing at the backs of her eyes as her body exploded with its release, unleashing her passion, yes, but also the deep love she held for the woman who was crawling back up her body.

Christian gathered her in her arms, raining kisses down on her face and lips. "I love you so much," she whispered.

Gray wrapped her arms around her, hugging Christian to her, her emotions still too high to speak.

※ ※ ※ ※

Gray sat on the ottoman, Christian's bare foot in her lap as the dancer relaxed on the couch, an ice pack on her troublesome knee. As her thumbs worked gently yet firmly on the foot in the way she'd been taught years before, Gray glanced up at the woman who sat with her head resting back against the back of the couch with her eyes closed.

"Baby?" she murmured softly, hoping against hope that what she was about to say would land correctly. "When's your contract up for this show?"

"Um," Christian said, the little wrinkle between her eyebrows appearing as it always did when she was in pain. "October. Why?" Her eyes just barely opened, gaze locked on Gray.

Gray shrugged, focusing back on her task. "This show is amazing, you're getting rave reviews for it." She shrugged again, *No biggie in what I'm about to say, right?* "I was just thinking that…your knee is getting worse. Hell, even Dr. Frye wants to try cortisone shots to help with the pain and deterioration."

Christian eyed her. "What are you saying?" she asked, her voice quiet, unsure.

"I'm saying, my love." Gray moved her thumb to work the ball of her foot, adding pressure where she knew it was needed. "This show is such a success. Why not go out with a bang rather than letting your body retire you?"

"You're saying I should quit," Christian said, her voice hard.

"No." Gray shook her head. "Baby," she began softly. "You're thirty-four, you've been the queen of the Broadway stage now for, what, five years? Six? You've blown away your critics, entertained and awed thousands upon thousands of people over the years. Look at all you've achieved," she continued, a smile of the wonder she felt for the woman before her. "Hell, you even got to reprise the title role in the movie version of *Angel* two years ago."

Though Christian hadn't said anything, Gray could see her eyes softening a bit.

"Christian, everything you set out to do you've done. Those awards over there say it all," she added, nodding toward the fireplace mantel. "Your Nanna would be so proud of you."

"I'm thirty-four years old, but falling apart," Christian said softly. "Is that what you meant to add?"

Gray shook her head. "No. I think if you continue on, that will be the case. Right now, your body is giving you a giant red flag warning. You're still in very capable shape of living a healthy, happy life, could still dance to stay limber, teach. Or," she added with a shrug. "Try something completely different."

"Like gardening?" Christian asked, an eyebrow raised.

Gray grinned, able to tell by her tone that, though not thrilled by the subject, she wasn't angry at the messenger. "Perhaps painting?"

"Or," Christian said, a twinkle in her eyes. "Maybe pottery? We can try the whole Demi Moore, Patrick Swayze thing."

Gray threw her head back as a bark of laughter escaped her throat. "Oh, yes. I so get to be Patrick."

"Well, you're taller, so that would make sense," Christian added.

"Always the pragmatist," Gray muttered, gently setting Christian's foot aside as she rose to her feet. She reached down and grabbed the ice pack. "Want another one, baby?" she asked.

"Please?"

Gray leaned over and snagged a quick kiss before heading into the kitchen. "I still haven't heard if Richard liked the profile or not," she called to the living room. "Or," she added with a smirk. "If he even read it."

"Oh, come on," Christian called back. "Do you really think he's not going to read that?"

Gray set the warmed ice pack on the counter and opened the freezer door to grab the next one. This game of ice pack switch-a-roo was nearly a nightly ritual now. She put the spent one in the freezer then closed the door. "Want anything while I'm here, baby?"

"Nope. All good. You know what I could maybe try?" Christian said.

"What?" Gray asked, noticing Brutus's water

bowl was low, so she walked over and grabbed it to dump it out and refill it.

"Maybe I should try motherhood," Christian said softly, so softly Gray wasn't sure she heard it right.

She paused for a moment, her brain trying to catch up to her ears. When it registered, she continued cleaning the bowl as it marinated in her brain and her heart. Bowl filled, she walked it over to their feeding area, Brutus meeting her there to lap it up and make a mess.

Standing again, she walked to the counter and grabbed the fresh ice pack before walking back to Christian, who was staring off into space. "Here, baby," Gray said, gently placing the pack on her knee. "Are you being facetious?" she asked, not entirely sure what to think.

Christian looked up, meeting her gaze. "No," she murmured. She let out a heavy sigh, sadness in her eyes. "Maybe," she began, looking to her knee for a long moment before returning her gaze to Gray's. "Maybe it's time."

Chapter Four

Gray had just turned on her work computer when her name was bellowed throughout the newsroom, heard above the police scanners, her colleagues chatting with each other and on the phones working their sources.

"Jesus H. Christ," she muttered, grabbing her notepad and pen before heading to Amir's office. "Yes?" she asked, resting her hand against the jamb of his open office door.

"Sit," he said, absently indicating the chair she usually occupied while in his office, his focus still on his computer screen.

Doing as bade, Gray plopped down in the seat, waiting for him to speak. She was nervous, as it had been four days since her profile had landed, and though she'd gotten rave reviews for it, the one person whose opinion she cared about hadn't said a word.

"Okay, sorry," Amir said, turning to face her. "Had to get that schedule out. So," he added, reaching to his printer and grabbing the page that was waiting in the printer tray. He slapped it down in front of her.

Brava, young Maestro.

Gray's smile was instant. She didn't have to look at the email address to know who it was from. She read the three words again, then a third time. Richard may as well have written an expansive serenade of praise for what those three words said to her, understanding his way.

"Good work, Rickman," Amir said, turning back to his computer.

Understanding that she'd been effectively excused, Gray took her printed page and left the office. If she hadn't been worried about tripping over something—because she was just that graceful—she would have skipped all the way back to her desk. Instead, she allowed her shit-eating grin to shine.

"How'd it go?" Holly, one of her colleagues and a reporter she'd worked on many stories with in the past, asked.

Gray grinned at her and handed over the email. Holly took it and read it, holding up her hand for a high-five, which Gray gave her.

❧❧❦❦

It was a warm evening as Gray stepped out of the large building on Eighth Avenue. She hitched her messenger bag higher onto her shoulder as she turned to head toward the subway. She noticed a black town car pull to the curb, the brakes squeaking slightly as it came to a stop. The back passenger window buzzed down.

"Gray," a man's voice called out.

Stopping, she looked over and realized it was Richard Cox who had called her name. Walking over to the sleek luxury car, she brought up a hand in a wave. "Good evening, Richard."

"And to you." He smiled. "Can we drop you? I'd like to speak to you."

She glanced around before meeting his gaze again. "Well, I guess I was able to trust you long enough for a lengthy interview, so why not?"

He chuckled and slid across the back seat so she could climb into the car, taking the seat he'd just vacated. "Where do you live?"

Gray gave her address to the driver, who nodded in acknowledgment before getting the car moving again in the dense New York City traffic. The car was beautiful with posh features and soft, white leather seats that a person sank into like a cloud.

"So," she said, placing her messenger bag on her lap. "I was pleased to see you liked the profile."

He nodded, glancing over at her. "I did. Very much. In fact," he said. "That's what I wanted to talk to you about."

She met his gaze, curious. "All right."

"Simon and Schuster has been after me for years," he began. "To write my memoir. I'm not a writer," he added, eyeing Gray with a little grin. "So, for years I've told them no, as I hadn't found a writer that I'd trust to write it." He reached over and slapped her knee once. "Until now."

Gray felt her stomach drop as her eyes saucered. "Wait, what?"

"I'd like to hire you to write it for me," he explained. "Your style is exactly what I'm looking for. A natural-born storyteller who has the thorough integrity of a top-notch journalist. Perfect combination for what I need."

Gray could hardly breathe as what he'd just seemingly offered sank in. "But, Richard," she said. "I'm not sure I'd have the time to dedicate to that. It's something I'd want to be able to investigate completely, talk to people who know you, see the places I'd be writing about, spend hours talking to you, getting stories, facts, memories—"

"All of which I'd pay you for," he assured.

"I..." She wasn't sure what to say.

"Listen," he said as the car pulled up in front of Gray's building. "Talk it over with your lady, come up with a list of any questions or problems, and then the three of us can sit down over dinner to discuss." He looked at her, eyebrows raised in an expression of compromise. "All right?"

Gray let out a long, shaky sigh and nodded. "Okay. I'll talk to her." She held out her hand as an acknowledgment of what would be a business agreement should she choose to accept it.

Richard looked down at it then wrapped his much larger hand around it, giving her a firm shake. "I'll be in touch."

"Thanks for the ride," she said, then gathered her bag and climbed out of the sedan, slamming the door closed behind her. She raised her hand in a wave as the car pulled away from the curb, leaving her standing there by herself.

She took the stairs as the elevator was out of service, feeling a little out of breath once she reached their floor and the door. She used her key to let herself in, a smile instantly touching her lips when she heard Sarah Brightman playing in the background. Christian sang along quietly, though it was hard to hear that above Brutus's excited whimpers and his nails scratching on the polished cement in his little happy dance that she was home.

"Hello, big boy!" she cooed, giving him his due attention. "Who's a g'boy?" She noticed a black-and-white blur that jumped atop the arm of the couch. "Hail, Caesar!" Brutus finally getting his fill, she was able to stand up from him and walk over to the cat. "You're a g'boy, too, buddy," she murmured, rubbing his head and his ears before heading to the kitchen where Christian had begun cooking. "You're a g'boy, too," she murmured, hugging the dancer from the back and nuzzling her neck.

Christian chuckled. "Yes, yes I am. After all these years I forget to tell you about one tiny thing."

"I don't know," Gray said into the warm skin of her neck. "I've been on the receiving end when you have that thing strapped on. Not so tiny."

Christian grinned and turned her head to give her a proper kiss. "You're early," she said as the kiss broke, reaching her hand back to run her fingers through Gray's hair. "Get a ride?"

"I did, actually." Gray patted Christian's shapely ass before moving away from her. She lifted the strap of her messenger bag over her head and set it down on one of the bar stools. "Stir fry smells amazing, baby."

"Thank you, love. Can you grab me the soy sauce from the fridge, please?"

"Of course." Gray fetched the bottle, twisting off the cap before setting it on the counter beside the stovetop. "Richard gave me a ride."

Christian glanced over at her, surprise in her eyes. "Really? Did he like the profile?"

"He did," Gray said, leaning against the counter perpendicular to the area where Christian was working. "He wants me to write his memoir," she said, deciding to just throw it out there.

Christian's head snapped in her direction, mouth open. "Seriously?"

Gray nodded. "Yeah." She shrugged, sheepish. "Go figure." The look on the dancer's face made her feel so much pride. She adored and admired Christian so much that it had become her goal in life to make her partner just as proud, to see the awe and love she saw in that moment. It was deeply humbling as so often she felt unworthy of the woman standing a couple feet away because of the incredible heart and soul Christian possessed.

One hand still on the wooden spoon she was using to stir the contents in the pan, Christian used the other to cup the side of Gray's head, leaning over to leave a soft kiss on her lips. "I'm so proud of you," she whispered. "You so deserve this opportunity." One last kiss left, she dropped her hand and moved back to her place in front of the stove, a smile on her face as she met Gray's gaze.

"Thank you, baby," Gray said softly.

"You're so talented, Gray," Christian continued. "What you do with words blows my mind. I'm lucky if I can string words together to make a sentence, yet you string them together on paper to create an entire story." She smiled. "Even if you're just writing about the new pizza place opening around the corner."

Gray's smile just wouldn't leave her face as she looked down, staring at her feet for a moment. Her chest felt like it would explode with happiness and a sense of...what was it? *Finally*, perhaps? Finally, all the hard work she'd put into her career, into her craft, maybe finally it was paying off.

"I do have to ask." Christian paused her stirring. "How will you do that? You work fifty-plus hours a week at the paper and barely have time now to work on your own projects."

Right, Gray thought. Time for logistics. She reached back and gripped the counter edge lightly on either side of her with her hands. "Well, I know the paper loves it when we publish," she began. "Amir is pretty supportive of it, too."

"You know," Christian said, turning to look at Gray. "What about a sabbatical? Like that guy, what was his name, Jamar, did a couple years ago when he went to Africa for six months?"

Gray nodded, feeling a bit of hope. "Yes, I remember that."

"I hate to ask, sweetheart, but what about a paycheck during that time? Sure, we have some savings, but you should be able to keep your insurance, right?"

Gray nodded. "Yes. Well, Jamar was able to." She crossed one foot over the other, leaning back against the cabinet. "Richard said he wanted to hire me to do this. He wanted you and I to figure out what makes sense for us, then we're supposed to have dinner with him to talk about it."

"Me too?" Christian asked, looking surprised as she tapped the spoon on the side of the pan before removing it off the heat and turning off the burner.

"You too."

Christian studied her a long time, then said, "It's a huge honor, Gray. What do you want?"

Gray considered for about three seconds before saying, "I wanna do it."

※ ※ ※ ※

Gray looked around the space she'd been given in Richard Cox's New York offices, which she had no idea he even had. He had many real estate holdings within the country as well as a robust involvement in American films. The people who took care of his American business were housed within the space, which took up an entire floor of an office building in downtown Manhattan.

The office was far bigger than the cubicle she'd had at the paper, which had been kind enough to grant a six-month sabbatical. To ensure the book was done right without financial worries, Richard had agreed to a stipend twice what she would have made at the *Times* for those unpaid six months, with all expenses paid for work she did on the book, including meals, travel, and incidentals.

She had her laptop set up on the desk alongside a stack of books she'd checked out from the library—all biographies of him written over the years, some authorized, some not. All she'd been doing over the last two weeks was to get a sense of what had already been written about him so she could form an idea of where she wanted to go. Considering her charge was a memoir and not a biography, the content would be different, but the research would still give her an idea of what sort of questions to ask him, determine what parts of his life felt the most important to focus on, decide where to travel to learn about his life as well as which people to talk to.

She lowered the book she was reading and reached over to her laptop, tapping out another name she'd come across in several of the books. The spreadsheet listed important people and information she felt needed follow-up with the primary source, which Richard had been more than generous to provide during their nightly call.

She was about to return her focus back to the

book when her cell rang. She looked at it, and though it was a local number, didn't recognize it. She set the book aside and answered the call.

"Gray Rickman," she said into the small device, learning long ago in her profession that calls often came in from sources or people wanting to give a favored reporter a scoop. This, however, was not a scoop. "What?" she asked, shooting up in the chair. "Where is she?" She grabbed her keys and wallet from the desk drawer she'd dropped them in, nearly tripping on the chair as she bolted out of the office.

❧❧❧❧

She'd been sitting in the waiting room of New York-Presbyterian Hospital's ER for more than an hour, her knee jiggling nervously as she waited for word. Finally, a scrub-clad woman appeared and called out for Christian Scott's family.

She was led back through the department to a curtained-off cubicle where Christian lay on a bed, her left knee, the problem child, terribly swollen and bright pink. Christian's eyes were closed, obviously in a great deal of pain. Silent tears streamed down her cheeks.

"Hey, baby," Gray said softly, walking over to her.

Christian's eyes opened and she looked over at Gray, the pain in her eyes not just that of her physical situation, but emotional as well. "It finally popped," she whispered.

Gray looked at the knee. "ACL?"

Christian nodded. "I just got back from the Lachman test. Doctor said I'll have to have surgery."

"I'm so sorry, baby." Gray reached out and took

one of Christian's hands in her own. She knew it was a fear that they'd both been holding their breath about.

"You know," Christian said softly, more tears falling. Gray used her thumb to wipe away the newest. "All I've ever wanted to do was skate or dance."

Gray nodded. "I know," she whispered, bringing up their joined hands and leaving a kiss on the back of Christian's hand. "I know, baby."

"I know we talked about me retiring," Christian continued. "And I know I hadn't fully made a decision, but…" She looked away, more tears coming. "I wanted to *make* that decision."

"I know," Gray said, kissing her hand again before resting their hands on the bed beside Christian's thigh. "I'm so sorry, Christian. Are you okay? Other than this, did you get hurt?"

Christian let out a heavy sigh and shook her head, bringing up her other hand to use to wipe her tear-streaked cheeks. "No. Well." She smirked. "Other than my ego and my ass."

Gray gave her a small smile. She noticed a box of facial tissue on the small table near the bed and reached for it, grabbing a few tissues and handing them to the woman lying on the bed. "Well," she said quietly. "Not much I can do for your ego, but I'm certainly willing to kiss your ass anytime and make it better."

Christian looked at her, a sad smile on her lips. "I'll take you up on that."

※ ※ ※ ※

Gray slowly closed the bedroom door, letting out a heavy, tired sigh once she did. She heard Michael in the living room talking quietly to Brutus and Caesar. When she stepped out of the hallway that led to the bathroom and bedroom, she saw him sitting on the couch with the animals.

"She asleep?" he asked, glancing up at her.

"Yeah. The pain meds the doctor gave her finally kicked in." Gray plopped down next to him. "Thanks for coming over to help me get her in. I really appreciate that."

"Of course." Absently petting Caesar, he asked, "What now?"

"Surgery."

"Yeah. Tonight the elevator here was working, but how often does it break down?" he pointed out. "What are you going to do? She's going to be in a wheelchair for a while at least, and then on crutches. I mean," he added. "We're talking like a year's worth of healing here."

"I know." Gray ran a hand through her hair, staring at Brutus as the wheels turned in her head. "I know."

Chapter Five

"Okay," Gray said, stepping off the final stair to the large space before her. She grinned into the camera before turning the tablet so the room could be seen by the viewer eighteen hundred miles away. "This, my sweet, is why I think this may be a really, super-duper good fit for us."

The semi-basement had its own entrance and large windows to produce plenty of light in the expansive space.

"This long wall here, I figure we can run mirrors and a ballet barre along. And," she said, turning the camera back to her. "But wait, there's more!" She shifted the tablet again and aimed it down at the floor. "Already wood flooring. Mom, if you would demonstrate, please?"

Bernadette, who had been wandering around the room, looking at this and that, went into perfect formation and pirouetted across the space to the applause of the audience of one back in New York.

Gray turned the tablet around so she was looking at the screen again. "Huh, huh?" She returned the smile she received. "And the real kicker? This house, all three bedrooms, one dedicated office, half an acre plot, and full, finished basement is two hundred thousand less than the most inexpensive house we looked at there."

"Unreal," Christian said, shaking her head.

"What do you think?"

Gray looked up when she saw Bernadette walk toward her. She left a kiss to her cheek and a quick finger wave to Christian before heading for the stairs, clearly wanting to give the two privacy to talk.

"Honestly?" Gray said. "I think this place is perfect. Great neighborhood, definitely getting our bang for the buck, though I'm shocked how expensive Denver has gotten since I've been gone. Even still, this is a steal compared to New York."

Christian was quiet for a moment as she sipped from a mug of coffee, Caesar just barely visible in the shot where he was lying on the back of the couch nearby.

"You said the master bedroom is on the main floor?" she said at length.

"It is. And, plenty of room in the open floor plan for a wheelchair or crutches so you can get around easily after the surgery."

"I'm worried about money, Gray," Christian said, looking into the camera again, concern etched on her beautiful features. "You'd have to leave the *Times*."

Gray nodded. "Yes, but with the money we'd be able to put down on this place, our mortgage payment will be manageable. We've got a great buffer with the extra Richard gave me, plus with the contract I signed with Simon and Schuster, I get a share of the advance. No royalties, but by that point, I'll hopefully be on with the *Post* or another paper here in Denver."

Christian blew out a breath. Finally, she nodded. "Okay. If we can get this done quickly, then I can have the surgery in Denver. Want to put in an offer?"

"No, that one goes over there," Gray said, directing the man who worked for the moving company, his arms loaded with boxes.

The new house was awash with activity, movers, and family helping direct traffic as well as keep Brutus out of the way. Caesar was locked in an upstairs bedroom so he wouldn't jet out of an open door .

The past month had been a blur of packing, dealing with finances, haggling over incidentals between buyer and seller, and finding a renter for the New York apartment. But, it had all finally been resolved and finalized and keys exchanged.

"Gray," Bernadette said, hurrying over to her with a box that hadn't been labeled. "Is Christian and your dad still unpacking boxes?"

"They are, Mom. Last I saw them they were in the master bedroom." She glanced down at the box, shaking her head. "No clue where that one goes and why it got left untattooed. Just give it to them and they can figure it out."

"Done," her mother said, nearly skipping as she left Gray in the kitchen.

Gray watched her go before turning back to her task of sorting through the boxes of furry kid supplies to find their food and water bowls. She wanted to set them up as soon as possible in their permanent spot to help Brutus and Caesar get used to their new digs faster.

As night began to fall, the movers cleared out, finished with their cross-country journey, the big moving truck gone from their driveway. Driveway. Such a strange thing for her to be looking out at. Since moving out of her childhood home for college, she'd only lived in apartments from Colorado to New York.

Truth was, she hadn't expected to ever move back to the Centennial State. There hadn't been a whole lot of time for it to sink in that that's exactly what they'd done, but just her surface feelings, looking out at the quiet neighborhood, the beautiful Rockies a magnificent backdrop, said she was happy.

"Hey."

Gray turned around to see Christian making her way over to her on crutches. "Hey, baby. Did the guys get the bed put together?"

"They did." Christian wobbled up next to her, Gray carefully moving to stand behind her, wrapping her arms around her middle. Christian leaned back into her. "I am so exhausted."

"Me too." Gray left a kiss to the side of her head. "Let's go to bed. We can get as much done as we can tomorrow before your surgery on Tuesday."

※ ※ ※ ※

Gray's fingers raced across the keyboard as she sat in her home office just across the extra-wide hallway from the bedroom where Christian was still asleep. Her desk looked much like Amir's with papers everywhere, open books, her tablet open to message conversations as she worked on the first chapters of the book.

Normally she had the French doors closed and her music going so as not to disturb the household, but it was the second day after surgery, so she was listening for any signs that Christian needed her. She still had an hour before she was due her next batch of pain medications. The biggest bit of advice Gray had been given from Christian's doctors and some of her peers in the dance world who'd been checking in regularly: keep up on the pain meds. Don't let the pain get away from you. So, Gray had made that her mission while working, her phone alarm set to every four hours.

The publisher wanted to see the first six chapters by the end of the week, so she had to plow through them while doing her best to care for Christian. Her mother had offered to help, which was a godsend, and she'd be over the next morning.

As she worked, she heard the telltale *click, click* of Brutus's claws as he wandered into the room, tail lazily wagging from side to side. She glanced down into the adorable face that looked up at her expectantly. "Yes?" she drawled, reaching out to pet his head. "Gotta do your bidness, big boy?" She smiled at his little cheek-puffing *woof.* "Okay, I feel ya." She pushed back from the desk. "Let's get you gone."

Together they padded down the hallway that was off to the side of the large main space, which consisted of the open living room and kitchen, a perfect space for spending time with family and friends. Gray couldn't wait to host their first holiday. Though the holidays were swiftly coming, with the move and Christian's injury, she wasn't entirely sure if the holidays would have to be put on hold for that year.

"Go on, buddy," Gray said, opening the back set of French doors off the living room. Brutus was still learning about this whole pooping-in-his-own-yard thing without an audience or a leash. He did, however, love sniffing around.

It was a nice day, so she left the door open so he

could come in at will and headed to the bedroom to check on Christian. She knew she'd have to wake her for her medication in a bit. To her surprise, the dancer was awake, lying in bed and staring at the ceiling.

The bedroom was about twice as large as the one back in New York, the bathroom suite alone about as big as the larger of the two bedrooms in the apartment she and Michael had shared before she'd moved in with Christian.

The four-poster bed was set up and the dressers were moved in, but the mirrors weren't mounted, and their clothing was still largely in bags on the floor of the massive walk-in closet. Gray intended to get all that taken care of within the day. She also needed to finish unpacking the bathroom, with its two-person tub and separate walk-in shower surrounded by glass.

Though the house still felt a bit empty due to lack of furniture to fill it and lack of their personal energy to change it, it was their dream home. Gray was determined to make it so. She smiled when she saw the lone figure in the bed.

"Well, hey there, gorgeous," she said, noting Caesar lying on Gray's side of the bed. His tail began to twitch at her voice. "Grumpy," she drawled, addressing the black-and-white brat.

Christian turned her head and looked at Gray, her expression guarded. "Hey."

Gray walked over to the bed and sat on Christian's side, mindful of her leg. "How are you feeling?"

Christian shrugged a shoulder. "Okay, I guess."

"Are you in pain?" Gray asked, ready to push up from the bed. "I can get you your meds now. Only about twenty-three minutes earl—"

"No," Christian said softly, reaching out and

placing her hand on Gray's leg, indicating she wanted her to stay. "I'm okay. I can wait."

Gray's eyebrows fell, concern filling her. As she looked at the woman lying there, she saw no spark. The amazing life-light she'd always had in her deep green eyes was dull and dim, and had been ever since the injury. Many of Christian's colleagues had reached out to her, wanting to do something special for Christian, be it on stage or privately to celebrate her run in the show that she had to leave prematurely, but Christian wanted no part of it. Gray hoped that she wouldn't come to regret that.

As she looked back at her fiancée, she could see that something was wrong, yet she didn't think it was something so easy or black and white to simply ask, *What's wrong?* She opted to sit quietly with her, her hand resting atop where Christian's still lay on Gray's leg. As suspected, Christian began to speak.

"I'm sorry, Gray," she said softly. She met Gray's gaze as she let out a heavy sigh. "I never saw my life going like this." She gave her a small smile. "I'm only pushing my mid-thirties, and I'm already useless."

Gray felt her heart break as she used her other hand to lightly caress Christian's cheek. "You're not useless, sweetheart," she said. "Not at all."

"I've taken you from your job, from your sources and colleagues." She looked away, so much tension in her face. "You've worked so hard at the paper. Taken you from Michael. Your life," she finished in a whisper.

"Baby?" Gray said, gently using her fingers to turn Christian's head so she was facing her again. "None of that matters. And, you didn't take me away from my life. *You* are my life." She gave her what she hoped was a winning smile. "As long as I'm with you, I'm home." She nodded toward the large windows in the bedroom. "The mountains out there are just a bonus."

Christian gave her a ghost of a smile but quickly sobered. "What about the paper?" she asked. "Your sabbatical is up in a few months."

"I spoke to Linda yesterday," Gray explained. "She's still at *The Denver Post* and was my boss before when I worked there. She said she'd be thrilled to bring me back on." Gray considered if she should share her news in that moment when Christian seemed so down and so unsure of herself and her place in the world. This was something she understood all too well. Pretty much her entire life pre-college was wondering who the hell she was and what she was supposed to do.

"What?" Christian asked gently. "You look like you're about to explode. Good news?"

"Yeah," Gray said, feeling shy. "Richard told me that when I head to Scotland next week to talk to his family, he wants to introduce me to some other folks who are interested in working with me on a book."

Christian's eyes widened and, for the first time in days, a genuine smile lit up her face. "That's wonderful, Gray!"

"Thanks." Gray felt a bit guilty delivering such potential for opportunity when Christian lay in that large bed looking so small and lost.

"I'm so sorry I can't go with you on your trip, Gray," Christian continued. "One country I've never been to."

"No, I understand, baby," Gray said, running her thumb over the soft skin of the back of Christian's hand. "You start PT next week, which is so important.

We gotta get you back on your feet, woman, so we can get married." She grinned. "Gotta put a ring on it before you realize I'm a pain in the ass."

Laughter escaped Christian's lips. "Oh, baby, I realized that when you were checking me out at the ripe old age of seventeen."

Gray chuckled. "Yeah, but you seduced me anyway," she said, stealing a kiss. "Want some coffee?" she asked, grateful for the lighter mood.

"That actually sounds amazing. And," Christian added. "Didn't you mention I have some pain pills coming my way?"

"I did." Gray scooted off the bed and pulled the covers back to the eternal annoyance of Caesar, who found himself beneath said covers. With a huff, he crawled out and glared at Gray before stretching and jumping down from the bed. "Crutches or chair?" Gray asked, channeling her inner Vanna White as she presented both items.

"Oh, chair," Christian murmured, slowly scooting her body toward the edge of the bed. "My armpits need a break."

"Chair it is, madam," Gray said, setting the crutches aside and grabbing the handles of the wheelchair to push toward the bed. "Want help?" She was trying to be more understanding of Christian's need for independence in her recovery rather than follow her natural impulse to take any burden off her partner.

"I think I got this," Christian murmured, concentrating as she got her one good leg under her and pivoted to turn around. Gray was surprised she hadn't seen the tip of her tongue poking out from the corner of her mouth, as she looked just like a little kid trying to climb down from a bed that was too high for short little legs.

Finally, after painstaking effort, Christian got herself lowered into the chair, held steady by Gray. "Excellent work, my love. By George, I think you've got this."

Christian let out a tired sigh. "Good Lord. It shouldn't exhaust me just to get into the damn wheelchair."

"Eh," Gray said dismissively as she got the chair turned around and headed out of the room. "Time, my love. Before long, you'll be good as new."

They made their way toward the kitchen, the rubber wheels of the chair squeaking quietly along the polished wood flooring. Brutus bounded into the house, tongue hanging out of the side of his mouth as he scampered up to Christian, butt about to shake off with the frantic wag of his tail in his excitement.

"Hey, big boy," she greeted, trying to duck his excited tongue. "I love you too."

Gray was amused as she set the brake on the chair, a lesson hard won after Brutus nearly sent an unsuspecting Christian down the basement stairs backward in her chair. "Okay, coffee on the way," she said, making her way to the kitchen. "Or, do you want your pain meds first?"

"How about you get coffee started, give me my meds while the coffee brews, then it'll be closer to being ready?" Christian suggested with a raised eyebrow.

"Smart girl," Gray muttered, moving around the kitchen to gather the things needed to make two mugs of coffee on their single-cup maker.

"What time is Bernie coming tomorrow?" Christian asked, Brutus's love attack ending as she wheeled herself toward the open back door.

"I think around nine." Gray hit the start button on the machine before grabbing a juice glass from the cabinet to fill with water. "What do you want to eat, baby? Gotta eat with these bad boys."

"Do we have any yogurt?" Christian asked, turning her chair and heading to the kitchen.

"No," Gray said apologetically. "We need to get groceries." She walked over to Christian and held her hands out, glass of water in one and pain pill in the other.

Christian plucked it off her palm with her fingers before popping it into her mouth, followed by a healthy drink of the offered water. "You know what?" Christian said after swallowing it down. "That's what Bernie and I will do tomorrow," she said with conviction. "We'll go grocery shopping."

Gray studied her for a moment. "Are you sure? I was going to go today."

Christian shook her head. "No, I need to get out of the house, Gray. I've barely done that since we moved in." She smiled up at Gray, reaching for her hand. "I think it'll be good for me."

Chapter Six

"Oh. My. God." Gray was all eyes as she ducked and weaved in the back seat of the sleek black 1954 Bentley to get a better view. The classic luxury car had picked her up from Glasgow International Airport and now was pulling up to a massive structure in the Scottish countryside.

The car drove down along a long cobblestone road that wound in front of a massive castle made of grey stone. The many peaks, towers and connected buildings were something out of a Medieval fairytale, though clearly the structure was in great repair and inhabited. Lights blazed from nearly every window, dozens upon dozens of them—perhaps even hundreds.

"What is this place?" she asked the driver, who had remained silent during their entire hour drive.

"This is Castle McCann, miss," the driver responded, his Scottish brogue apparent.

That told her absolutely nothing. "Is this the hotel?" The man holding a sign with her name on it at the airport had told her he'd be taking her to where she'd be staying.

"No, miss," he said. "Mr. Cox's residence."

"Holy shit," she whispered, face nearly glued to the window as she tried to take it all in. There were a couple cars parked out front, but there were no people around. The long, winding drive was like a racetrack, where the Bentley could stop in front of the stone steps that were about one hundred feet wide, then continue on around another curve to head back the way it had come, the two tracks parallel to each other with lush greenery landscaped along the length between them.

The double doors at the top of the stairs were huge, arched and wooden, and ribbed with iron. When the doors were closed, as they currently were, they looked like a drawbridge protecting the massive front wall of the structure. The windows in the front wall even resembled arrow slits, though presently they had been outfitted with glass.

The car pulled to a stop and the driver got out, walking around to her side in the back and pulling open her door. "Your luggage will be brought in for ya, miss."

"Thank you," she said with a polite smile, climbing out of the car.

She felt hugely intimidated as she walked up the stone steps, wondering just exactly whose footsteps she was walking in. As she reached the ten-foot doors, one side swung inward, revealing, to her surprise, a sizable courtyard surrounded by the outer wall of what seemed to be the exterior of the main structure.

A smaller, human-sized door was located on the opposite side of the courtyard, which was open to the nighttime Scottish sky, ablaze with stars. The courtyard was filled with beautiful landscaping, potted plants, and fountains that released their calming melody as they did what fountains do. Tables and chairs were set out for people to sit and chat, or read, perhaps. She thought it would be a wonderful place to write, especially at the bench settled near what looked to be an ancient fireplace, its stone face smoked black from centuries of use.

She made her way along the stone path to the door, and when it opened, Richard was standing on the other side.

"Greetings, young writer!"

Gray smiled. "Hello, Richard. Some place, you've got here." She was relieved to see him, as it had been a very long trip of strangers in a strange land.

"Back to my roots, at least on my mother's side of the family," he explained, ushering her inside. "Believe it or not, this castle was abandoned for nearly as long as your country has been the United States." He glanced at her as he led her through a maze of dark hallways and corridors. "I purchased it nearly forty years ago, and it's been a four-decade love affair with bringing her back to life."

"This place is like something out of a movie," Gray murmured, looking at a suit of armor mounted to a stand. No doubt it was authentic. "Wow."

"Indeed. I hope you don't mind that I have you set up here," he said, leading her into a circular tower, the stone stairs spiraling round and round as they corkscrewed their way upward.

It was so easy to imagine lit torches or candles in the stone nooks as opposed to the can lighting currently shining down on small art pieces of metal or glass.

"So, would it bother you if this place ended up in a book someday?" she asked.

He chortled. "Of course not! If you need information on it, just ask."

They left the fourteenth century and entered a present-day hallway with regular walls, a rug runner over the stone floor, and modern light fixtures. The only nod to the castle's historical roots were the two doors on either side of the corridor, elaborate and arched and ribbed with iron, much like those at the front of the building.

"These are our guest rooms," he explained, taking her to the last one on the left, the door standing open in invitation. "Please, get refreshed as I have a few people here who would like to meet you."

She looked at him, surprised. "Oh?"

"Yes. Some are the people you'll be meeting with this week, while others are friends of mine who are interested in perhaps pursuing your talents. So," he added, stepping away from her. "When you're ready, simply join us downstairs."

"Um," Gray said, glancing back the way they'd come. She'd seen nothing that would take her anywhere that made sense.

"That way," he said, pointing toward the opposite end of the hall from where they'd entered, not far from her own door. "Those stairs will take you directly down to us."

She ducked her head forward and to the side. "Oh. Okay." She smiled at him, then stepped back into the room, closing the thick, heavy door.

The bedroom was a suite, replete with sitting room and ginormous bedroom with large, chunky furniture that belonged in a king's bedchamber. She had her own fireplace which, if it hadn't been lit, she could have easily stepped inside of. To her shock—and confusion—her luggage was already placed neatly near the oversized armoire.

The bathroom was something she couldn't help but think would have Christian nearly giddy. She seemed to like their master bath back home, but considering a peewee league of football players could hold a scrimmage in the one she now stood in, she figured she should take some video to send home.

Thirty minutes later, with her clothing changed, face washed, and teeth brushed, Gray felt somewhat presentable and headed downstairs. Sure enough, the long, grand staircase led straight down to a huge open area flanked on all sides by twenty-foot arches, presumably gateways to other parts of the castle.

The open area seemed to be an inner sanctum of the castle, designed to either work as a hub for the other six directions to choose from, or to act, as it currently was, as a large space for get-togethers.

A couple dozen people or so were gathered in various stages of finery from the casual pair of jeans to the obviously custom-tailored suit. They mingled, many carrying wine glasses or tumblers of various types of liquor or mixed drink.

She reached the bottom of the stairs and was met by a uniformed waiter carrying an empty silver tray. "What can I get ya, miss?"

"Oh," she said, unsure. "Um, do you have white zinfandel?"

With a curt nod, he turned on his heel and disappeared through one of the archways. She saw Richard standing with a small group, a peel of laughter garnering her attention there. She felt nervous and completely out of her depth as she recognized some major stars of the film industry, a couple men she thought were NFL players, and a handful of well-known singers. She also saw an extremely attractive woman wandering around by herself, an impressive camera dangling from her neck by a strap. She seemed to be eyeing the crowd looking for a good shot.

"There she is." Richard walked over to her,

brandy snifter in hand, and placed an arm around her shoulders. "Everyone! Can I have your attention," he said, his deep baritone echoing off the stone of the carved ceiling above, marble floor below, and cavernous space around them. "I'd like to introduce you to our guest of honor, all the way from Denver, Colorado," he announced, glancing over to one of the guests. "Your old stomping ground, Mr. Hall-of-Fame," he added cheekily. "Gray Rickman!"

Gray felt shy as a round of applause sounded. She raised her hand in a small wave of acknowledgment. "Hello."

"Our young writer here hails from *The New York Times* before moving recently to Colorado for personal reasons. And now," he added. "Here she is. All the way in Scotland to help my big mouth become even bigger on paper."

Gray grinned with the laughter that filtered through the gathered group.

"Now, she's had a very long day of travel, so go easy on her," Richard advised. "I need her brain fully intact this week." He squeezed her shoulder in good humor. He raised his hand, waving someone over with his fingers. The woman with the camera Gray had noticed made her way over to them. "Hello, Fatima."

The woman, who had Middle Eastern features with darker hair, olive-tone skin, and beautiful large, hazel eyes, smiled. "Hello," she greeted Gray.

"Hi." Gray's attention was grabbed by the waiter who zoomed over to her, a single chilled glass of wine upon his silver tray. She smiled as she took the crystal goblet. "Thank you." As he walked away she turned back to the woman and Richard.

"Gray, this is Fatima Darmandi, the amazing

photographer I've used for years. She's taken many of my headshots and will be taking the pictures for our little tome that you're currently hatching."

Amused by his choice of words, Gray chuckled. "Nice to meet you, Fatima." She extended her hand that wasn't holding the wine.

"You, as well," the photographer said, shaking her hand. "Richard has invited me here for a few days to snap shots of you working, the people you'll be interviewing, you and Richard talking, and the like."

Gray nodded. "Okay, wonderful. Just let me know what you need from me as I am anything but photogenic," she added with a nervous laugh. Truth was, she hated being in pictures or on film.

Fatima smirked. "Oh, I doubt that," she said, then moved out of the way as other guests began to surround Gray. She was taken off guard by the comment but didn't have a chance to give it much thought as the newcomers politely clamored for her attention.

❧❧❦❦

The grounds of the castle were just as incredible as the inside. It sat on hundreds of private acres, seemingly endless rolling Scotland green. Gray strolled with Richard in the gardens up closer to the compound.

"So," he said, hands clasped behind his back. "Do you feel you got all the access you needed this week?"

"I do," she said, nodding. "Your first wife was going to get back to me before I leave tomorrow regarding your son who…Um…"

"Died," he offered, giving her a sincere but sad smile. "It's all right to say. We tried everything we knew how with Martin, but those opioids kept calling his name, like a siren's song. He was gay, you know," he added.

Gray met his gaze, eyebrows raised. "Really?"

"Yes. I think that was part of his using, to be honest." He let out a heavy sigh. "It was the eighties," he said. "Things were different back then for those of you in the LGBT community."

"Sadly, yes," Gray added. "It's not easy today, either, but I certainly concede it's much better than it was forty years ago. But I'm truly sorry, Richard. That must have been terrible to lose a child like that."

They walked in in silence for a moment, the cool day threatening to give way to more drizzling rain. Gray had never been anywhere that was placed under such a perpetual sprinkler. Richard looked up into the brooding, overcast heavens and raised the hand that had been using his umbrella as a walking stick, the umbrella flicking open with a *thwoop*. He changed it from his right hand to his left so the canopy covered them both as the rain began to fall.

"So," he said. "What's left for you to do for the book, then?"

"Well," Gray said, grateful for the cover as the temperature seemed to drop by several degrees as the skies above began to weep. "Once I get home, I need to organize the hours and hours of interviews I've done while here. Listen to them all and figure out exactly where they belong, how I can interlace them all together to create your story, based on your own words, impressions, and stories."

"Have you enjoyed the process?" he asked, leading them back toward the castle.

"I have. Much more than I ever thought, honestly." She grinned, shoving her hands into the pockets of her jacket. "It's kind of like if journalism and all its research, and fiction writing with all its story-weaving, had a love child, your memoir would be it."

He threw his head back as a bark of laughter escaped his lips. "I love it." He placed his arm over her shoulder in his fatherly way. "Come. Let's go get warm."

⁂

Gray started, not entirely sure what had awoken her as her eyes blinked a few times. She found that she lay on her left side in the massive bed made to sleep about eight. As much as she was looking forward to getting home to Christian, she was loath to leave the bed that was like sleeping on a cloud.

Wakefulness coming stronger, she felt a bit of a chill and realized that in the night the tank top she slept in had gotten strangely twisted, the strap fallen, leaving her shoulder bare and sticking out from the covers.

Figuring that was probably what had woken her, she turned to her back and stared up at the underside of the bed's canopy for a long moment, trying to gather her wherewithal for the day's journey home. It had been a long, productive, and amazing week, but she craved having Christian next to her at night and waking up to her in the morning. She missed her smile, her kisses, and just everything *her*.

Finally, she shoved the covers off her and made herself leave the warm cocoon to shower and finish packing. As she padded her way across the room, there was a soft knock on her bedroom door, which she knew was actually quite a firm bang to be heard through the thick wood at all.

She partially hid behind the door after pulling it open as she was only dressed in the tank top, since straightened and adjusted, and a pair of mesh shorts. Fatima stood on the other side, sans camera—the only time Gray had seen her without it. The two hadn't spoken again after that initial introduction, the woman like a phantom that seemed to appear and disappear at will, snapping away to get the perfect picture for the book.

"Hey," Gray said, a question in her eyes.

"Hi. Hope I didn't wake you?" Fatima said. When Gray shook her head, she continued. "Richard just called. He's sending Roger to pick us up in the Bentley to take us to the airport in about an hour." She glanced down at her phone. "Or, a little less now. So, figured I'd let you know."

"Great, okay," Gray said, nodding. "I was just getting my wits together for the day, so great timing." She returned the other woman's smile. "Thanks for the heads-up."

"No problem. See you in a bit." With her message delivered, Fatima turned around and headed back down the hall to her own room.

Chapter Seven

"Hello, Mom!" Gray allowed herself to be enveloped in one of Bernadette's bone-crushing hugs. As small as the woman was, she packed a wallop when it came to the art of the embrace. "How are you?"

"I'm good," Bernadette said, grabbing one of Gray's bags and rolling it to her SUV, back hatch open and waiting. "Been a busy week." She stood by as Gray loaded her other bag into the back before slamming the hatch down, the two walking to their respective sides of the vehicle to get in.

"Oh, yeah?" Gray asked, getting herself settled and buckled in.

"Your father got his newest rendition of the Dennis-mobile." Bernadette glanced at the rearview mirror before she pulled away from the curb, a taxicab honking at her as it rushed past her. "Asshole," she muttered. "Anyway…"

Gray listened as she prattled on and on about the new show they were getting ready for, a new crop of dancers that had signed up for classes, the plumber they hired who seemed to be an idiot, the changing of the season. One thing, however, that her mother hadn't mentioned was Christian.

"So," Gray began, watching as the familiar landscape passed by, including the God-awful Denver Devil Horse.

It was a mammoth sculpture of a rearing bronco painted blue with glowing red eyes. It was meant to honor the state's football team, the Denver Broncos, but to Gray all it did was make those about to fly leery of perhaps a curse put on them by the demonic creature, or make those arriving eager to leave the airport grounds.

Taking her eyes off the horse, she returned her focus to her worries. "How's Christian?"

Bernadette let out a long sigh and remained quiet for a moment. Then she finally said, "She's okay." She glanced over at Gray. "She had a bit of a setback."

"What?" Gray exclaimed. "Why didn't you tell me? I spoke to one or both of you almost every day."

"Well," Bernadette said. "I didn't want to worry you."

"What happened?" Gray asked, her heart pounding.

"Brutus got a little excited and knocked her down."

"What?" Gray was upset now. "Why didn't you tell me? I would have come home—"

"Which," Bernadette said firmly, though her voice softened as she continued. "Was why I didn't tell you." She met Gray's angry gaze with the look only a mother of many years can give. "She had us."

"And, she's okay?" Gray asked, calming, though only slightly.

"MRI showed no tearing or damage, but unfortunately, it had a bad effect on her emotionally and mentally."

Gray ran a hand through her hair, deep concern hitting her square in the gut. "So, what now?"

"I think it's going to take some time, Gray,"

she said gently. "Christian was hitting the end of the road in her career, at least at the level of dancing she was doing, but she still wanted it to be her choice to make." She let out a sigh, shaking her head. "Here's the rub for someone like Christian," she continued. "She had an endless well of talent, amazing genetics, and it seemed like the possibilities were limitless. So this woman, who in chronological age is in her thirties, has the face of a woman in her twenties, and knees, ankles, and hips of a woman in her seventies." She shook her head again. "So damned unfair."

"I know there were some women in the latest show who were clearly vying for her spot," Gray said, feeling sad.

"Oh, no doubt," Bernadette agreed. "Though you may share a bond and camaraderie with your castmates, it's a dog-eat-dog industry, Gray. That aspect I never did miss."

Gray nodded and was silent for a long moment as she watched the scenery pass, evidence of a recent snow on display. "I wonder if spending some time with Dad would be good for her. I mean," she said, glancing over at her mother. "If anyone knows what it's like to have a career cut due to injury, it's him."

"I've considered that too," Bernadette said. "I think it would be good for her. But," she added, reaching over and slapping Gray on the leg. "What she needs more than anything is you, sweetheart. I'm glad you're home."

≈≈≈≈

Bernadette pulled into the house that had yet to truly feel like a home to Gray, regardless of the fact that the woman she loved, the animals she loved, and all of her belongings resided inside. Their short time in the structure hadn't yielded the homeness to make it feel like theirs—yet. She knew that would be a matter of time.

Climbing out of the SUV, she and Bernadette each took a roller bag as they headed up the unoccupied side of the driveway and to the three steps that landed on the expansive front porch and door.

Through the beveled glass panes, she could make out the image of Brutus loping toward the front door, his deep, resonating barks heard. She smiled at the thought of getting loves from her pup, even as she dreaded likely being pinned against the wall. This was one of the longest times she'd been away from the big guy since she'd moved in with Christian.

"Come here, Brutus. Brutus! Come."

Gray smiled at the sound of Christian's voice calling the big dog back to corral him into another room while Gray and Bernadette entered. Once the all-clear was called out, Gray unlocked the dead bolt—the setting of which was a habit ingrained after living in New York for so long—and pushed the door open.

"Hey, Caesar," she greeted, the black-and-white cat sitting primly in the middle of the entryway hall, staring up at her. "How are you, sweet boy?" She set her large roller bag aside and bent down to give him proper loves, Brutus's anxious whimpers not far away.

Not wanting to chance the powerful bullmastiff hurting Christian again, she made sure Christian was safely seated before letting the canine free. She quickly gave him the attention he made so pitifully clear that he needed.

"Hello, buddy," Gray said, bending over and

giving him love. "Who's a g'boy?" Once he'd had his fill, Brutus trotted off to curl up in his bed by the window and plop down with a groan. Amused, Gray shook her head before turning her attention finally to the woman she loved. "Hey, baby."

"Hey, yourself," Christian murmured, a smile on her face as she stood and took Gray into a tight, all-encompassing embrace.

Gray's eyes fell closed as she absorbed her warmth and scent, so familiar, so comforting. It felt like it had been a month since she'd last touched Christian, even though it had only been six days. The hug ended many moments later and Gray cupped Christian's jaw.

As Bernadette had pointed out, Christian was a woman in her mid-thirties, but to Gray, she'd always be that twenty-three-year-old who had first captured her eye, then her imagination, and finally, her heart. She smiled, lightly caressing the soft skin of the dancer's face before leaning in for a kiss, which was returned.

Once they parted, Gray was able to see that Christian stood with no crutches, her left leg wrapped in the large, cumbersome brace that reached from nearly mid-thigh down to her lower shin.

"How are you feeling?" she asked, looking into Christian's eyes. "Mom told me about Brutus."

Christian nodded, giving Gray a small smile and shrug. "Guess it happens, huh? I'm okay. Doing my best to abide by Dr. Bowman's many, many rules and my home PT assignments."

"Good." Gray looked down at her brace and smiled at her. "It's so nice to see you upright. When I left, you were still on crutches."

Christian grinned. "Yes, well, the good doc took those away."

"Bad, Dr. Bowman," Gray murmured playfully. Gray had been so lost in Christian, she'd forgotten her mother was even there until she wheeled one of Gray's suitcases past the couple. "Mom, I'm sorry," she called past Christian, who turned to follow Bernadette's progress past them and toward their bedroom. "I'll get that."

"No worries, honey," her mother called back to her. "You two catch up."

"Think we grossed her out with our exuberant hello kiss?" Christian asked with a shy grin.

Gray returned the grin. "Hey, coulda been way worse," she said, reaching around and playfully goosing Christians glorious ass, which earned her a gasp and a swat to the arm.

"Okay," Bernadette said, coming back from dropping off the luggage. She gave Christian a quick peck on the cheek, then one for Gray. "I'll leave you two be. Dinner," she said, pointing at them both in turn. "Our house. Tomorrow night. I'll call with details. Love you!" trailed behind her as she headed for the front door.

Gray watched her go then turned back to Christian with a raised eyebrow. "Did everything go okay while I was gone?"

Christian nodded. "I think she's letting us have time together. That being said, care to join me while I take my meds?"

Gray snapped to attention, heels of her boots clicking together next to Christian. With military precision, she squared her shoulders, puffed out her chest, then, almost as an afterthought, she extended her right arm to the side before bending at the elbow. She waited until Christian, who was giggling, placed her hand in the crook of her arm.

"Who says chivalry is dead?" Christian muttered.

"Not this girl," Gray said dramatically.

☙☙❧❧

Opening her eyes, Gray realized she was alone. The room was still dark, other than moonlight coming in through the window, painting a window-shaped beam across the floor of the bedroom. Further inspection revealed that Brutus, too, was gone, which meant Christian had been gone for a bit and wasn't just in the bathroom.

Sitting up, the covers fell to expose naked breasts to the middle-of-the-night chill. Climbing out of bed, Gray tugged on her discarded sweats and sweatshirt from the night before and left the bedroom.

Brutus met her in the hall, looking up at her with his big brown eyes, a little whine coming from him before he turned and led the way to Christian, who was sitting on the couch, her braced leg stretched out to rest along the cushions while her good leg was pulled up against her chest. She sat somewhat sideways on the couch, her back cradled in the corner between the back cushion and the arm.

The lights were off, much like the bedroom, only the moonlight coming in through the window to show the way. She walked to the couch, running her fingers through Christian's hair once she reached her. Christian said nothing, but leaned into the touch.

"What can I do?" Gray asked softly.

Christian looked up at her. "Coffee?"

Gray smiled. Not exactly what she meant, but at least it was something tangible that she could make happen. "You got it." She bent down and left a kiss to the top of a blond head before making her way to the kitchen. "Mind if I turn on the light, baby?"

"No."

Gray flicked on the light as she readied the single-cup coffee maker. She glanced over at the couch several times, her eyebrows drawn. Christian had always been a quiet person—it was just her nature—but not as quiet as she had been since Gray's return from Scotland. They still talked, interacted, and had even made love for the first time since the surgery. But this quiet, a quiet of soul, was new.

New, and unsettling. It was a quiet not born of peace, but a quiet like the calm before the storm. She knew Christian dealt with things internally before she was ready to talk about them, and though at times that could be frustrating for Gray as she always wanted to help, she'd come to understand and accept that fact about her fiancée. She wasn't sure this time, however, if Christian was trying to work through things or just burying them.

While the coffee brewed, she walked over to the opposite end of the couch and oh-so-gently lifted her outstretched leg to rest in her own lap as she sat down. She looked over at her love, who looked back at her. "Hi."

Christian gave her a small smile. "Hey, baby."

"Talk to me. What's swirling around in that gorgeous head of yours?"

Christian shook her head. "It's stupid."

"Christian," Gray said gently. "If it's bothering you, it's anything but stupid." She placed her hand on

Christian's foot. "Please talk to me."

"I've watched you," Christian began softly, resting her head against a closed fist as her elbow rested against the back cushion. "Over the years. From a teenager who had no clue who you were to a woman who really found her stride at the paper." She smiled, a genuine smile that reached her eyes. "So confident in yourself, your leads, your stories." Her smile broadened. "It was insanely sexy to watch you on CNN, talking about some massive story you broke that they picked up."

Gray grinned, feeling a little shy. "You never told me that."

"Oh, yeah," Christian admitted. "If I could, I'd bring it up on my phone during rehearsal and watch my friends ohh and ahh over you as you did your thing. I was very proud to be your biggest fan. Still am."

"But?" Gray asked, uncertain.

"No but," Christian assured. "It's just, I watch you now, so dedicated to your work, closed up in your office for sometimes thirteen hours a day, pounding out Richard's book. It's so wonderful to see you so focused, so excited about this. And you've been telling me all about your trip, the people you met." She looked away, out into the night through the French doors that led to the backyard. Clearing her throat, she said softly, "Who am I? Compared to all of those people."

"That's easy," Gray responded, waiting until Christian looked at her again. "You're my biggest fan and the only one I care about." She tried a winning smile, but quickly let it go as she knew what troubled Christian was beyond that. "You told me once that you felt so lost after everything happened with your figure skating career when you were young. You were taking classes from Mom and dancing at that club."

"Oh, Lord," Christian said, rolling her eyes. "Don't remind me of that place."

Gray smiled. "Hey, I happen to have some pretty damn good memories of that club."

"Okay, fair," Christian said, a sly grin on her lips.

"Anyway, I didn't realize it at the time because I didn't know you that well, but when we first met, you had this quiet, almost dark thunderstorm rumble to you. Like, at any moment you could break open and explode."

Christian nodded. "Also fair."

"What I didn't realize back then was that thunderstorm was you being confused. Confused because you'd just lost everything you'd known. Forced to start over."

Christian looked down at her lap, nodding. "Again, fair."

"Baby?" When Christian looked up at her, she said, "I hear the distant thunder." With a gentle touch, she caressed the foot, her hand rested atop. "Why don't we start getting you out a bit?" she suggested. "You've been cooped up now for a couple months, both back in New York and since we've moved here. You're more mobile, and the doc said it would be good for you to be up and around more anyway, so..." She shrugged.

Christian nodded. "Okay. I think that would be good."

Chapter Eight

"So," Gray began, thinking back to what she'd just witnessed. "According to your torture master, you could be totally healed by spring," she said, bringing her giant mug of mocha breve with whipped cream to her lips. "Right?"

Christian smirked. "Torture master. You are not wrong. And, from what she said, yes." She also lifted her mug, blowing over the surface to cool the chai tea within.

Gray sipped her breve, noticing a woman standing near the door behind the man she'd been sitting with. He was pulling the door open for them to leave. The woman seemed to be in her forties perhaps, with short brown hair a bit of grey streaking the strands.

She and the man had been sitting just a few tables behind them, Gray and the woman facing each other. The woman had looked over at them often, particularly when Christian was speaking or laughing. Gray didn't recognize her, nor did she see any real recognition in the woman's brown eyes toward her. So, she had to wonder if the woman perhaps thought she knew Christian.

"Do you know that woman?" she asked, nodding toward the door.

Christian turned, but by the time she looked, the door to the coffee shop was closing, the couple gone. She turned back to Gray. "Who?"

"She left. Forties," Gray explained. "Brown hair with some grey. She kept looking over here."

Christian looked again, obviously to no avail. She shook her head with a shrug. "No idea. Maybe she's seen me at PT or the doctor."

Gray nodded. "I hadn't even thought of that. Probably. So," she added, eyebrows lifted in question. "I was thinking if your knee is up for it, wanna head to the mall and look around? It'll be all decorated for Christmas and isn't all that far away."

"Yeah, let's do it." Christian's smile was beautiful.

※ ※ ※ ※

Gray loved the holidays. The mall was fully decorated, Christmas music piped in to deck the halls with holiday joy. Red, green, silver, and gold was plastered over anything that would sit still, the big man in red sitting on his throne in the winter wonderland created just so the kids of the area could give their Christmas wish list.

Hand in hand they strolled, taking it as slow as Christian needed to. In Gray's opinion, the dancer looked gorgeous in a holiday-red sweater and multicolored broom skirt, which was a creative way to cover her leg brace. She felt self-conscious of it and couldn't wear it under pants, so the skirt was the best option for an outing.

"I really don't know what to get her," Gray said, the handles of the bag carrying the gift they'd bought for her father held snugly in her hands. "Mom is so damn hard to buy for."

"I'll pry," Christian said with a conspiratorial

grin. "See if I can find out what she wants or needs."

"Oh, by all means, yes," Gray responded. "I guess if all else fails, we can go the bubble bath route. I know she loves to soak—"

"Chrissy?"

Gray and Christian both stopped at the female voice coming from behind them. Gray looked to her partner to see a look of confusion on her face. When Gray looked to the owner of the voice, she was shocked to see the woman they'd seen less than an hour ago at The Mean Bean.

"Chrissy Scott?" the woman asked.

Christian stared at her for a moment before she gasped, a hand coming up to cover her mouth, eyes huge. "Oh, my god," she whispered behind her hand.

Gray looked from Christian to the woman and then to the man with her, who looked as confused as Gray felt. She and the man met eyes for a brief moment before turning their attention back to their respective ladies, who clearly knew each other.

Christian let out a small sob, then threw herself at the woman who eagerly accepted her embrace. After several moments, the women parted, the taller, older woman holding Christian at arm's length as she took her in.

"Good Lord! Do you ever age?" she asked, excited laughter in her voice.

Christian wiped at her eyes with her sleeve and chuckled. "Trust me, I do." She turned to Gray. "Gray, this is Yancy Pritchard. She and I were on the same Olympic team." She turned back to look at the other woman. "The last one I was on." She smiled then looked back to Gray. "But, we knew each other for a bit before that."

"Yeah," Yancy said. "This little shit took *my* place when I was still skating singles back in oh-two." She grinned. "You're why I went into pairs skating."

Christian burst into laughter, the sound music to Gray's ears, so hungry for some joy in her partner. "Not my fault." The woman looked to Gray with questions in her eyes before looking back to Christian, who clearly got the point. "Yancy, this is my fiancée, Gray Rickman."

Yancy smiled and extended a hand. "Nice to meet you, Gray." The woman indicated the man with her, who stepped forward. "This is my husband, Tony." She studied Christian for a long moment, shaking her head. "I can't believe it. The last time I saw you was—"

"The trial," Christian said, finishing the sentence for her.

Yancy nodded. "Yeah." She pulled Christian in for another tight hug before releasing her. "Okay, we have to get going," she said. "Just came to grab a quick gift for our son. But..." She pulled out her cell phone from her purse and looked at Christian expectantly. The dancer gave her her phone number, which the older woman tapped into her phone. "Got it. Gray, it was nice meeting you," Yancy said, smiling at her before she and her husband quickly headed off.

Left alone, Gray looked to Christian, who seemed to be caught up in a whirlwind of emotions. "Are you okay?" she asked softly.

Christian nodded, then looked up at Gray. "Can we go home?"

༄༄༄༄

Christian was quiet as they drove through the

busy streets to get back home. Gray said nothing, which was hard as all she wanted to do was ask questions. It was clear this Yancy person, seeing her again, had a profound effect on the dancer. Why?

Gray's thoughts were interrupted when her phone rang. The Bluetooth in their new SUV, which they'd had to buy upon moving back to Colorado, played the caller's voice through the car speakers.

"Hello?"

"Gray, it's Janice." The somewhat piercing voice belonged to her high-octane editor for the Cox book. Her exuberance filled the cabin of the SUV.

"Hey, Janice," Gray greeted, the smile on her lips reflected in her tone. "What's up?"

"How many chapters have you completed since we last spoke?" Janice asked, never one to miss an opportunity to dive right in.

"Uh," Gray said, thinking. "Four, nearly finished with the fifth."

"Okay, well I need you to double, triple, and quadruple your output," Janice said. "Mr. Cox has announced he's retiring after the release of his new movie in early spring, and, in their infinite wisdom, the powers that be here have decided to push up the release of the book to coincide."

Gray felt her stomach fall. "Oh, hell," she muttered. "Okay. So, how long do I have to get this done?"

"Just over a month," Janice said with an exasperated sigh. "And, I need you to send me every chapter as you finish so I can keep us going on edits."

Gray ran her hand through her hair. She felt like she was going to throw up. "Oh, boy. Okay. Yeah, I can do that, okay."

"Great. Get to work. Talk soon." With that, Janice

was gone.

"Shit," Gray muttered, suddenly feeling very nauseous, indeed. She felt a hand move to rest on her thigh. She glanced over at Christian.

"You can do this, baby," Christian said softly. "I've seen you pull an entire story out of nowhere at the last minute for the paper before." She squeezed Gray's thigh and gave her a small but reassuring smile.

Once they got home, Gray felt a bit overwhelmed. She knew she needed to just go into her office and make a plan. Her time to write this book had been nearly cut in half. Though she was a fast thinker and fast writer—years in the journalism industry had taught her that—the book was a whole different animal and she wanted to do it right.

She knew that how well she did this, how it was perceived, would outline the rest of her professional career as a writer. With a kiss to the lips and promise of dinner brought into the office, Gray was sent away to work.

She went to the bedroom first and changed into her comfy flannel pajamas, then headed into the office. Standing in the doorway, she looked over the room, with her desk back in the corner. Mounted to the wall behind it was an ornate shadow box her father had made. Inside were Christian's two Olympic medals, polished to a gold and silver shine. There were also the awards Gray had won over the years for journalistic excellence, as well as Christian's theatrical awards.

It was proof of a professional life well-spent, accolades well-earned. Besides her desk, there was a small couch. It was large enough for her to flop down on and rest her eyes as she worked out a problem in a project, but not exactly what one would want to use to get a good night's sleep. It was mainly where Caesar plopped himself while Gray worked, if he wasn't sprawled out in the spot of sun that came through the French doors in the living room.

Very little had been hung on the walls outside of the shadow box, as she hadn't had much time for that. Once she finished the project, she intended to truly do her part to make the house a home for them. She knew Christian wanted to paint and add other cosmetic touches, but with her leg at the moment, things along those lines were a bit too much for her to tackle alone. She was, however, now allowed to remove the brace once she got home and move around freely, only to put it on for bed and leaving the house.

Hands on hips, Gray's attention turned back to her desk, her computer sitting there silently, waiting for her fingered command. Blowing out a long breath, Gray turned around and closed the French doors, closing her off from the rest of the house. It was time to work.

Sitting at her desk, she turned on her laptop, the computer logging on and doing its thing as she opened a drawer and retrieved the little tape recorder she'd used for all her interviews. She had a few files left to download on the computer, but for the most part they were all there, ready for her.

Gray grabbed her earbuds and stuck them in her ears, finding the files she wanted to start with on her computer and hitting play. She listened as she downloaded the other audio files off her recorder before opening her manuscript.

As the voices of many flowed through her head, Gray could see their faces, remember their facial expressions and gestures. She could still smell the perfume on one woman, the strange cologne of a man. She could see the roses that had been placed in the crystal vase near where their chairs had been arranged in the parlor of McCann Castle.

She got lost in their stories about Richard, weaving their tales into her narrative. Be it a family member or friend, his wife Eva, or a fellow actor who worked with him on a movie or in charity work, each person shared their unique take on the knighted actor. Using these many brushes, Gray painted a portrait of the man she'd come to know, seen through the eyes of those who knew him best. Minutes turned to hours, and hours turned to days.

Once she got to Richard's audio, she really began to burn fuel. As days turned to weeks, Gray's fingers continued to fly over the keys as, like with the other interviews, she was easily able to transport his own reflections to the page.

It was easy, that is, until it wasn't. Richard, though incredibly generous with his time, had provided so much material that it all started to sound the same. Over the last couple of days Gray had spent hours working in his perspective on the actor's role in politics, only to have that entire thread completely contradicted by another anecdote recorded later. It all suddenly seemed overwhelming, like her quest to produce a coherent story was futile. And then, the doubts came. Maybe it wasn't a matter of too much material, maybe it was just that *she* wasn't talented enough to pull it off. Too green. Lacking finesse. Simply, not good enough.

Pounding away on the keyboard, she noticed movement out of the corner of her eye. Glancing up from the screen, Gray saw Brutus staring at her through the panes of glass in the closed French doors, his tail swinging lazily back and forth. About to return to her work, she thought better of it and instead decided to stop, take a break, and stretch. She also realized she needed to pee something fierce.

She stopped the recording and removed her earbuds, using a finger to reach in and scratch an itch caused by the inner part. A shiver passed through her body at the feeling as she pushed up from the chair.

Her ass hurt, her eyes hurt, and, when she stopped and thought about it, her stomach hurt. She was hungry. She tried to remember if she'd eaten breakfast that morning or not. And, to her shock, it was nearly eight o'clock at night.

"Christian?" she called out, pulling open one side of the French doors. She was confused when she saw that the house was dark, save for a light that had been left on over the stove. "Babe?" She was about to take another step when she realized she'd stepped in something soft, and very smelly. Flicking the nearby light on, she looked down. "Son of a bitch," she muttered.

Brutus was already hiding behind the couch, peeking around the corner at her with a little whimper.

"God damn it, Brutus," she muttered, glaring at him. "Why the hell weren't you let out?" She reached down and removed her shoe, hobbling along on the other and one sock-clad foot on her way to the kitchen sink, eyes peeled for any other landmines along the way. Shoe dropped off, she made her way to the back door, pulling it open. "Go on, Brutus. Go out."

With another whimper and tail tucked between his legs, Brutus scurried out into the backyard. Gray sighed, irritated. Where the hell was Christian? Why hadn't she let him out? When she walked back into the kitchen area she noticed that Brutus and Caesar's bowls were empty. Neither had been fed, which should have happened two hours before.

Caesar appeared out of nowhere when she opened his can of wet food and dumped the slop into his bowl, dropping a scoop of Brutus's hard food in his before cleaning up the mess on the floor.

As she scrubbed her shoe in the sink, she heard the front door unlock and open, then close again. Shortly Christian appeared holding a white Styrofoam food container and a couple shopping bags.

Gray glanced over her shoulder at her, irritated. "Where were you?" she asked. "Why didn't you tell me you were leaving?"

Christian met her gaze as she walked to the large kitchen island. "I did," she said with a raised eyebrow, setting the container on the island as well as the two shopping bags before shrugging out of her leather jacket.

"When? Brutus just took a shit on the floor," Gray griped. "How long ago was he let out? And, their food bowls—"

"Slow your roll, Gray," Christian said calmly. "I told you at three I was going Christmas shopping and to dinner with Yancy. We have Christmas dinner tomorrow with your parents and we still hadn't finished shopping. So," she added, nodding toward the two bags. "I finished up tonight."

"Who's Yancy?" Gray asked, eyebrows drawn. She was tired, she was irritable, and she was in a terrible mood.

Christian stared at her for a moment, a confused expression on her face. "What do you mean? The woman we met three weeks ago at the mall, from my Olympic team. I've mentioned her to you off and on since then, and she was even over here last week for coffee."

Gray could only stare at her, feeling like she was stuck in an episode of a TV show she'd never seen before. Running a hand through her hair, she grumbled a tacit "Oh" before turning back to her shoe in the sink.

Christian walked around the cooking island to stand beside her. "Gray," she said softly. "You've been putting in twelve, fifteen-hour days, seven days a week." She brushed some hair out of Gray's eyes, a small smile on her lips. "You didn't even go get your hair cut on Tuesday."

It was disconcerting, as normally Christian could pull her out of whatever wretched headspace she was in. Not tonight. Not with this much riding on her financially. Worse, she'd convinced herself that Richard and the publisher would hate the book and she'd never work again in that field. She was so anxiety-ridden, so worried she was in over her head, that even the balm of Christian's voice couldn't soothe her. She didn't want to think about what would happen if she permanently lost that ability.

Chapter Nine

Gray shoveled another spoonful of mashed potatoes into her mouth. It was one of her favorite foods, and frankly she thought her father's gravy should be its own food group, but she barely tasted it. Her mind was on chapter twenty-nine, considering if she should—

"Gray!"

Her head snapped up, eyes wide to see her mother glaring at her across the table. "What?"

"Pass me the green beans, please," Bernadette said, clearly exasperated with her.

Gray cleared her throat, feeling stupid. "Sorry," she muttered, handing the side dish over. She made a conscious effort to pay attention to the conversation around the table.

"So," Dennis said to Christian, who sat to Gray's left and across from him. "Yancy played a large part in you getting out of that slimy bastard coach's house, then?"

"She did," Christian said, buttering a roll. "She was absolutely instrumental in helping me get out of that situation until my Nanna flew in to help."

Gray stared over at her for a moment. "Why didn't you tell me that?" she asked softly, confused and hurt.

Christian met Gray's gaze, her green eyes cool, just this side of aloof. "You haven't been interested in hearing about it, Gray," she said matter-of-factly. "You've been...busy."

Gray looked away, feeling anger bubbling in her gut. If she were being honest with herself, which she didn't want to do in that moment, she'd know the anger was at herself. She was failing miserably at balancing the massive project and her obligations at home. *Obligations* wasn't even the word she meant. Christian was her life, and their animals were her babies. But, right now, in the thick of it, they all felt like a heavy weight around her neck.

She ran a hand through her hair as she sat numbly chewing her Christmas dinner. Her favorite. Her father had become an excellent cook over the years, and his food was amazing. Her morose thoughts were interrupted when her phone rang. Setting her fork down, she reached for it to see that it was Janice.

"I need to take this," she muttered, pushing back from the table and ignoring the irritated look her mother gave her. She quietly retreated into the other room to take the call.

※ ※ ※ ※

Later that night, Gray called Brutus in after he did his business once they returned from her parents' house. "Come on, big guy," she said, locking up the back door before heading to the pantry to give him his nightly chewy.

Tossing it in the air, the big dog grabbed it out of midair then trotted off toward the bedroom, where Christian was already settling in. Gray stopped at her office to send the file she'd promised Janice during her brief call during dinner.

Running a hand through her hair and letting out a tired sigh, Gray booted up her laptop and got herself to the correct file and section. She saved the requested chapters into a new document and sent them on into the night and invisible highways of the internet.

The bedroom was abuzz with the nightly news playing on the TV, which wasn't much of a surprise to Gray. Lately she'd gone to the bedroom to change into her jammies for a late-night writing session to see Christian lying in bed with the animals—usually asleep on Gray's side—watching TV or a movie. They never used to use the TV in the bedroom—or rarely, anyway—both agreeing the bedroom was a sanctuary reserved for sleep, making love, or pillow talk.

Walking to the closet, Gray stripped out of her clothing and tossed the garments into the laundry basket before donning a T-shirt and loose shorts to sleep in. She walked to the bathroom where Christian stood at her sink brushing her teeth. Gray walked over to her own sink and used a headband to pull her bangs away from her face. She glanced at Christian's reflection in the mirror for a moment before looking away.

"You really should call your parents tomorrow and apologize," Christian said softly around her toothbrush.

Gray's gaze flew back to the reflection. "Why?"

Christian bent down to spit her spent toothpaste into the sink, then rinsed her mouth and the sink bowl before standing erect again. "They put a lot of work into today." She wiped at her mouth with a tissue from the box on the counter before turning to look at Gray the person rather than the Gray the reflection. "Dennis was so excited that it was our first Christmas back in Colorado."

"Yes, and I was there, Christian," Gray said, defensive. "I was there opening gifts. I played board games and I ate dinner."

"And," Christian added, irritation in her voice. "You took a phone call." She stared at Gray. "In the middle of dinner, Gray. In the middle of goddamn dinner, which you barely touched. You barely said more than two sentences to anybody all day."

Gray stared at her. "What are you talking about?"

"Don't play stupid, Gray." Christian's voice was low and warning. She walked over to the water closet, leaving the door open as she pushed her pajama pants down and sat. "You couldn't have been more distracted if you tried."

Gray rolled her eyes, tossed down the hand towel she'd been holding, and marched into the bedroom, grabbing her cell phone. She found what she was looking for then marched back in, holding out her phone for Christian to see her call log, including the call from Janice at dinner.

Christian looked at it then up at Gray. "Why the hell was Janice calling you?"

"Because she finished the chapters I sent her this morning and needed more," Gray explained, as if that explained it all. She walked back over to the vanity and set her phone aside to start washing her face.

"But it's Christmas," Christian retorted, finishing her business and flushing before walking back to her sink to wash her hands. "It's friggin' Christmas, Gray."

"She's Jewish," Gray muttered as she leaned over the sink, rinsing off the face cream.

"But you're not, Gray!"

Surprised by the passion in Christian's voice,

Gray glanced over at her, eyebrows shooting up. She finished what she was doing before turning the water off and patting her face dry. Lowering the towel, she met Christian's gaze.

"Whoa," she said quietly. "You understand I have to get this done, right?"

"Don't you dare patronize me, Gray." She turned and left the bathroom, where she angrily tossed the first throw pillow she grabbed to the chair where they lived overnight.

Gray followed. "Damn it, Christian, I thought you understood what this project means."

"I very much understand," Christian said, sending another pillow flying, this one overshooting the chair and landing on the floor next to it.

"No, I don't think you do." Gray reached for Caesar, who had already parked his black-and-white butt on the bed. The cat hissed at her before jumping off the bed and disappearing into the darkness beyond the open bedroom door.

"I've barely seen you for a month, Gray," Christian said, turning to face her, the large expanse of the bed between them.

Gray let out an irritated sigh. "Damn it, Christian. We talked about this."

"Yes, the book. The book, the book, the book. I get it. And I understand you have to finish it, I truly do. But I've seen you on the knife's edge of a deadline before. Like, a your-job-depended-on-it kind of deadline with the paper." She shook her head. "It was nothing like this has been. We've barely spoken. I can count on one hand the nights you've actually slept in the bed as opposed to me finding you sprawled out on the couch in your office." She indicated Gray as a whole. "You've lost weight. You've subsisted on coffee, essentially."

Gray looked away, rubbing the back of her neck. She'd also been surprised to find most of her clothing had begun to hang on her.

"You're on edge all the time. Either you're bitching at me because I'm being too loud, I'm being too quiet, I'm not here, got home too late, the dog shit on the floor, I didn't wake you up." She threw her hands up in exasperation. "I've been walking around here on eggshells. Poor Brutus doesn't know if he's coming or going because his favorite playmate wants nothing to do with him."

"I have to get this right, Christian," Gray said softly, trying to keep her own emotions under control. It never ended well when they both lost control. "I need you to understand that."

"I know you're a perfectionist," Christian said. "You always have been when it comes to your work—"

"If I don't get this right, Christian, we're fucked!" Gray's words hung in the air like a little dialogue balloon, both women frozen in time, staring at each other. When the balloon popped, Gray looked away, ashamed at herself for blurting it out that way even as she was relieved that it had been said. "Look," she continued, voice a bit softer. "We have one more month tops that Richard is paying my salary to get this done. Yes," she added, "we still have some in savings from the advance, but that's it." She sliced her hand through the air to emphasize her point. "It's not as expensive here as it was in New York, but it's still not cheap."

Christian turned her back to Gray, slowly perching on her side of the bed. Every single ounce of body language in her screamed defeat. "I'm sorry I dedicated thirty years of my life to an industry that labels you no longer viable by age thirty-four," she began. "I didn't mean to get hurt, Gray."

Gray's eyes fell closed, her own fear of their immediate future nailing her feet to the ground where she stood, even as her heart ached for the hurting woman so close, yet so terribly far away. It felt like they were a galaxy apart.

Christian's head fell for a moment before she pushed to her feet and walked toward the bathroom. "Don't worry," she murmured. "I'll have a job by Monday."

"Wait, baby," Gray said, finally shaking free of her stupor. She turned to follow the dancer but came face-to-face with the closed bathroom door instead.

Chapter Ten

Carry-on backpack in place, Gray trotted down the stairs to the basement where she found Christian sweeping the expanse of the floor with a broom. Caesar and Brutus were both lounging, Brutus chewing on a bone and Caesar grooming.

"My ride's here," Gray announced, standing just at the bottom of the stairs.

Christian glanced over at her. "Okay. You know I offered to drive you…"

"I know," Gray said. "I told Richard, but he didn't want to bother you, with it still tough for you to drive."

Christian nodded. She leaned the broom against a nearby wall before walking over to Gray. The air between them was thick and heavy, as it had been since Christmas. She looked Gray in the eye briefly before taking her in a hug.

Though the hug was tight and meaningful, Gray was unsettled by it. For so many years a hug from Christian had settled her like nothing else could. Now, in that moment, she felt like a stranger.

"Be safe," Christian said softly, pulling out of the hug. "Good luck."

Gray nodded. "Thanks." She leaned in for a kiss, receiving a small peck. Gray met Christian's gaze, but again, only briefly before Christian looked away, heading back to her broom. "I'll call you," she said weakly.

"Okay," Christian said, grabbing the cleaning tool. "I'll be here."

Gray nodded, turning to the stairs. She stopped at her name, glancing back over her shoulder.

"I love you," Christian said quietly.

A small smile graced Gray's lips. "I love you too."

✦✦✦✦

Richard and his town cars. It seemed like wherever he was on the planet, he managed to find one. He could be in the middle of the Sahara where the locals get around on camels, and he'd still find a polished, black town car to plow through the sand.

The town car he'd sent to get her to the airport pulled up at the departure terminal. The female driver got out and opened the door for Gray before gathering her single piece of luggage out of the trunk and rolling it to the outside check-in for her. The woman tipped her hat and headed back to the car before driving away.

Gray stayed distracted with the long, drawn-out process of getting through security, basically having to undress and do the hokey pokey before turning herself around to put her shoes back on and hurry deeper into the airport to get to her gate. It would be a long flight to New York but a short visit. Well, it wasn't even a visit, it was for a photoshoot for the book.

The publisher was taking the unusual step of doing a small bio of her, the would-be ghostwriter. Typically, they were just that: writers without public-facing names or credit doing the heavy lifting on celebrity memoirs and the like, but known within the industry and pimped out when needed by agents for their busy clientele. Richard had strongly suggested she get an agent herself, which made her a bit nervous. Richard said that was one thing he wanted to work with her on during her three-day trip.

She hated having to pack so much for what amounted to a long weekend, but was told to bring several clothing options for the pictures. Sitting in the uncomfortable chair waiting for her plane to board, she glanced out the large windows that overlooked the tarmac. She watched the workers scurrying to and fro doing their respective jobs, including the guy driving the mini choo-choo with its curtained cars filled with luggage to be loaded into the belly of the 737 parked at the end of the passenger boarding bridge.

She'd asked Richard if she could bring Christian with her, wondering if perhaps getting out of town, a change of scene for a bit, might do them some good. He'd told her Christian would either be off by herself or stuck in a hotel room the entire time as their schedule was filled with appearances, appointments, and the photoshoots themselves.

So, she'd decided to not even bring up the possibility and just go alone, do her job, and get back home. As soon as she returned, she was going to contact her old boss at *The Denver Post* to talk about a staff position. She was beginning to have dreams about her financial worries, and it was stressful. Innately, she knew they'd be fine. Her parents had prepared her well regarding money, and Lord knew Michael had preached to her enough.

Running a hand through her hair, she tried to relax back into the seat and wait for her plane.

※※※※

Sure enough, Richard picked her up in a town car with a driver behind the wheel. She smiled, glad to see him as they hugged and the driver loaded her luggage into the trunk. He held her by the arms, looking her over. His heavy eyebrows fell.

"You've lost so much weight, my dear," he said, looking her in the eyes. "Are you unwell?"

"No," she said, laughing off his concern. "No, just crazy busy trying to get your book done, sir." She poked him playfully in the chest.

He smiled. "Well, then, good thing you'll be joining us for dinner tonight, isn't?"

Gray climbed into the back of the car, Richard following.

※※※※

Dinner was at one of New York's most exclusive restaurants, and Gray and Richard were joined by Richard's wife Eva, his longtime assistant Bryce, who would be basically heading the next three days to make sure everything went off without a hitch, and Fatima Darmandi, who would be taking all the shots for the photoshoot.

Gray reached for her glass of wine when Fatima, who sat to her left, leaned over to speak to her.

"Since everyone is just getting into town tonight and the real hit-the-ground-running work doesn't start until tomorrow, I wanted to ask you if you'd come to my place after dinner. Everyone here is already well aware of the process." She smirked. "Except for you."

She nodded toward Richard. "He's been involved in all this since God was a boy, so it's completely understandable you're the newbie. We'll be working out of my apartment for the shoots, so I wanted to get some lighting measurements of you to cut down on time later."

Gray nodded. "Okay. I can do that."

Fatima smiled, which lit up her entire face. Gray noted that she truly was a beautiful woman. "Wonderful."

⁂

Gray walked into the massive apartment that took up two floors. The style was industrial, a prototypical mixed-use space, looking more like something out of a movie than real life. The larger portion of the apartment was her studio, which they entered into.

Gray walked over to the inside wall, comprised of naked brick like so many of the apartments in Manhattan's older buildings. It was lined with framed black-and-white pictures of the famous people she'd shot over the years. There were entertainers, politicians, humanitarians, and faith leaders.

"Believe it or not," Fatima said, startling Gray as she was suddenly standing right behind her. "The Bush family were some of the nicest people I've ever shot. Fun bunch."

"Really?" Gray said, moving farther down the row of pictures, putting a bit of distance between them. Protective of her personal space outside of Christian, she struggled when people invaded it.

"Yes." Fatima walked past Gray to an area that opened up to where all the work happened.

A large tube of sorts was strung about eight feet above the ground along a wall, several little silver pull handles hanging down. It reminded Gray of the white projection screen in classrooms at school, the teacher reaching up to pull it down from its home, the satisfying *thwack* when the spring-loaded roll retracted. She figured it was likely the backdrops Fatima could use for her shots if she didn't employ a greenscreen and add them in later digitally.

Gray figured there was a light for every type of setup imaginable. Fatima had various props tucked away in a small cage in one corner of the room, as well as several types of furnishings—an armchair, ottoman, chaise lounge, and wooden stump.

"This place is great," Gray said, eyeing everything, hands shoved into the pockets of her pants.

"Thanks." Fatima walked over to a large black cabinet set in a recess in the wall opposite the photo set. "A whole lotta magic has happened here," she murmured, glancing over her shoulder and smirking at Gray.

Gray said nothing, simply turned away, rubbing the back of her neck with her hand. "So," she said, clearing her throat. "What do you want me to do?" She faced the photographer again, who was bringing out a camera from the cabinet.

Fatima glanced up at her as she walked over to a small table nestled against the brick wall. "Hold tight and be your gorgeous self," she said as she dealt with the piece of equipment. "Actually, you don't wear makeup, right?" At the shake of Gray's head, she said, "Go upstairs into my loft and wash your face in the bathroom. Just use the soap I've got up there."

"Okay."

Gray was directed to use the spiral staircase made of wrought iron that went up to the second-floor living space. It wasn't as expansive as the first floor, but still large with an open floor plan for the kitchen and living room area. Basically, it was a much, much bigger version of Christian and Gray's New York place that they still owned and rented.

The living room was tastefully decorated in lots of black leather and chrome, but the bedroom, which was nearly as large as the one they had in Colorado, was the showstopper. Not her taste, but certainly an eye-catcher.

More black leather, including the padded black leather headboard mounted to the wall, adorned the room. The bed was huge and covered in leopard print with a mass of black satin throw pillows. There were sturdy hooks protruding from the cement walls and the ceiling, and she absolutely did not want to know what they were for—even as the image of a sex swing popped into her mind.

Shaking the thought and image away, she went into the en suite bathroom. She quickly washed her face, wanting to get out of Fatima's personal space and back downstairs where things were more professional and less uncomfortable.

Fatima glanced at her once Gray rounded the corner into the studio area from the stairs. She smiled. "It's just not fair," she said, turning back to adjust the lights.

"What's not fair?" Gray asked, wandering over to her.

"Well," Fatima began, reaching up to change the angle of one of the barn doors on the light to focus it more. "Stand over there, please," she said, indicating the two pieces of blue tape that formed an X on the cement floor. "And," she continued, walking over to Gray and standing in front of her, hands on Gray's hips. "Over just a little bit," she murmured, urging the move with pressure from her left hand. "You're naturally gorgeous," she said, meeting Gray's eyes. "I think the camera will love you."

The two were standing so close together that Fatima's breasts nearly touched her own. She felt trapped where she stood. She didn't want to be rude and back up, but she felt incredibly warm and uncomfortable where she stood. Clearing her throat, she forced a smile.

"Yes, well." She smirked. "You should see me first thing in the morning."

The arched eyebrow and look of interest on Fatima's face made it quite clear that what had been meant as a joke of self-deprecation had instead landed dead center where it didn't need to land.

Clearing her throat again, she gave Fatima a shy smile. "So, what do I need to do? For the light test stuff?"

≈≈≈≈

"I'm glad you squeezed me in for a few minutes," Michael said, sipping coffee they picked up before hitting Central Park.

"Of course," Gray said, holding her own paper cup with the shop's logo proudly printed on the side. "I'm just sorry I don't have time to make you guys dinner at your place. Super short trip packed with a lot of stuff."

"Good stuff," he offered. "Important stuff." He

smiled over at her as she met his gaze. "I'm proud of your stuff."

Gray chuckled. "Thanks. My head is spinning a bit, I won't lie. Leaving that brunch this afternoon…" Her face scrunched up in a bit of confused disgust. "Who the hell does brunch for a meeting?"

Michael grinned. "Really rich people. I deal with them all the time working in finance."

"Yes, the people I had brunch with today certainly fit into that category. But I really liked Natalie," Gray said, thinking of the woman in her sixties that Richard and Eva had brought her to meet.

"Yeah? Do you think you *need* an agent? That's what she is, right?" At Gray's nod, he said, "What would she do for you?"

"Well," Gray said, bringing her cup down after taking a sip. She licked a bit of wayward mocha breve from the corner of her mouth with her tongue. "*If* she took me on as a client, she'd promote me to publishers for freelance gigs, negotiate any signing bonuses, coordinate if anyone wanted to interview with me for a project, pimp me out to authors who need a little help with their book…" She shrugged. "That kinda thing." When Michael remained quiet, she glanced up at him. "What?" she said. "What are you thinking?"

He grinned down at her. "Look at you," he said. "My bestie, who didn't know her asshole from a hole in the ground for the first eighteen years of her life, and look at you now. Not even thirty, and hot shit."

Gray rolled her eyes. "In that heap of dung there's a seed of compliment somewhere."

He draped an arm over her shoulders, his hand dangling at the wrist. "It's too bad Christian isn't here to see all this."

It was an innocent comment. Gray hadn't filled him and Kevin in on what was going on at home. She didn't want them to worry and, honestly, wasn't ready to talk about their problems out loud. Instead, she remained silent, trying to push her emotions down. Michael was the one person on earth she needed to talk to, and she didn't feel she could. Not yet.

Unfortunately, Michael knew her better than anybody on the planet, save for perhaps her own partner. Using his arm over her shoulders as a bit of a rudder, he got them headed to a bench where he urged her to sit with him.

"Okay. What's got my little hummingbird's feathers ruffled?"

"Damn it, Michael," Gray muttered, looking away and wiping at one of her eyes. The soothing tone of his voice could make her cry when she needed to and just couldn't quite get there herself.

He said nothing, simply used the hand that had been on her shoulder to run through the back of her hair, a calming touch. Gray didn't let herself go fully, but she did allow some tears to fall, let a bit of the pressure out from under the lid.

After several long moments, Michael's hand stilled, moving back to her shoulder. He leaned over, resting his cheek against her head. "If you need to get away for a bit, doll," he said softly. "You know you always have a place with us." He left a kiss where his cheek had been. "You or Christian. No judgment, no questions."

❧❧❧❧

"Like this?" Richard asked, whipping his leg up

and across Gray's body as though she were about to catch him as he jumped into her arms.

Amused, Gray played along, wrapping her hand beneath his leg, making them all laugh harder. Fatima, all the while, snapped away on her camera, moving around them.

"Well, she said act friendly toward each other," Richard griped good-naturedly, lowering his leg as he grinned at Gray.

"I don't think she meant a post-wedding pose." Gray laughed.

"You two just talk," Fatima said from behind the lens. "You have such a wonderful relationship and connection. Just interact."

Richard turned to Gray, clearly comfortable with direction from a photographer after years of being on film sets and photoshoots surrounded by cameras. Gray, on the other hand, was struggling a bit. She felt awkward, like she was under a microscope.

"Natalie was quite impressed with you," he said.

Forgetting about the camera for a moment, Gray's eyes widened. "Really? I thought I acted like a spaz, I was so nervous."

Richard raised a bushy eyebrow as he cocked his head to the side. "Not entirely sure what a 'spaz' is, but I'll assume it's not good." His grin made Gray smile. She heard a series of shutter clicks at that moment. "Even so, you acted superbly," he continued, unfazed by the shots taken.

"Whew." Gray wiped imaginary sweat off her brow as she smiled up at him. "She didn't hate me, huh?"

"Hated you? Rubbish. She only wants to take a quick looksee at the full, edited manuscript. Which," he added, leaning in as though to conspire. "I talked our dear publisher into letting her do. If she gets what she expects to get, she wants to represent you."

"Holy shit!" Gray exclaimed, throwing herself into his arms, her shock and excitement taking over any decorum.

Richard hugged her back, though briefly. A typical Brit, as he would say, who wasn't keen on public displays of affection.

"All right, you two," Fatima said, lowering her camera. "We got it. Got our posed shots and now some good candid shots." She gave them both a winning smile before walking over to the table where she set her camera down. "I'm quite pleased."

"Wonderful, then." Richard looked to Gray. "I believe this wraps up our week." He reached for Gray, this time giving her a quick but robust one-armed hug. "Proud of you, my darling," he said. "You've outdone yourself in this project, and you should be proud."

"Thanks, Richard," Gray said softly, touched.

Richard's inside sport coat pocket began to sing "Fly Me To The Moon." He excused himself as he pulled his cell phone out. "Must take this," he said, heading to the stairs and up into the living area of the apartment.

Left alone, Gray walked over to her belongings, which were set on a stylistic chair in the corner. She turned back when she was called over to the cabinet where Fatima was dealing with her camera. The beautiful photographer opened the other cabinet door to reveal a computer monitor inside, as well as shelving filled with photo equipment.

"I wanted to show you some of the shots I got of you the other night," Fatima said. "Want a little peek?"

"Uh, sure." Gray moved in closer

Fatima typed this and that on the laptop's touchpad before several thumbnail shots appeared, all of Gray from the night of the lighting check.

"Look at this," Fatima said, double-clicking on a shot so it filled the screen. "Look at those cheekbones." She glanced over at Gray, a twinkle in her eyes. "I knew the camera would love you, and it does." She minimized that picture and brought up another one. "Here. This was a candid shot." She met Gray's gaze. "What were you thinking just then? This was when you were waiting for me to finish setting up. I saw the look on your face and just couldn't resist."

Gray studied the image. It was a three-quarter of her face in black and white. She was staring off into the distance. The expression on her face and in her eyes spoke of unseen troubles. Gray had to look away, as that image was the outside version of what she'd been feeling for so many weeks. She felt Fatima's gaze on her and remembered there was a question on the table.

"Um." She cleared her throat. "Probably just thinking about the coming few days, you know?" she said, giving her a weak smile.

Fatima studied her for a long moment. "Hmm. Interesting." She braced a hand against the wall next to Gray's head. "I was thinking," she began. "Why don't you stay and have some wine with me? I'd love to shoot you more." A sexy little grin spread across full lips. "See all your facets." She ran her fingernail down along Gray's cheek and her jaw.

Like a jolt of electricity rushing through her, Gray jumped away from her, nearly stumbling back over her own feet. Once she got her balance, she stared at the other woman, shocked. "Somehow I don't think my partner would approve," she said, her voice breathy from her surprise.

Lips pursing and the seduction in her eyes turning to dark anger, Fatima crossed her arms over her chest. "Well," she said dryly. "She's not exactly here right now, is she?"

Disgust filled Gray as she raised her chin a bit, almost defiantly, though she said nothing. There was nothing to say. She could only hope Richard finished his call soon so they could leave.

※ ※ ※ ※

Gray rinsed her toothbrush and set it aside before she swished water in her mouth, spitting the frothy liquid into the sink before rinsing it out. Even though it was a hotel and would be cleaned after she checked out, she still couldn't leave a mess.

Using a towel to dab at her face, she heard her phone go off. Christian's ring. She walked over to the dresser where it lay and picked it up. "Good morning, baby. How are—" Her eyes shot open. "Wait, wait, what? You're crying too hard. I can't understand—" She felt her face pale. She walked over to the bed, barely making it before her legs gave out. "What?" she whispered. "What are you saying, you don't want me to come home?" She ran a shaky hand through her hair, emotion stinging the backs of her eyes. "Wait, Christian, don't hang up, wait—"

When the line went dead, all she could do was stare straight ahead. She couldn't think, could barely blink. She could hear her heart pounding in her ears, feel it throbbing in her throat. She jumped when her phone dinged.

She opened the text from Christian and tapped on the link, her hand flying to her mouth in horror.

"Oh, my god!"

Chapter Eleven

Looking around, Gray felt lost, sad, and deeply hurt. How on earth had her life become a backpack and a guest room in her best friend's house? She turned to look at him, and clearly he saw something in her eyes because he gently removed the backpack straps from her shoulder, setting the bag aside before he took her into a long, warm hug.

"It'll be okay, Gray," he murmured into the hug. "We'll get you through this. Stay as long as you need to, okay?"

She nodded, unable to speak.

He gave her a final squeeze before letting her go. "I'll leave you alone," he said. "Michael will be home in a bit, and I'll send him up, okay? Or," he added, hand on the doorknob. "Would you rather be alone and maybe try to sleep?"

"No," she said, shaking her head. "Send him up, if that's okay."

"Of course." Kevin gave her a kind smile before leaving the room, closing the door softly behind him.

Left alone, she looked around the room again before deciding to go to the bathroom. She wanted to wash her face, try and feel somewhat human after such a horrific day. Sure enough, she found everything she needed where Kevin said it would be, plus her own toothbrush and toothpaste she grabbed from her carry-on.

The cool water felt good against her heated skin as she splashed her face. Her hanging bangs got wet in the process and dripped into her face before she pushed them back with a hand. Looking at her reflection, she barely recognized the woman staring back at her. Her eyes were red from hours of crying, the surrounding skin chafed from tissue rubbing to quell the waterfall.

She looked as tired as she felt—emotionally, mentally, and physically. She turned off the water and was drying her face on a hand towel when she heard a knock at the bedroom door. "Come in," she called out, hoping it was loud enough to be heard across the bedroom and through the wood door.

The bedroom door opened and Michael's reflection appeared in the mirror behind Gray's. The sight of her oldest and dearest friend sent the floodgate dams packing, and the tears fell anew. Michael took her into his embrace, letting her cry it out. They both knew that once the dam broke and she got the initial wave of emotion out, she'd be ready to talk.

After several minutes and deep breaths, he pulled away from her just enough to bring his hand up and use his thumbs to wipe away some of her tears. "Want to come downstairs and have a cup of coffee and talk?" When she nodded, he smiled. "Okay. Kevin has it brewing. Would you prefer he leave us alone? He offered, so don't worry about hurting his feelings."

Gray gave him a sheepish grin. "If that's okay, yeah. I love Kevin, you know that, but—"

"I get it, sweetie. And, so does he." He drew his eyebrows down, all serious-like. "You clean all this up," he said in a dramatically deep voice, indicating her tear-streaked face. "And I'll have a cup of joe waiting for you."

She gave him a weak smile. "Yeah, yeah. Okay."

He lightly cupped her face then turned and left the room, leaving the door open. She took a deep, cleansing breath once she was alone and ran her hand through her hair. She could do this. After cleaning up her mess in the bathroom, she descended the stairs until she found herself in the kitchen on the main floor.

Sure enough, Michael's husband was nowhere to be seen. She loved Kevin, but the situation was so deeply personal that she wanted only Michael. She was grateful the sensitive and empathetic attorney understood that, evidenced by his absence.

Michael was just setting down two filled mugs of coffee at the eating nook in the kitchen when she walked up. Still dressed for work, he plopped down in the kitchen chair before loosening his tie and pulling it off. He tossed it to the table before unbuttoning a couple buttons on his dress shirt. "Sit."

Gray did as bade and sat to his right. "Thanks," she said softly, wrapping her fingers around the handle of the large mug.

"Of course. So." The light that shone down on the table turned his handsome features garish. "What happened?"

Gray opened her text message from Christian that morning and slid the phone across the table. Picking it up, he tapped on the link Christian had sent to Gray.

His mouth fell open just before his hand came up to cover it. He looked up at her before looking back down to the screen. He rubbed his chin and the neatly trimmed goatee that grew there, a bit darker red than the hair on his head.

"'My week with Gray Rickman,'" he read, which was the title of Fatima Darmandi's social media post. "So," he continued, still looking at all the pictures. "She essentially starts at the beginning of the week, depicting an exuberant greeting between you two." He glanced up at Gray, who nodded.

"Yeah. She was quite huggy, to my surprise."

"And as the week goes on…" He paused, looking at more pictures. Some were candid shots taken by guests at McCann Castle, others from the official photoshoots. "We end with a nice shot of you," he said, again looking at Gray. "Naked in bed."

Gray felt a wave of nausea wash through her. "I wasn't naked," she said quietly. "I was wearing a tank top. The strap came down either in my sleep, or she did it."

He nodded, quietly setting the phone down before taking a sip from his coffee. His expression told Gray he was ruminating on what he'd seen. "Gray, I've known you longer than I've known anyone in my life, except for my family. I want to say I know the answer to this, but I have to ask—"

"No," Gray said adamantly, shaking her head. "I did *not* sleep with that woman. I didn't even come close."

"Okay. How did she get that picture of you sleeping?" he asked carefully. "Did Christian take that at some point? Did Fatima take it from your own social media account?"

Gray shook her head. "No. I'm just positive that was taken when I was in Scotland."

His eyebrows fell. "Scotland? How did she get into your room? Did you two share a room?"

Gray shook her head, sipping from her coffee, hoping the warmth would bring her some comfort, a kind of hug from the inside. "No. We both were staying in Richard's castle. Her room was down the hall from me. I have no idea when she came in and took that."

"Jesus," he muttered. "Creepy. Have you spoken to Richard? I mean, she's his personal photographer, right?"

"Well, they work together a lot."

"Have you spoken to him? Asked him to call off the dogs?"

Gray's eyes grew wide. "No!"

"Why not?" he asked.

"What if he thinks I did this?" Gray tapped the darkened screen of her phone with a finger.

Michael stared at her for a long moment, slowly shaking his head. "Gray, listen to yourself. Who gives a flying fuck what Richard thinks? Your *fiancée* thinks you did this. Priorities, babe."

As much as she wanted to argue with him that it wasn't like that, his words hit her between the eyes, and the tears came anew. "You're right. God." She looked into the depths of her coffee. "You're right. I'll call him."

"How did Christian get this? Have you talked to her since?"

"I have no idea where she got it. I couldn't understand half the things she said, she was crying so hard. But I've tried reaching out. She won't answer the phone, my texts, nothing."

"And your mom? Has she called?"

Gray shook her head. "No. Not a peep. This tells me Christian hasn't told her, which scares me a little."

"Gray," Michael began, head slightly cocked to the side. "What on earth would make Christian believe this bitch," he said, tapping Gray's phone. "Instead of you? Is this what was going on the other day at Central Park?"

Gray shook her head. "No. This hadn't even happened yet. This all happened this morning." She could feel his eyes on her, so she met them. In their depths was sadness and concern, making her look away again or chance brand-new sobs.

"How long have there been problems?" he asked gently.

Gray let out a long, shaky breath. "I'd say since before we left New York, if I'm honest with myself. Once her knee was beginning to really give her problems and it was becoming clear decisions would have to be made."

He nodded, sipping from his coffee. "And then your new career began to take off."

Gray sighed again and nodded. "Yeah." She shook her head, so unsettled with everything. "I feel like a stranger in my own life, Michael."

"Honey," he responded, his voice gentle. "You two met when you were so young. A lot has changed. People change. Sometimes love can change, too."

She considered his words, tasted them, but ultimately shook her head. "No," she said firmly, meeting his gaze. "Love was never the issue, Michael. Ever."

"Then, what happened?" he asked.

"We stopped talking."

☙☙❧❧

The Uber pulled to a stop, Gray's heart racing

to the point she was worried she'd have a heart attack. She glanced over at the quiet house, Christian's car parked in the driveway. She'd texted to let her know she was coming home, as she couldn't hide in New York forever.

"Thanks," she said, climbing out of the car and dragging her backpack with her as the driver popped the trunk. She retrieved her larger roller bag, shut the lid, and waved the driver off.

Standing on the sidewalk outside of the house, Gray sucked in a long, deep breath of fresh Colorado air to garner the courage to walk up the driveway, along the path, and finally up to the porch and inside.

It was a pleasant day, winter not completely behind but not yet spring. Some of the windows were open and the house smelled strongly of cleaning products. Gray groaned inwardly. Not a good sign. She was surprised she wasn't met by a barking Brutus, yet she saw Caesar trotting his way over to her.

"Hey, bud," she said, allowing her backpack to slide off her shoulder as she set it down next to the roller bag. It was nice to feel the black-and-white cat's soft fur beneath her fingers. "How are you?" He purred as he rubbed his head and face all over her hands and her bent leg. "Missed you too, sweet boy. Well," she amended with a small smile. "At least right now."

Pushing to her feet, Gray left her luggage where it was for the moment, as she had no idea what would happen once she found Christian. It didn't take long. She was in the kitchen, scrubbing down the inside of the emptied-out fridge, all the perishables on the cooking island.

"Hey," Gray said softly. It was then she saw

Brutus in the backyard, the French doors closed, undoubtedly so Christian could do what she was doing without worrying about him taking off with the ketchup bottle.

Christian didn't look at her but kept cleaning. "Hello." Her tone was as cold as the air coming from the fridge.

Gray grabbed a bottle of salad dressing that she didn't recognize. She wondered when they'd gotten it. "How are you?" she asked lamely, not entirely sure what to say. Tears were threatening, yet again, to burst forth.

"Just fucking peachy, Gray," Christian said, still not looking at her as she continued her frantic cleaning. Gray had learned long ago that cleaning, especially deep cleaning, was Christian's coping mechanism for strong emotions.

"How's your knee?" Gray asked.

"Can we please stop with the pleasantries?" Christian bit out, finally looking at her. "Please?"

"All right," Gray said with a nod. "Then let's go straight to it. Nothing happened."

Christian glared at her, so much hurt and anger in those vibrant green eyes. "How dare you?" she asked, her voice low, dangerous. "How fucking dare you, Gray?"

"Christian, I'm telling you—"

"I saw it with my own two fucking eyes!" Christian slammed the spray bottle of cleaner and the rag she was using onto the counter next to the fridge. "How stupid do you think I am?" She stared Gray down, one hand braced on the counter, the other on her hip. "Now I understand why this entire thing has been so hush-hush with you. Why you never wanted me around with this whole book bullshit. Why you didn't want me to go to New York with you. Now I fucking get it."

"That's not true, Christian," Gray said, her own anger building. "I have not lied to you once throughout any of this. Not once!"

"Except when you were fucking your photographer."

Christian's words hung in the air, growing heavier and heavier by the second. "I didn't sleep with her," Gray said quietly. "I did *not* sleep with her," she added, slapping her palm on the stone cooking island top with each word.

"I don't believe you." Christian crossed her arms over her chest. "The person you've become over these past few months, so aloof, so distant, so…" She looked around as though searching for the words. "So, 'I don't give a shit.' Now I know why."

Frustrated, Gray ran her hand through her hair. "Damn it, Christian." She sighed. "Why won't you believe me? You've known me for how long?"

"Yes," the dancer said. "Yes, I've known you for a long time and I truly thought I knew you, Gray. But that picture…" She looked away as her eyes filled with tears and her voice cracked.

Heart breaking, Gray took a step toward her only to have Christian move away.

"Don't touch me," Christian whispered, tears falling.

Gray fought her own tears. "I don't know what else I can say." Her voice was quiet, defeated. "I've never lied to you, and I'm not lying now."

"I don't want you here," Christian said, her back turned to Gray, seeming so small as she hugged herself tighter.

"Where would you like me to go? Every dime we have is sunk into this place. I'm not going to stay with my parents over something I didn't do." Gray looked down when she felt Caesar rubbing against her leg. He looked up at her and she smiled down at him. "I'll stay in one of the guest rooms upstairs," she finally said.

Not waiting for Christian's response, Gray reached down and scooped the cat up in one arm before heading to the entryway to gather her luggage.

❧❧❧❧

"Yes," Gray said into her phone, lying on the double bed in the spare bedroom upstairs. Caesar lay next to her, purring softly as her hand absently ran through his fur. "I turned her down. Told her I had a partner. Clearly," she added with a sigh. "She wasn't happy."

She listened as the voice on the other end responded, anger in his voice. She was so grateful for his reaction, and even more grateful for the little guy vibrating against her hip. She needed comfort, and Caesar seemed more than willing to offer it.

"I know. Total bullshit," she agreed. "The thing is, Richard, I don't care if Fatima got pissed at me. Fine, so be it. Who likes rejection? But the fact that she went after my relationship..." Yet again, she felt the emotion threaten. "It's not good, Richard. Christian is devastated, and honestly? So am I." Her eyes squeezed shut as she tried to regain her slipping composure.

She reached for a tissue from the box on the bedside table, wiping at her eyes as his soothing voice calmed her just a little. He made it clear he wasn't about to abandon her now, wasn't going to take Fatima's side and throw Gray and her burgeoning career to the wolves.

"Thanks, Richard," she whispered. "Means a lot to me." Letting out a heavy sigh, she added, "I wish like hell I could go back to a year ago. Divert all this."

Chapter Twelve

"There're some new faces around," Linda said, leading the way through the maze of desks. "But you should recognize most of 'em."

Gray nodded as she followed behind, looking around the large newsroom of *The Denver Post*. Finally, they stopped at the rear of the room next to a desk, a chair, and a small table set against the back wall.

"So," the editor said, indicating the desk. "Here we are, lady."

Gray noted her new, empty real estate, which she knew would soon be filled with her notes, papers, calendar, sticky notes, and coffee cups. Nodding, she looked at her old-boss-turned-new-boss. "Thanks so much, Linda. I truly appreciate this."

Linda waved her off. "Glad to have you back, kiddo. See you *mañana*."

"Good night, Linda." Gray watched the older woman weave her way back toward her office before looking around again.

The newsroom was largely empty as it was pushing the end of the day. Most reporters were already gone or still out working a story. She hadn't figured she'd get hired today, but Linda had brought her directly here after her interview with the higher-ups.

Just to be able to leave something of herself

there until she returned to work the following day, she dug into her messenger bag until she found a tube of Chapstick. Hey, it was something. She dropped the lip balm into the top drawer, where it landed with a thud. Pushing the drawer closed, she headed out.

The newspaper was about a fifteen-minute drive from the house, which was nice. And, she had to be in by six thirty, so she'd miss the morning rush hour, too. She was looking forward to getting back to work, getting settled back into a routine. She had no further freelance projects to work on, and worried that ship had sailed thanks to Fatima Darmandi.

Being that she was leaving the paper after five, the evening rush-hour traffic was in full swing. She pulled her SUV to a stop behind the car in front of her, both waiting in a long line of folks trying to get home after a long day.

She bobbed her head with the music on the radio when she noticed a car in the northbound traffic, leaving where she was headed. It was a black town car, windows heavily tinted, exactly like the one she rode in with Richard that day in Manhattan. Too bad that was never going to happen again.

The house was quiet when she arrived home, but it didn't take long to hear the muffled barks of Brutus out back and Christian's voice as she talked to him. It was such a bittersweet moment as Gray walked to the living room and the French doors heading out back. She watched through the panes of glass for a moment. Christian was raking up the dead grass and leaves from the winter. Though they weren't out of the woods quite yet for winter weather, things needed to be done to prepare for warmer temperatures and the coming summer.

As she watched the woman move around the yard, she felt a deep longing. Christian was so beautiful, moving far more gracefully now as her knee continued to heal. As she watched, she ached. Her arms ached to hold Christian. Her hands ached to touch her. Her heart ached. She was losing her best friend, and she had no idea how to stop it.

Steeling her spine, she took a deep breath and pulled open one side of the French doors. Brutus ran over to her, all excited puppy dog, bridging the chasm between his two mommies in his mutual love.

"Hey, big boy," Gray greeted, nearly knocked over backward in his exuberance and excitement. This, of course, got Christian's attention. Gray glanced up, meeting her gaze. "Hey." It had been three days since she'd returned from New York, and the frosty tension seemed to have morphed somewhat into resigned cohabitation.

"Hey. How'd it go?" Christian asked, standing across the yard, her hand topping the rake handle as she stood the yard tool upright.

"Well," Gray said, a small grin on her face. "Linda pulled a bit of a bait and switch. Hired me on the spot, so…"

Christian returned the smile with one of her own. "That's great, Gray. I'm happy for you."

Gray nodded but had to look away. Once upon a time, Christian would have run over to her and given her a huge hug and kiss, excited for the good news. Now, the two stood an entire yard apart.

"Well, um, I was going to do some laundry and ironing," Gray said, hitching her thumb back into the house. "Get ready for my early start tomorrow. But, if you need help out here, I'm more than happy—"

"No," Christian said, shaking her head. "No, Brutus and I pretty much got it." She gave Gray a small smile. "Go ahead and get ready for your big day."

Gray nodded. "Okay." She walked toward the house, then stopped when she heard her name. Turning back to Christian, she saw that she'd taken a step forward.

"It's really great news," she said softly.

Gray met her gaze for a long moment, then nodded. "Thanks," she replied, then headed inside.

Closing the door, she paused at the entrance to the master bedroom, intending to go in and grab some outfits to take upstairs for her work week. It had been a while since she'd worn most of her work outfits, and with the move, no doubt they needed to be ironed, a job she hated to do.

Looking inside, she saw that the bed had been made to perfection, everything as it should be. Well, that is, everything except the fact that it was no longer her bedroom. In that moment, she just couldn't do it, so she headed upstairs instead. She had an "aw, shucks" moment when she saw Caesar curled up on her bed. He'd stayed by her side since she'd returned from New York, while Brutus was desperately trying to bring everyone back together with his antics.

Walking farther into the room, she saw that the cat wasn't the only thing on the bed. A tall cylinder lay against the pillows. The paper it was wrapped in was a matte black, and there was a small card attached, which read:

I hope it helped. If not, perhaps this will.
R

Confused, she tossed the card to the bed and grabbed the package, unwrapping it. Inside was a bottle of twenty-one-year-old Glenlivet, Richard's favorite. Baffled, she stared down at the box, which opened up like the ends of a jacket to reveal the bottle of the aged whiskey within.

"I wondered what that was."

Gray glanced over her shoulder to see Christian standing at the open bedroom door. She turned to face her. "Was he here?"

The dancer nodded. "He was. Left about half an hour before you got home."

Gray nodded, looking down at the package in her hand. "Oh." She wasn't sure what else to say.

"Can we talk?" Christian asked hesitantly. "For a minute?" Her voice wasn't exactly friendly, but it didn't have the ice-queen tone of recent days.

"Yeah." Gray smirked. "Do I need to open this for this?"

"Well, he did bring a six-pack of ginger ale also, so I'm assuming it goes with that?"

Gray nodded. "It's pretty good. I had it in Scotland."

"With her?" Christian bit out.

Gray looked at her for a long moment, trying to keep her emotions in check. Finally, she shook her head. "No. With Richard and Eva."

Christian tucked in her bottom lip and looked away before meeting Gray's gaze again. "Sorry," she whispered. "Let's go downstairs."

Taking the scotch with her, Gray followed her to the kitchen. Without a word, Gray pulled two small glasses from a cabinet while Christian retrieved the ginger ale from the fridge and set the cans on the counter. "Ice?" Christian asked, taking the glasses from Gray.

Gray nodded and removed the bottle from its cylindrical box, opening it to allow the smooth yet strong fragrance to reach her nose. She poured a smidge in both glasses of ice before Christian added the soda.

Finally, they took a seat at the kitchen table, sitting across from each other. Gray took a drink, letting the liquor go down before she looked at Christian, the stinging remark still burning in her brain. "What did you want to talk about?"

"I need you to do something for me," Christian began softly. Her hands wrapped around the tumbler that held her drink. "Okay?"

Gray nodded. She wasn't sure how to feel. She'd been happy to see Christian at her door, hoping maybe Richard had straightened everything out, but then that comment had cut her to the quick and made her furious with Fatima all over again. "Yeah. Okay." She took another small sip of her drink.

"Okay. I need you to take me back to the very first time you met that woman." Christian's voice was flat but held none of the same bitterness as her quip upstairs. "I need you to explain how every picture came about. Every single one."

Gray nodded, actually quite glad for the request. She had nothing to hide. "Absolutely."

While Gray told her story, outlining every single interaction she'd ever had with Fatima in great detail, Christian listened, giving her full attention to Gray. Christian asked a few questions, which Gray answered with ease, as there just wasn't a lot to tell.

"Yes," Gray said to the latest question. "She did

join us at dinner that night, but I was there with Richard, Eva, and Natalie."

"The agent lady," Christian clarified.

Gray nodded. "Yes."

Christian looked down into her glass. "And that last picture?"

She didn't need to elaborate, as that last picture had been the elephant in the room since Gray had gotten home. "I've looked at that picture a million times," Gray said. "Trying to figure out when she got in my room to take it, and I think I've figured it out. That bed I was sleeping in was in Richard's castle in Scotland. Again, Fatima and I were both staying there, in separate rooms." Though the repetition was likely unnecessary, she wanted to make sure it was understood.

"Okay," Christian said, acknowledging the specifics.

"That last morning, the day I flew out, I remember waking up—no, something had woken me," Gray explained. "I wasn't sure what it was, but just shook it off, no big deal. I also remember realizing my tank top strap was down. You know me, I'm not a wild sleeper, so it didn't make sense that it was pulled down, but I just shrugged it off." She gave her a sheepish grin. "No pun intended."

"And you think she went into your room and took that picture?" Christian asked. "You're saying, she went in, uninvited, and perhaps even staged it?"

"That's exactly what I'm saying," Gray said. "She was never in that room with me, Christian. While I was awake," she added. "Never."

"And you said she did proposition you? That last night."

"Yes, she did, and I immediately shut her down. Told her I had a partner."

Christian studied her for a moment, then grabbed her drink and took a sip, her mouth working as she seemed to be moving it around, tasting it, contemplating. Finally, she nodded. "Okay." Her tone was noncommittal as she met Gray's gaze. "Thank you."

⁂

Gray lay in bed awake, the sun still hiding below the horizon. Her alarm was set to ring any minute, so she reached for her phone and turned it off before it disturbed Caesar. Task complete, she rested her hand, still wrapped around the phone, on her stomach and stared up at the ceiling.

It was her second day of work, and her mind just wasn't in the game. She'd dreamt all night of Christian, the dreams ranging from the two of them making love to Christian stabbing her in the back with a ten-inch blade. That one had sent Gray into wakefulness with a gasp. She could still see the hatred in those deep green eyes.

Squeezing her eyes shut, Gray took a deep breath as she tried to let go of the emotion the montage had evoked in her. As it was, her waking hours weren't a hell of a lot better, though they had become civil. There was tension for sure in the house, but the anger and bitterness seemed to have waned a bit on Christian's end. For Gray, it was building. She was doing her best not to snap at Christian or cop an attitude, even though deep inside she was beginning to seethe.

Where had her life gone? Where had her relationship gone? How could one vengeful bitch do this to them? How far adrift had they been before now for this to even have any possibility of gaining a foothold?

Letting out a huge sigh, Gray decided to push it all aside for the time being so she could get her mind where it needed to be, and that was ready for work.

Thirty minutes later, Gray headed downstairs, freshly showered and dressed. She was planning to make coffee, but Christian had beat her to it.

"Good morning," the dancer said, pulling down two mugs from the cabinet.

Gray eyed her, a bit confused. Civil over the last couple days hadn't quite extended to solicitous. "Morning."

"I was going to heat up a breakfast sandwich real quick before I head out to Colorado Springs," Christian said, walking over to the fridge and grabbing the coffee creamer from inside. "Want one?"

"Uh," Gray said, her brain not quite awake enough to keep up. "Sure. Springs?"

"Yeah." Christian set the bottle of creamer on the cooking island. "Yancy works down there at the Olympic training center." She smiled, the first real smile Gray had seen in far too long. "Full circle, huh? She wants me to come look at a new girl she's training."

For just a moment, every bit of anger and confusion evaporated out of Gray and she felt like her old self. She looked at Christian, her eyes tearing up a bit at the wonder she saw in Christian's face, heard in her voice. "That is so wonderful," she said softly, a bit emotional. "I couldn't be happier for you."

Christian looked down at her hand, playing with the creamer bottle. "Thanks," she said softly, almost shy. She cleared her throat. "I probably won't be home for dinner, so…"

Gray nodded. "That's fine. I'll likely do what I've been doing since my trip, just eat a snack and go up to my room." The words had a little more bite than she intended, causing a heavy silence in the room for a moment.

"Um," Christian said at length. "I can call Bernie if you want. I'm leaving in the morning for a couple days. Your mom can come over and let Brutus out during the day since you're back at work."

Gray felt her stomach roil but couldn't bring herself to ask questions. "No, it's okay. I should be able to run home during the day and let him out."

"Okay." Christian stood at the island for a moment before moving over to the coffeepot, which was gurgling to a finish.

Chapter Thirteen

"Hey, Michael," Gray said into her phone, which she cradled between her ear and her shoulder as she continued to type her notes from the interview she'd just done. "Just working, my friend. What's up? Can't really talk."

She was only half paying attention as she continued to work, but the mention of Christian's name caught her attention.

"Yeah, she left for a couple days," she said. "No clue where she went, though. Why?" Her eyebrows drew. "What do you mean you think you found her? I didn't think she was necessarily lost." Gray stopped typing and listened fully to what he was saying. "Oookay. Let me log in to my account."

She quickly clicked out of the work program and logged in to her personal social media account. Sure enough, there was a private message from Michael. She clicked the screenshot he'd sent her and recognized the profile picture of the photographer immediately.

I want to clear up an unfortunate misunderstanding from a post I made a while ago. Some took my post regarding author Gray Rickman as though we had a relationship that was anything other than professional. That's just not the case. So, my apologies to Gray and her partner, dancer Christian Scott, for any trouble it may have caused. Gray and I have never been anything more than colleagues working on a project for the amazing Richard Cox.

Gray read it three times before it fully penetrated. She agreed with Michael and felt Christian had indeed been behind the post to clean up the massive mess that had been made by Fatima's spitefulness. Christian came off as sweet and kind, which she was, but what the average person didn't know was just how scrappy she could be. When she felt she'd been wronged, God help the person she held responsible. Gray knew all too well as she camped out in the spare bedroom.

"Wow," she murmured. "Yeah, yeah, I'm here," she said into the phone. "No," she said to Michael's question. "I'm not sure how I feel. I gotta go. Bye."

Setting her phone on the desk, she studied the post. No, she wasn't sure how she felt at all.

Licking the spoon and looking down at her empty bowl with a sigh of lamentation, Gray pushed up from the couch in the living room where she'd been watching TV and eating ice cream and ambled to the kitchen.

For just a moment she considered getting a second bowl but went to the sink instead and rinsed her bowl and spoon before placing them into the dishwasher. As she finished, she heard Brutus begin to bark and whine as he scurried to the front door.

Sure enough, moments later Christian let herself in and greeted her very excited pup. Gray paid attention to make sure Brutus wasn't going to knock her down again. Though Christian was several months past surgery, a bad fall could undo all her progress.

Brutus began to settle down when he realized Mommy #1 was staying, then trotted off to plop down on his bed in the living room. Gray closed the dishwasher and began to clean the cooking island top with the spray cleaner and paper towel as Christian headed to the master bedroom with her roller bag. She was in the bedroom for less than five minutes before returning sans luggage and shoes.

"Hey," she said, padding up to the cooking island.

"Hi." Gray had had an entire day to mull over what Michael had sent her earlier and still wasn't sure what she thought of the entire thing. "Good trip?"

The dancer nodded. "Yes. More of a mission, really. Accomplished."

Gray nodded. "So I saw."

"I had to confront her, Gray." Christian's voice was firm. "I'm not going to let that bitch get away with what she did. The lies. She could have done some serious damage to us."

Gray stared down at the paper towel gripped in her hand. "I understand why you confronted her," she said quietly.

"But yet," Christian said. "You don't seem happy about it. Please don't tell me I just threatened to ruin a woman's career who was telling the truth the first time."

Gray's gaze snapped up to meet Christian's. "No," she said, her voice low. "She was telling the truth this second time. Nothing happened."

"Then why do you seem so upset that I did this?" Christian asked. "I miss 'us,' Gray." She looked into Gray's eyes, her own pleading. "Don't you?"

"Of course I miss 'us,'" Gray said. "But I miss

the 'us' when you trusted me, when you believed me over someone you've never met. I miss the 'us' when you would have talked to me rather than kick me out of my own house. Certainly my bedroom." She glared at Christian, her anger finally reaching a point of no return, her voice raising as her temper did. "I miss the 'us' when you would have asked me questions, not throw accusations."

"I was shocked, Gray," Christian exclaimed. "I didn't know what to do."

"Talk to me!" Gray slammed her palm down on the stone island top with each word. "Talk to me."

Christian looked away, tears brimming in her eyes, though Gray wasn't sure if it was hurt, anger, or sadness. Perhaps a mixture of all three.

"Why did it take Richard showing up and telling you what really happened before you finally deemed me worthy of asking?" Gray demanded. "Was it checking my story? Making sure it matched Richard's?"

Christian hugged herself, looking down at her socked feet for a long moment. Finally, she raised her head and said quietly, "I'm sorry for that. You're right. I should have talked to you." She nodded at her own realization. "I was just so hurt, so utterly devastated, I was worried if I said too much to you, I'd tell you we were done."

Gray felt her stomach drop at those words, her breath stolen from her. She remained silent, even as her heart was breaking.

"I feel like you're a million miles away from me," Christian continued, her voice cracking with emotion. "Like, we're a million miles away from each other, and I don't know how to fix it."

Gray's anger drained out of her, leaving profound sadness behind in its wake. She nodded in agreement. "Can it be fixed?" she whispered, terrified at the answer. "Do you want it to be?"

Christian nodded immediately. "Yes. I love you very much. I can't walk away from that." She let out a long, heavy sigh. "Maybe we need some help, someone to talk to. Are you willing?"

"What, like a marriage counselor?" Gray asked, smirking as she looked down at the island again. "Not like we're married," she muttered.

Christian didn't say anything for a moment, clearly Gray's quip hitting its mark. Finally, she cleared her throat. "Okay. I'll look for someone."

※ ※ ※ ※

Gray was leaving the newspaper to go interview the couple for her upcoming story for *The Denver Post* when her phone dinged. She climbed into her car before opening Christian's text:

Hey. I heard back from Stacy Callhoun. We have an appointment with her at 6:30 tonight. I've added the address below. I hope you'll meet me.

Gray rested her head back against the seat as she sat behind the wheel. She considered the message, could almost hear the hope in Christian's voice as though she'd spoken those words and hadn't sent them with her fingertips.

She looked at the address to get a mental image of where the place was. The office was on the other side of town from her afternoon interview, but she would brave the traffic to save her relationship. Yes, of course, she would go.

"How do you feel about Christian's assessment of the last ten months or so, Gray?" Dr. Stacy sat in a wingback chair in her office, opposite Gray and Christian. She was a small woman—shorter than five feet, Gray figured—and in her fifties perhaps. She seemed nice enough, and kept things professional even as she always had a smile in her blue eyes.

Gray adjusted herself on the comfortable flower-patterned couch. "Well, I suppose I'd agree with most of what she said."

"What don't you agree with?" the therapist asked, her pen in hand and at the ready with a pad of paper resting on her thigh.

"I don't think it's accurate at all that I wasn't there for her when she got hurt or while she was healing. I mean," she said, incredulous. "I was willing to move our entire lives for her, to start over."

Dr. Stacy looked to Christian, an eyebrow raised. "How do you feel about that, Christian?"

Christian turned to Gray. "You were there for me physically, Gray," she conceded. "But mentally, emotionally, you checked out. Your mom was the one who was there for me. Who I largely cried with."

Gray stared at her, mouth opening and closing for a few moments before she looked away, hugging herself defensively. "That's crap, Christian."

"Gray," Dr. Stacy chastised gently. "Remember, this is a bubble to be honest here without fear of recrimination. Whether you agree with it or not is perfectly fine and your right. But, perception is reality, and Christian is giving you her perception of that shared reality."

"Understood," Gray muttered.

"We're almost out of time, but there is an exercise I want you two to practice at home. I call it, 'There's a rock in my shoe.' Gray, when something small starts to bother you, I want you to look at Christian and say, 'Christian, there's a rock in my shoe,' and tell her about that small thing. Christian, you should do the same to Gray."

Gray looked at her, baffled. "Why a rock in my shoe?"

"Because when a rock gets in your shoe, it's a small annoyance that can be easily dealt with—the rock removed and tossed aside. But," she added, holding up a finger. "If you don't take it out, another one gets in, and another one, and another. Eventually, you can't walk, crippled due to too many rocks." She smiled at both women. "It's about learning to communicate, no matter how small the issue."

"Ah," Gray said, nodding. "Okay."

"And," Dr. Stacy added. "When someone says this, it's a bit of a safe word. It's that person's turn to talk out an issue without interruption, without dispute. All right?"

"Makes sense," Christian said.

"Good. Now, let's continue."

※ ※ ※ ※

"Thank you very much," Gray said, accepting the paper bag filled with their food order and cardboard tray of drinks. She secured it on the passenger seat before pulling out of the drive-thru.

After they left Dr. Stacy's office, they decided that Christian would head home to let Brutus out since he'd been in for several hours already, and Gray would stop and get them dinner. She pulled into the driveway and reached up to push the electric garage door opener. As the door buzzed upward, Christian's car came into view.

As she sat there, her own car idling as she waited for the door to fully open, she allowed herself a brief moment of happiness and peace to see that other car, indicative of the woman who shared the house with her.

They were still in separate bedrooms, and they'd been honest with their therapist about that. Dr. Stacy had recommended they continue doing what was comfortable for them both, but also start to consider if it was helping or hindering their shared goals. It was a lot to think about.

Christian was setting the table when Gray let herself in, Brutus in the backyard barking at something. Without a word, the two women got things ready, the silent communication of the truly connected who had years of history between them. Finally, they were sitting at the table eating their respective burgers.

"So, what do you think?" Christian asked, her tongue sneaking out to grab a glob of ketchup that had escaped to the corner of her mouth.

Gray smiled, grabbing a takeout paper napkin off the pile and handing it to her. "I like her. I think the whole 'rock in my shoe' thing is kind of strange, and it'll take some doing before I can say it with a straight face, but I see the point of it."

Christian dabbed at her mouth, nodding. "Agreed. There's some benefit there. And it's nice that the phrase triggers actual engagement, so we don't miss it when the other has something to say."

Christian was quiet for a moment as she took a sip from her soft drink. "You know, one thing I did like that she recommended was us taking the time to go over our day."

"Me too," Gray said, nodding. "We used to do that all the time." She met Christian's gaze. "Remember? We'd either talk while getting ready for bed or while lying in bed."

Christian gave her a sad, wistful smile. "I do," she said softly. "I used to love that. Why did we stop?"

Gray shook her head. "I think we just got too busy. Lame as that sounds."

"Okay, so, let's do like she said," Christian suggested. "You tell me one thing about your day, and I'll tell you one."

"All right." Gray finished chewing a bite of burger as she thought about what she'd share. Swallowing, she wiped her mouth with a napkin and said, "My desk is near our sports reporter, Alec, and that guy farts like every three minutes, I swear."

Christian's eyes opened wide, and she brought her napkin up in front of her mouth, obviously trying not to break into laughter.

"Today," Gray continued, "I'm sitting there on the phone with the couple I'm doing a story about and, *phoof!*" she said, making the sound of the near-silent sound. "Then suddenly, I'm like, Oh, my gawd!"

Christian was smiling full-on, now. "Oh, no..."

"Oh, yes," Gray assured. "I can see why the desk was open and why Linda was so eager to shove me into it." She grinned. "So, your day?"

Christian cleared her throat, obviously trying to get rid of her giggles. "Well," she finally said. "Not quite as odorous as your day, but Yancy has officially asked me to join her coaching team."

Gray stared at her, blinking a few times. "Wait, what?" she asked, the wonder she felt in her voice.

Christian nodded, looking at her a bit shyly. "I wasn't sure what you'd think of it. But she's gone into coaching Olympic hopefuls, and she thinks the girl she has right now can make it all the way. She wants to stay as the head coach on the team, the one dealing with the ice and such, but she wants me to work on her with dance."

Gray sat back in her chair, needing to gather herself for a moment. At one time she would have taken Christian in her arms and kissed her and told her how proud of her she was and how much she loved her. Not that she didn't feel all those things now, but it just wasn't appropriate anymore.

Instead, she smiled and said, "You know, I used to think that about you, the way you dance. Long before I knew your history. I used to think you glide across the floor like you're on ice or something. To me, it makes perfect sense that she'd want you to teach this girl that incredibly beautiful, unique way of movement. I have no doubt it'll make her a better figure skater, Christian."

A small smile touched Christian's lips just before she looked down, but not before Gray saw a glint of emotion in her eye. "Thank you," she said softly.

Gray looked away before she was tempted to do something stupid. She preoccupied her hands with her food. "Thanks for getting the therapy appointment all squared away."

Christian nodded, glancing up at her. "Thanks for getting dinner."

Chapter Fourteen

It was a gorgeous day, and the paths and trails around the Aurora Reservoir were filled with joggers, walkers, and people walking their dogs, as Gray was doing with Brutus at the moment, Dennis wheeling along beside them.

The workers were in the house installing the mirrors and ballet barre in the basement, finally turning it into the dance studio Gray had envisioned from the moment she'd first seen the house. They decided it would be a better idea to get the bullmastiff out of the house or risk a lawsuit from a worker dropping dead of a heart attack with Cujo staring them down.

Dennis, wearing his fingerless black leather gloves to protect his hands from blisters and the rubber tires of his wheelchair, was chattering on about his newest recipe that had flopped spectacularly. Gray's eyebrows fell. "My question is, on what planet did you think raspberry jelly and shrimp was a good idea?"

Dennis chuckled. "Pretty much what your mom said."

Gray was quiet for a moment, glancing down at Brutus to see him trotting proudly beside her. Finally, she garnered the courage to ask a question she'd been wanting to ask for the past couple weeks. "Dad," she began. "After you got hurt and could no longer dance with Mom, were you…Did you…" Her brow wrinkled as she tried to formulate exactly what she was wanting to say. "Did it change how you felt about Mom? In a bad way? Meaning," she added, realizing that wasn't exactly what she was trying to say. "Did you find yourself on the defense, or not trusting?"

"Oh, my goodness, yes," he said without hesitation. "Listen, Gray, this might be a bit more than you were after, but even though I could function as a man in the bedroom, I didn't feel like one. When I lost the use of my legs, I also felt I'd lost the ability to be a husband to Bernie or father to you and Ivan. See, it was all tied into dancing—who I was as a person, how I defined being "a man," a provider. Without that, I was nothing. Nobody."

Gray listened, saddened as the story of what had happened to him when she was just four months old hit far too close to home. "Did it affect your marriage?"

"Very much so. We damn near divorced when you were about six or seven."

Surprised, Gray glanced down at him as they walked. "Wow," she muttered. "Why?"

"Honestly? Me." He chuckled. "My self-esteem and self-worth were in the toilet. I was suspicious of every man—hell," he added with a snort. "Every *woman* your mom talked to. Surely they could give her what I couldn't."

Gray swallowed down emotion that threatened to sneak past her eyes and down her cheeks. "What was that?"

"A whole person," he said simply. "With my legs went my identity, Gray."

"Did you ever accuse her of cheating on you?" she asked, unable to keep the bitterness out of her voice.

"I did," he admitted. "Not with a specific person, but in general. It was all my own insecurity."

Gray looked down when she felt his hand on her forearm. She tugged lightly on Brutus's leash, stopping their forward progress as she looked into her father's eyes.

"Honey," he said softly. "Give her time. It's always been Christian the dancer and Gray the writer. It's still Gray the writer, but now it's just Christian." He gave her a loving smile. "She's got to figure out not only who she is as a person, but who she is with you."

※※※※

Gray turned on the couch and looked at Christian, who met her gaze. "Okay. Um, Christian, I have a rock in my shoe."

"All right," the dancer said quietly.

"It felt to me like you didn't take my job working on Richard's book seriously. Like it meant little to you." She looked down at her hands, which rested in her lap. Initially she'd said something because that's what Dr. Stacy had just instructed her to do, but as she said it, she realized just how hurtful it had been. "Um," she continued, taking a deep breath and meeting Christian's gaze again, which she'd been told was part of the exercise. "I felt like you didn't support me in finally achieving my dream of being a published author, even if it is just as Richard's ghostwriter."

For just a moment it looked as though Christian was going to refute what Gray had said, but instead, she nodded. "Okay. So, what I'm hearing you say," she said, per the therapist's instructions. "Is that you feel that, while your dream was coming to fruition, something you felt was deeply important to you, I did not take it as seriously, or understand what it meant to you. Right?"

Gray nodded with a smile. "Right. And," she said, glancing over at the therapist. "I'd like to add something, if I can?"

"Of course, Gray." Dr. Stacy waved her on.

Gray turned back to Christian. "Thank you for what you just said, and I want to add that I'm sorry for not speaking up. You can't fix what you don't know is broken. That part," she said, placing her hand on her own chest. "Is on me. I should have spoken my truth and not expected you to be a mind reader."

Christian gave her the softest smile, the look in her eyes just a ghost of the woman she'd known for so long. "I love you," Christian whispered shyly, then her eyes fell.

"I love you too," Gray whispered in return. It was the first time they'd said those cherished words in ages, though to Gray it was still scary to say, no matter how much she meant it. She looked back to their therapist, unable to look at Christian anymore. She was feeling a closeness to her that was making her feel uncomfortable. She wasn't there. Yet.

"This is our third session," Dr. Stacy said. "How are you ladies doing with getting Gray back into the bedroom?"

Gray said nothing, as it had been Christian who had kicked her out in the first place. She stared down at her hands once again.

"Um," Christian finally said, her voice soft. "I'd very much like to start that process."

"How do you feel about that, Gray?" Dr. Stacy asked.

How did she feel? Gray considered that question and, though she was still unsettled by recent events, she knew they had to move forward. Finally, she nodded. "I agree," she said, still looking at her hands.

❧ ❧ ❦ ❦

"This is the last of it," Gray said, a pile of folded T-shirts hugged to her chest. She walked over to her dresser and pulled open the drawer the shirts belonged in. Placing them inside, she hipped the drawer closed and surveyed the large master bedroom.

It looked as it always had, nothing had been added or subtracted—except her—but somehow it felt different. Christian appeared in the bathroom doorway. She'd gathered all of Gray's toiletries from the upstairs bathroom while Gray had moved her belongings from the spare bedroom. She met Christian's eyes.

"Still feel okay about everything?" the dancer asked.

Gray looked around the room again, hands on hips. Her gaze fell to the bed, knowing it was more comfortable than the one upstairs. Finally, she nodded, looking back at Christian. "Yeah. I do. You?"

Christian pushed away from the door frame and walked into the large room, a fair distance from Gray. "I do. Um, I'm going to jump in the shower, if that's okay. I have a really early morning tomorrow." She gave Gray a shy smile. "Erika is coming here for her first lesson with me now that the studio downstairs is ready, so…"

Gray nodded. "Okay." She gave her an awkward smile, not entirely sure what to do. "Sounds good."

Christian nodded before heading back into the bathroom. Gray let Brutus out for his final time of the night, then headed into the bathroom to get ready for bed.

The shower was still running when Gray entered the room, which was warm and soap scented. The air very much smelled like what Christian's neck smelled like when she used to bury her nose in it. Such a comforting aroma. Now, it was just confusing.

Standing at her sink brushing her teeth, Gray made the mistake of glancing up into the reflection of the bathroom. Just off over her right shoulder was the glassed-in shower stall. Though the glass was steamed, it wasn't hard to make out the glorious figure moving within.

Gray's actions slowed as she absently and mindlessly did the motions it took to brush her teeth. Her focus was completely on the naked body of the woman Gray had always thought was the most beautiful she'd ever seen.

Her body compact but extremely strong. With well-muscled thighs, a washboard stomach, and a strong back that Gray used to love running her tongue down, Christian Scott was stunning. Even with a muscled physique from years as a top-notch athlete, she was all woman. Her breasts were small yet perfectly shaped, with extremely responsive light rose nipples. She had hips that flared out just enough to drive Gray crazy and an ass that was as soft as it was firm.

Gray shook herself out of her thoughts, which was making her body want things that just weren't possible yet. Finishing her nightly routine, Gray hurried from the bathroom to change and get into bed, hoping to be asleep by the time Christian joined her.

She first settled into her default position, lying on her side with her back to Christian's half of the bed. Suddenly, she wondered if Christian would find that rude, like she was shutting her out, so she moved to her back, staring up at the ceiling. The adjustment made her feel out of sorts, like a stranger in her own home. When would anything ever feel easy, familiar, or comfortable again? She knew it was all in her own mind and she needed to work on reinstating herself in her own life. It would just take time.

Christian got settled in on her side of the large bed, the mattress shifting as she reached over and turned off the lamp on the nightstand, the room going dark. "You're off tomorrow, right?"

"I am," Gray acknowledged. "Why?"

"Well, and, if you don't want to, it's okay," Christian rushed to say. "But I was wondering if you'd mind filming Erika's lesson with me. It's only an hour. I want her to be able to study it."

"Of course," Gray said, not thinking twice. "Whatever you need."

"Thanks." Christian reached over under the sheet and took Gray's hand. "I'm glad you're here."

Gray looked over at her, just barely able to make out her face in the dimness. "Me too."

☙ ❧

Erika Abubakar was a lovely sixteen-year-old girl who had immigrated to the United States from Nigeria with her parents six years before, largely to pursue her dream to skate.

It had been nearly eight months since Christian's surgery, so her doctor gave her permission to teach, though she had to, in her doctor's words, "Let the students do most of the work."

As Gray filmed the entire hour's worth of training, she couldn't help but smile. In those sixty minutes she saw the light return to Christian. Saw the joy in her eyes, the lightness in her manner, heard the easy laughter in her voice, even as she was a strict teacher. She had Erika moving, sweating, but most importantly, learning.

It was delightful to see the *Ah-ha!* moments on Erika's face and the pride in her eyes when Christian excitedly clapped at her nailing the difficult move she was being taught. The young woman reminded Gray a lot of Christian back when Christian was in her early twenties dancing at Bernadette's theater. Her talent was palpable and almost scary, but she was clearly raw in some aspects, a rough stone begging to be polished.

Now, Christian was the silicon carbide to polish this beautiful gem, and it was touching to watch.

"Ready for a break?" Christian asked Erika, who was all but panting. At Erika's nod, Christian turned to Gray. "Baby," she said softly. "Would you mind running upstairs and getting us some water?"

Gray was surprised to hear the term of endearment that she hadn't heard in a long time. Despite her trying not to let it, it managed to wiggle its way directly into her heart. She smiled and nodded. "Sure."

Christian held her gaze for a long moment, the silent communication that had eluded them for far too long passing between them. Finally, the dancer smiled. "Thank you."

"It is such an amazingly beautiful day," Christian said, Brutus's leash in her hand as he trotted along with them at the Aurora Reservoir. "Not too hot yet," she said, smiling over at Gray who walked along with them.

"I agree. Really gorgeous day. Uh-oh," she said, noting a group headed their way down the path with a dog. "Want me to take him?"

"Yeah." Christian handed Brutus's leash over, as Gray was bigger and able to keep Brutus on a shorter leash, as it were, than Christian. Plus, they'd been extra careful since her surgery.

The powerful dog whined and whimpered, pulling at the leash as he wanted to go say hello to the other dog and passing people, but Gray did her best to stand her ground and keep him within a few feet of her. She wouldn't grab him by the collar unless he began to jump.

"Calm down, Brutus," Gray warned. "Calm down."

Gray smiled and nodded at the group of two men and a woman, who was also trying to keep her dog under control as they passed each other. Finally, the tension eased as the people and beagle passed and Brutus began to relax.

"Good boy," Gray said, rubbing his head. "You were a g'boy." She got them moving again when Christian called out to her.

"Hold on," she said. "I've got a rock in my shoe."

Gray stopped and took a deep, centering breath to brace herself for whatever Christian may need to talk to her about. They'd made great progress, but she was hoping today they could just have a nice afternoon walk.

Turning around she saw Christian a few steps behind her. "Okay," she said calmly. "What's up?"

Christian looked at her, confusion on her face for a moment before she burst into laughter. "No, I really have a rock in my shoe. Get over here so I can lean on you and get it out."

Gray felt the giggles start before they morphed into a full-on belly laugh that she just didn't seem to be able to control. She made her way over to Christian, who put her hand on Gray's shoulder but was laughing too hard to do much else. Gray's hand went to Christian's waist, and it was as if in that moment, many months of anger, hurt, tension, and confusion evaporated, a glacier of ice broken through

Somehow, Christian ended up in her arms, Gray's arms wrapped around her. The laughter died down, leaving the connection as their bodies were pressed together in the warmth of the full-body hug.

Gray's eyes fell closed as she buried her face in Christian's hair, which she'd let grow and now reached just below her shoulders. She'd missed the softness, the scent, the feel of it against her skin. The way Christian embraced her, almost in a desperate hold, Gray knew she was feeling it, too.

For months they'd been working with Dr. Stacy, clawing their way back up from the rock-bottom pit they'd found themselves in. As hard as it had been to face some fundamental truths about her own personal shortcomings, ways Christian felt she'd let her down and vice versa, during that quiet moment, a first physical touch of any real measure, she felt hope.

Gray felt a hand gently cup the back of her head,

such a loving move that she hadn't realized how much she'd missed until it was done. After several moments, Brutus got their attention when he whined from where he sat dutifully next to the couple.

Gray pulled away just a bit, distant voices getting closer on the path. She met and held Christian's gaze for a long moment, the dancer cocking her head to the side just slightly. The softest of smiles spread across full lips, so much unsaid in Christian's expression, though Gray understood it completely.

Bringing up a hand, Christian cupped Gray's face for just a moment before her hand fell away. "Let's go home. But, I still have a rock in my shoe."

Chapter Fifteen

Gray hipped the car door closed after pulling into the garage and headed into the house. She was already ready for the night's production at her parents' theater, so took the time to get a bouquet of flowers to present to her mother as a congratulations for the summer production.

Gray was dressed in a lightweight women's suit, casual but a step up from her mesh shorts on a warm summer night. It was opening night, and though she was happy for her mom, she was nervous. How would Christian feel, watching a production she hadn't been involved in? Is that what retirement looked like?

It took her much less time to get ready, so she decided to get out of Christian's way as she showered and did her magic. Walking into the kitchen, she set the two bouquets that she'd purchased from a nearby flower shop down on the cooking island..

She entered the walk-in pantry in search of the crystal vase she knew they had when Christian came padding into the room. Gray's movements, and her heartbeat, stopped.

Christian's hair was still wrapped up in her bath towel, turban-style, after her shower. She wore nothing more than a pair of thong underwear—no panty lines in her dress—and a strapless bra. Her body of absolute perfection was on full display.

Their years living in New York had turned them

into vampires with pale skin, not a lot of sun on the sidewalks of the concrete jungle, but now, with the yardwork they'd both put in, especially Christian, her skin was sun-kissed. She was beautiful and beyond sexy.

There was a time when Gray would have grabbed Christian, heaved her up to sit on the cooking island, and had her way with her. Hell, back in New York, that had happened many times. But now, even as Gray's body burned and she knew they had time before they had to leave, she froze.

Standing there, her hand on the pantry door, she felt impotent and incompetent. Why couldn't she just go over to her? Even tell her how amazingly beautiful she was? Why? She didn't have long to ponder that question as Christian grabbed a bottled water out of the fridge then sauntered out of the room, hips swaying ever so gently, just enough to capture Gray's attention. Like always.

Gray's head hung for a moment as she wrestled with her confusion. Maybe she needed to go back and see Dr. Stacy by herself to get past this hump of her own making.

※※※※

The show had been a total success, and Gray couldn't have been more proud of her mother and her students. It had been a small, low-budget play written by a local playwright that, together with Bernadette and Dennis's mastery of movement, had been turned into a magical production including dance and even a few musical numbers.

Gray stood with Bernadette and some of the cast members, as well as audience members who had bought a premium ticket or were season-ticket holders, which allowed them to hobnob with the cast after the show on opening night.

It was one of the very few shows Gray had watched purely as an audience member, rather than working as an usher or some such position as she'd done since childhood. Now, as she stood there sipping her glass of champagne, she looked around and realized that at thirty years old, she was older than many of those in the cast. Christian, who had just walked up to join their group, was thirty-five, a downright elder among the athletically talented. Where had the years gone?

"So, what did you think of Brianna?" Bernadette was asking, the question pulling Gray out of the morose direction her thoughts were headed.

"The lead?" Gray clarified. "I thought she was beautiful," she said at her mother's nod. "Very talented." Gray glanced across the group to see Christian staring down into her champagne.

※※※※※

The drive home was quiet, Christian mostly looking out the passenger-side window as Gray drove. She glanced over at the dancer from time to time but said nothing, not sure what to do. Was Christian was bothered by being at the show, perhaps, because she was not able to do them herself anymore?

They arrived at the house and parked in the garage, still silent as they headed inside. Gray glanced at her again as they headed into the kitchen once the puppy attack ended. She had bought two bouquets of flowers earlier, one for Bernadette, and one for Christian, though at the moment, she wasn't sure if it was a good idea to give them to her or not.

"Gray?" Christian finally said, after letting Brutus out to the backyard.

Gray looked at her from where she still stood in the kitchen. Her stomach dropped, as the quiet tone warned there might be trouble coming. "Yes?"

"Are you still attracted to me?"

Gray stared across the large space at her. Surely, she wasn't serious.

"Wait," she said, a bemused smile on her face. "Is this a rock-in-shoe thing?"

The carefully guarded expression in Christian's eyes turned dark, and the storm clouds rushed in. "Why, yes it is," she growled, reaching down and removing one of her high heels. She threw it to the floor, followed by the other. "A giant goddamn rock!"

Gray's eyes widened as she fully realized the significant misjudgment she'd made. "Why on earth would you even ask that?" she asked, confounded and a little hurt.

"Why won't you answer the question?" Christian pushed, walking over to Gray, near murder in her eyes. "Come on, you had plenty to say about Brianna Keebler, a goddamn dancer who's eighteen years old, yet I've all but thrown myself at you naked and not a fucking word! Not a fucking touch!"

Gray looked on in stunned silence as Christian advanced on her

"What?" Christian said, stepping into Gray's personal space. "Got nothin' to say? You supposed to be a writer or somethin'?"

"Stop this, Christian," Gray warned. She wasn't sure whether she should laugh, cry, or get angry.

"Stop what?" Christian asked, bringing her hands up to push against Gray's chest, sending her back a couple steps. "Stop what?" she asked again, eyebrow raised. "An eighteen-year-old kid more attractive to you? Or, is it the dancer part?" Another push, sending Gray back into the fridge. "Is that it, Gray? Was that where the attraction stopped? When I could no longer be your personal ballerina?"

Aghast, Gray stared at her. "Stop this." When Christian went to push her again, Gray grabbed her wrists. "Before somebody gets hurt."

Christian looked her dead in the eyes, tears beginning to well. "It's too late for that, Gray." She turned to walk away, but Gray held her wrists. Glaring at Gray, she tried to yank them away, but Gray held strong.

Something inside her snapped, and she knew in that moment that everything she'd been trying to do had backfired catastrophically. She loved this woman with every breath in her body, and goddamn it, she wanted her.

Gray tugged on Christian's wrists, forcing her back to her, their bodies colliding from the inertia. She leaned down, taking Christian's lips in a vicious kiss. Christian tried to pull away, so Gray used one hand to hold slender wrists, cupping the back of Christian's head with her free hand to hold her still.

She knew that Christian was strong as a damn ox, and that if she wanted to get away she would. Knowing she might very well find herself flat on her ass on the floor, Gray kept forcing the issue. It took a moment, but finally Christian sank into the kiss, which then became frantic, two dying women getting their first drink of life-preserving water.

Christian's hand was buried in Gray's hair, fingers taking the short, dark strands into her fist as she consumed Gray's mouth. Gray wanted her, and she wanted her now. Never breaking the kiss, she reached down and hiked Christian's emerald-green, knee-length dress up before yanking the thong down, Christian kicking it away once it slid down strong legs.

With almost superhuman strength, Gray cupped Christian's naked ass and heaved her up onto the countertop. Christian's head banged back against the upper cabinets, but neither cared as she took Gray's lips again in a hungry kiss.

Needing more, Gray broke the kiss and bent down, Christian groaning low in her throat as Gray forced her legs open wider and pushed her dress up and out of the way. Her mouth watered as the heated scent of Christian's need met her nose.

The first taste of Christian's desire garnered a long moan from Gray as she wrapped her arms around the dancer's hips. Christian was soaked, and Gray knew it wouldn't take long. Her tongue went directly to a swollen clit. She could hear Christian's whimpers and cries from above, her hands in Gray's hair, holding the strands painfully tight as she tried to buck her hips in rhythm with the quick laps of a firm tongue.

After a few moments, Christian cried out as her orgasm rocked her body, her hands slamming down onto the countertop on either side of Gray's arms to brace herself. Gray heard the bang as once again Christian's head fell back against the cabinet door.

One final slow lick all the way up Christian's seam to her clit, and Gray stood erect. She was immediately taken into a bear hug that included Christian's rock-hard thighs as well. She didn't care; it was the best hug of her life.

"Love me, Gray," Christian whispered breathily. "Please, just love me."

Gray pulled away just enough to look into Christian's face. She gave her a smile that she hoped captured all the love she felt in that moment. She gently swept soft blond strands behind the dancer's ears. "I love you with all that I am, baby," she murmured. "I have since I was seventeen years old and will until the day I die." She cupped her jaw, lightly caressing her cheek with a thumb. "So sorry I ever made you doubt that." She left a lingering kiss to full lips, then lightly kissed both eyelids that fell closed just before Gray saw tears welling once more. "I don't care if you're a dancer, if you're not a dancer, if you're cleaning toilets, or sitting on the couch watching soap operas. You're the love of my life, my soulmate."

Christian hugged her to her again, a bit less aggressively than before. She buried her face in Gray's neck. "I love you, Gray. So, so much."

"I love you, too, Christian," Gray responded, gently running her fingers through Christian's hair. "What do you say we take care of the animals then head to bed so I can really show you just how much?"

Brutus and Caesar fed and watered, and the kitchen counter sprayed and wiped down, the two headed hand in hand to the bedroom. Christian's kisses were soft, sultry, and deeply arousing as she undressed Gray. Truth was, Gray had no idea how she'd gone without for so many months after living on a steady diet of them for years.

Gray was softly instructed to climb into bed, which she did. Christian followed once she tugged her dress off over her head and removed her bra. Gray watched her partner crawl over to her and a jolt of anticipation shot through her body, landing squarely between her legs. She reached for Christian, guiding her on top as their lips met again.

The feel of Christian's skin against her own was heaven. She ran her fingers down along Christian's strong back, the muscles moving beneath the soft skin. As they kissed, Christian maneuvered to straddle one of Gray's thighs, Gray's skin instantly slick with her renewed need. Christian urged Gray's other thigh to move, opening her up to deft fingers.

Gray's gasp was swallowed by Christian's mouth as two of the dancer's fingers gently entered her. The kiss broke, though Christian stayed close as she gently rocked her hips against Gray's leg while making love to Gray with firm thrusts that matched the rhythm of her hips.

Eyes falling closed, Gray's free leg fell to the side, allowing Christian all the room she needed. Even as the thrusts were slow and deep, her pleasure was rising. Hearing Christian's little whimpers and sighs only added to it, knowing they were feeling much of the same thing, giving as they took, connected through their endless passion for each other.

Christian gasped loudly, her hips bucking against Gray's thigh as her orgasm seemed to overcome her quickly. Her fingers stilled inside Gray for just a moment as her brain caught up to her overwhelmed body. After a moment, she got her bearings back and quickly changed her position, keeping her fingers inside Gray as she moved her body down between Gray's legs.

Gray groaned deep in her throat as the thrusting began again as a tongue flitted against her clit. Her back arched and her breasts heaved as the pleasure began low before it exploded throughout her body, exiting her mouth as she cried out, loud and long.

She tried desperately to catch her breath as the final wave of her orgasm rippled away. She felt light-headed, as if everything her body had been holding in for the last half a year had finally burst forth in one, long go, leaving her spent.

Christian crawled back up beside her, lying on her side facing Gray. After a few moments of deep breaths, Gray turned to her side to face her. Legs entwined, Gray rested her hand on Christian's thigh and looked into the beautiful green eyes that she adored. She saw so much love and peace there, something she hadn't seen in a long, long time.

"I've missed you," Christian said softly.

"Me too, baby," Gray said, thumb lightly caressing the soft skin of Christian's thigh. "Can I tell you something?"

"Of course you can." Christian glanced over when the bed shifted slightly as Caesar jumped up. She grinned as the cat surveyed the scene, eyeing them both. "Guess he feels it's safe now."

Gray smiled, reaching out her hand to the feline who climbed over their entwined bodies to get to his place up near the headboard. Gray refocused her attention back on the woman she loved, even as Caesar purred against the top of her head, which was amusing and a bit distracting.

"Anyhoo," Gray said dramatically, making Christian grin. "Watching you work with Erika," she said, an instant smile coming to her lips. "It's so beautiful."

Christian's smile was shy. "Really? I mean, you don't think it's pathetic, that I'm the teacher? Rather than being in rehearsals for something."

"Oh, god, no!" Gray caressed Christian's cheek, hoping her eyes held the love and adoration she felt for her. "Baby," she began gently, keeping in mind what she'd learned over the months in therapy. "You're the best dancer I've ever seen in my entire life. And, I've said that to many people for many, many years. Honestly, you're one of the greatest of your generation." She smiled. "Erika's family has been through so much, of course back in Nigeria but also just to get her here to train and have a chance at success. What better person to teach her? Honestly, I think it was a brilliant move on Yancy's part."

Christian's smile was genuine, her eyes twinkling. "Thanks, baby," she whispered. "I really want you to get to know Yancy. Would it be okay if we had her and her husband over for dinner or something?"

"Of course," Gray said without hesitation. "I'd really love that." Gray's phone rang from her bedside table—Michael's ringtone. About to ignore it, she saw the deeply mischievous look on Christian's face. "What?"

"Gimmie," Christian said, holding her hand out. "Let's give a gay boy a big ol' lezbo hello." Christian tapped the button to decline the call. With perfect calmness, she went into Gray's incoming log and called him back using the FaceTime app.

"Oh, no," Gray said, a deep chuckle in her throat. "You're not."

"I am," Christian said, glancing up at her from the phone.

Gray could hear the sound of the video call being sent, then picked up.

"Hey, there!"

"Hey, Michael," Christian answered with a smile as she rolled over onto her back and as close to Gray as she could. Gray could see the screen: a close-up of Christian's face, leaving it a mystery for Michael to determine where she was. "Gray was occupied so she couldn't grab the phone," she fibbed with a grin. She widened the shot just enough to add in Gray's face as well.

"Hey," Gray greeted with a smile, fully in on the gag now. "Sorry, we were busy."

Christian brought up the phone a bit, showing their heads and bare upper chests and shoulders. "Yeah," Christian echoed. "Busy."

Michael's eyes grew huge and his hands came to cover his mouth. "Oh, my god!" he gasped excitedly. "You two had sex!"

"Just finished, actually," Gray said casually, though she was dying laughing inside. She'd kept Michael abreast of their situation over the weeks, as he'd been deeply concerned.

"Oh, god!" He gasped again, this time as realization hit his face. "I didn't need to know that!"

"Oh," Gray said, looking down the length of her body, which was of course out of frame of the video call. "I'm almost dry, now."

"Ew! Wait, was that a boob?"

Christian grinned. "Well, between the two of us, there *are* four of them here, so," she concluded with a smile. "It's entirely possible one of the little buggers popped in a cameo."

The call went dead, the screen blank.

Christian cackled in delight as she reached past Gray to place the phone back on her bedside table before taking Gray in a deep kiss.

Chapter Sixteen

Gray was humming as she got out of the shower. It had been a wonderful start to a lazy Saturday. She'd awoken to kisses and caresses, which of course she could never refuse. After a very sensual morning, Christian had gotten up to make coffee and care for the animals while Gray showered.

She'd invited the dancer to join her, but they both knew they'd never get out of the house if she did, and they had plans to head to the farmers' market and get some fruits and vegetables.

She quickly dried off, hung her towel, and padded naked to the bedroom to get dressed. Panties and bra on, she'd just sipped on a pair of cargo shorts when she heard the doorbell ring and Brutus go nuts.

"Crap," she muttered, quickly grabbing her tank top and tugging it on.

"Thank you," Christian said loud enough to be heard over the dog, then heard the front door close.

Gray slid her feet into some flip-flops and began to run her fingers through her damp hair as she headed out of the bedroom only to be met by Christian and Brutus in the open doorway.

"Everything okay?" Gray asked.

Without responding, Christian took one of Gray's hands in hers. "Come with me."

Gray was led to the kitchen where a FedEx box sat on the cooking island. She saw that it was addressed to her with a return address from Richard. Surprised, Gray gripped the box and, from its heft, had a good idea what it might be. She glanced up in time to see Christian walk back over to her with a knife.

Heart racing, Gray sliced through the tape. One flap up, two, three, then four. Atop a covering of crinkly brown paper, which she already had in mind for Caesar, was a card, the same type as had been included with the scotch.

A quick glance to Christian, she set the knife down and opened the card. Gray read his neat, bold script aloud: "'Dearest Gray. I'm not pleased with the fact that this was omitted from the contract, but be that as it may, I buck the system once again.'" She smiled, not even knowing what he'd done. "'Share your gift, my darling. And I extend an invite to you AND your lady to join me for a book signing and a weekend of wonders in New York. Below are the dates available, as I know you two are busy bees. Cheers! R.'"

Setting the card aside, Gray once again met Christian's gaze. They two shared a smile and a shrug before Gray turned her attention back to the box. She removed the brown paper and revealed two even stacks of books, the hardback version of *Call Me Sir*. Richard never used his knighted designation, which had become a bit of a joke in the press, so the publisher thought it was a perfect title.

The cover of the book was a black-and-white photo taken by Fatima, a close-up of his face. His ever-present smile was in place, his eyes full of mischief. But what caught Gray's eye and made her gasp just a little bit was how her name had been included. She'd expected a subtitle along the lines of: *A memoir by Richard Cox with Gray Rickman,* with her name in point-three font. But, no. Instead, all in large, bold script, it read: *Mumblings by Richard Cox and those who embarrass him the best as told to Gray Rickman.*

"Oh, Gray," Christian breathed out.

Gray could hardly breathe herself when it registered that he'd essentially given her complete writing credit, not just as a ghostwriter. She reached in and picked up one of the copies and, as she held it in her hands, it felt just like holding her own newborn baby. Tears came to her eyes as she stared down at a lifelong dream, realized. She wiped at the smooth book jacket with her fingers, unable to speak.

"It was all worth it, baby," Christian said softly, so much pride in her eyes.

Gray met her gaze and nodded, letting out a long, shaky breath. "What do I do with all these?" she asked with a shy chuckle, pulling out the ten copies from the box.

"Are you kidding me?" Christian said, grabbing one and hugging it to her chest. "I, for one, am going to read it!" She held it out. "Sign it for me?"

Touched, Gray smiled. "Sweetheart, you honestly don't have to read that. Please don't feel obligated." Gray recoiled a bit when that one eyebrow slowly slid upward.

"When you went to my shows," Christian began quietly. "Was it out of obligation?"

"God no," Gray exclaimed. "I loved watching you dance."

Christian said nothing more, simply held the book up with that eyebrow arched.

Gray smiled, nodding. "Point taken." She leaned over and left a lingering kiss on soft lips. "I hope you like it."

"Gonna love it," Christian insisted. "So proud of you."

Gray felt like she'd just won the lottery. "Thank you," she murmured. "And, about the trip…I want you to go with me, Christian. But, if you don't want to, or can't…" She shrugged. "I know you just started up with Erika and Yancy. But," she added, "Let me be clear. I want you with me." She'd learned her lesson—boy had she. She wanted absolutely no questions about motive or lack of communication.

Christian met her gaze for a long moment before she set the book down gently on the island top then turned to Gray, grabbing both her hands and looking up into Gray's face. "I know we're both still a little bit leery of things, trying to step carefully after everything that happened. Richard told me that you'd asked if I could go on that last trip, and that it was *him* who told you it wasn't a good idea because of the short trip and busy schedule."

Gray nodded. "Yes."

"I know that we covered this a bit in Dr. Stacy's office, but I never really spoke to you privately, apologized to you privately, and you deserve that." She tilted her head slightly, looking deeply into Gray's eyes, into her very soul. "I'm so sorry about my behavior. About believing a woman who you'd already mentioned was a bit odd and inappropriate. You were honest with me from the start." She continued with a heavy sigh. "I allowed my own insecurities and self-doubt to allow me to play right into her hands. Forgive me?"

Gray's heart melted right across her lips in a smile. "Of course I do, baby."

"You've never lied to me, never given me *any* reason to doubt you. I'm so sorry."

Gray took her into a warm embrace, just holding her. "We both played our part in that mess, baby," she said into fragrant blond hair. "I'm sorry too." Her eyes fell closed. There was literally nowhere on earth she wanted to be in that moment but exactly where she was. "I want you to come with me,' she whispered. Despite what Christian had just said, she knew she really could have pushed it with Richard and found a way for her and Christian to have some time in New York together, even if it was after her book obligations. She'd made Christian feel unwanted, unimportant, and left out. Never again.

"I'd love to go," Christian said into the hug, her words somewhat muffled against Gray's neck. "Maybe we can take in a show?" she asked, pulling away and looking at Gray's face.

Gray studied her face for a long moment. "Will you be okay to do that?"

Christian nodded. "I think so. See what's on Broadway." She smiled. "Go to dinner with Michael and Kevin, if Michael will ever be willing to show his face again." She gave an evil grin. "See some of my friends from the show days."

Gray smiled and nodded. "I think it sounds amazing."

※ ※ ※ ※

"Okay," Christian said, walking out of the bedroom in the massive suite Richard had arranged for them. "This place is no joke."

Gray grinned, pulling the bottle of champagne out of the ice bucket it had been chilling in. "No, it is not," she agreed, reading the label of the bubbly. "And unbelievably generous of our own Sir Richard."

"There's a clear heart-shaped tub in there," Christian said, thumb hitched back toward where she'd come. "I honestly thought something like that didn't exist outside of Vegas."

Gray lifted the bottle and an eyebrow in invitation. With the nod she got, she stepped away from her partner and unwrapped the foil around the top before untwisting the wire cap. When it popped off, both women let out a little cry of surprise before the laughter came.

Crystal flutes filled, Gray set the bottle back into the ice and held up her glass. "What shall we toast to?"

Christian stared into the golden depths of her glass before meeting Gray's gaze. "To us. To amazing opportunities during this trip, and to new beginnings in all ways."

Gray nodded in agreement and tapped her glass against Christian's before taking a drink of the best champagne she'd ever had. "Now, *that* is seriously good."

"I agree." Christian pulled up the silver cloche next to the ice bucket, revealing beautiful red strawberries. "Oh, my," she murmured. She gave Gray a side-glance. "When do we have to meet them for dinner?"

"Seven thirty."

Christian hugged the bowl of strawberries to her side and turned away. "Let's go give that Jacuzzi tub a try."

༺༻

"I'm so glad!" Gray said with a smile. "You made

my day, ma'am."

"Will you please sign this to my son?" the woman asked, pushing a second book in front of Gray. "He's fourteen and really wants to be an author someday too. I think it would mean everything to him to get an autograph from an actual author."

The title alone sent a little thrill through Gray, even as a stack of the books with her name on them sat next to her on the table set up for her and Richard. "What's his name?" She penned a quick note of encouragement to the teen and handed the book back to his mom with a smile.

As the woman walked away, Gray looked past the next person stepping up to the table and saw Christian standing back by the Self-Help section with two women she recognized from the dancer's years on stage. The three friends were going to lunch while Gray had her signing. Christian had her phone out and seemed to be recording Gray signing books and talking to people.

She smiled, somewhere inside feeling dorkishly excited that Christian was seeing her sign books and talk to these people as an author. It might be her only chance to ever do this, and she wanted Christian to be proud of her.

Later that night they had tickets to see *Phantom of the Opera*, which was Gray's favorite production ever—outside of anything Christian had done, of course. She knew a couple of Christian's close dance friends were in the show as well. Life was good. Life was damn good.

Gray was on her feet, hands stinging from the long minutes of clapping, her cheeks still wet from crying at the entire last part of the show. Her face hurt from smiling, her chest still expanded as it was filled with all the emotions the show always made her feel.

The charismatic actor/singer who played the Phantom came out for his curtain call, the last of the cast to do so. The troupe came together at the apron of the stage in a long line, holding hands, and did a round of bows together.

As the applause began to die down, Gray was ready to gather their things when the woman who had played Christine Daae began to speak. "Ladies and gentlemen," she called out. "First, I'd like to thank you all for coming tonight. It means the world to us to have you in our house." She gave a brilliant smile as she scanned out over the audience. "If you don't mind, we'd like you to join us in a special moment." She paused as the audience cheered. "Yeah? Are you all right with that?" The applause grew louder as the man who played the Phantom walked up beside her. "Wonderful!"

"Someone very special is in the house tonight," the Phantom said. "Our friend, and for many of you who are theater and dance fans, a name you love, Christian Scott!"

Thunderous applause rent the air as the spotlight began to dance along the heads of the audience members.

"Heeeeeeeere, Christian, Christian, Christian," the female singer prodded, audience members laughing. Finally, the spotlight found the row where Gray and Christian sat, eight rows back from the stage. No surprise, considering Christian's friends in the show had gotten them tickets. "There she is! Stand up, lady!"

Christian met Gray's gaze, her eyes wide with surprise, but she stood, turning to the audience of nearly seventeen hundred people, and raised her hand to wave. Gray applauded with the rest of the crowd, so proud as she looked up at the dancer who she felt very much deserved the love she was getting.

"Come up here, Christian!" Phantom called out, waving her over.

Christian looked down at Gray, holding her hand out to her. Gray looked down at that hand then up at her in confusion. "Come on," Christian shouted over the thunderous sound.

Her stomach flipping, Gray took her hand and was pulled from her seat. The two made it down the aisle and around the orchestra pit to the stairs stage left. Gray's eyes were wide as they got closer to the entire cast, still in costume, clapping and smiling at them. She'd been around performers her entire life, but somehow, for some reasons, this felt different. Feeling like a fish out of water was a gross understatement.

Gray hung back once they reached the stage, giving space for Christian's moment to shine. One of the young women playing a ballerina in the show ran back onto the stage from the wings with a microphone, which she handed to Christian.

Gray crossed her arms over her chest, watching with a smile on her face as Christian addressed the audience. She looked out over the masses and had to admit it was pretty spectacular. She could see how it would be quite addictive to have so many people focused on you and your singular talent.

"My happiest moments as an adult have been on the stage," Christian was saying. "Playing dress-up as an adult is the ultimate rush."

Gray smiled at that. Though she'd been with Christian for more than seven years and had seen her on the stage hundreds of times, she'd never seen her interact like this. Her quiet nature disappeared and suddenly the performer appeared. She was full of life, cracking jokes, the charisma oozing from her. She was beautiful, she was sexy, and, as Gray grinned at the thought, she was hers.

"I'd like to introduce you all to someone," Christian said, turning to Gray. She held out a hand to her.

Gray swallowed and glanced back out into the massive house, most of the people in darkness but she knew they were there. She felt a small push on her back and knew it was one of the cast members she'd been standing near.

Reaching Christian, Gray looked out over the crowd again, nervous. She was more than fine watching from the side.

"Everybody, this is Gray Rickman. She's an author, my partner, and the love of my life." She met Gray's gaze and smiled the smile that was reserved for Gray. "You see," she continued into the microphone. "About eleven years ago I was taking lessons in dance from an amazing dancer named Bernadette Rickman."

Somewhere in the darkness someone let out a loud cat whistle, which garnered Gray's attention. Her grin grew as she wondered if that was somebody who remembered her parents.

"Wasn't she amazing?" Christian asked in the direction of the whistle. "So," she said, glancing over at Gray again. "This beautiful woman is Bernadette's daughter. A feisty, cocky seventeen-year-old at the time." She brought up a hand to shield her mouth from Gray as she spoke "conspiratorially" to the audience. "She used to spy on me while I danced," she stage-whispered, laughter rippling through the audience and those on stage.

Gray buried her face in her hands, which brought even more laughter and a few pats and squeezes on the shoulder from those around her.

"So, here we are," Christian continued. "All these years later. I'm going to do this right this time."

Gray dropped her hands and looked up in time to see Christian fall to one knee. Gray gasped, at first worried that her knee had given out, but when she saw the look in Christian's eyes as she reached for Gray's hands with her own, Gray's heart began to race. A loud gasp went up collectively as understanding hit the audience members.

"Gray," Christian began, one of the cast members holding the microphone for her. "We've been through so much together. Good, bad, and everything in between."

Gray nodded at the truth of those words.

"Through it all, I've fallen in love with you even deeper." Christian smiled up at her. "So, would you be my wife?"

Gray could only nod, her words choked up with surprise and love. Finally, she managed into the microphone that was aimed at her: "Yes."

The theater erupted, the entire audience on their feet as Christian got slowly to hers. She took Gray into a bone-crushing embrace, Gray burying her face into her neck.

Chapter Seventeen

Gray looked down at the ring on her left ring finger yet again, unable to resist as she waited for Natalie to finish with her phone call. After they'd left the theater the previous night, Christian had surprised her with the engagement ring, which she'd bought before they'd even moved back to Colorado. But, after Christian's injury and the subsequent implosion of their relationship, the ring had remained stowed away safely and secretly in Christian's jewelry box.

The ring was beautiful. It was a simple yet elegant gold band with three inlaid diamonds separated by both Christian's and Gray's birthstones. She couldn't stop looking at it, its slight weight on her finger a comfort and constant reminder of what almost wasn't.

"Okay," Natalie said, cradling the phone with a heavy sigh. "My God, that woman is seriously trying. So." She refocused on Gray, who sat on the opposite side of Natalie's desk in the small but beautifully appointed office. "Contract stuff done. You're good with it all, right? Do you need me to go over anything?"

"No, ma'am," Gray said, shaking her head. "I understand everything, and we're good."

"Good thing." Natalie smirked. "Since you already signed it. Okey dokey, so down to business." The middle-aged bottle-blonde had a smoker's rasp. "So, as you know, my role here as your agent is to parse through any offers for your writing services, appearances, and all that jazz, as well as act as your negotiating voice and submitter to publishers for any original work you want to try and get a publishing deal for."

Gray nodded, butterflies in her stomach at the mention of everything. It blew her mind that she was sitting in the office of one of the best agents in the business. Sure, Richard and Natalie were old friends, but Gray knew the woman wouldn't put her reputation on the line as a favor. No pressure.

"I have offers. Shall we go over them?" Natalie asked.

&.&.&.&.

"Okay, so you're telling me your options right now are, either you sign a contract with Simon & Schuster to essentially be a ghostwriter for a certain number of books for a certain period of time," Michael said as he, Christian, and Gray strolled through Central Park. "This would give you a guaranteed income, and a pretty darn good one, though no royalties, no real credit per se, and no part of the advance."

"Correct," Gray said, sipping from the fruit smoothie they'd picked up before entering the park.

"All right. And," Michael continued. "The other major offer on the table is another publisher who wants to sign you for a one-book deal, which of course would be royalties and a small advance."

"Also correct," Gray said with a nod.

"Royalties are quarterly, so could be a good payout, but are you allowed to work on your own book if you take the ghostwriter gig?" he asked.

"Oh, hell." Gray laughed, glancing at Christian briefly. "I wouldn't have time, considering the time Richard's book took."

"Fair statement," Michael said. "You asked for my advice, and as your financial advisor, I'd advise taking the sure thing for the time being."

"That's what we were thinking too," Christian chimed in. "I figure while doing the other contracted projects, she can learn the ins and outs of the industry before writing her own book."

"I agree—" Michael cut himself off as he glanced over at Gray, stopping their momentum with a hand to her arm before he grabbed her left hand. "What is this?"

Gray gave him a sheepish grin. "Yeah, um, about that…"

"When?" he asked, eyeing both women. "And you *must* let Kevin and I help plan."

Gray burst into laughter. "We don't know yet. We just kind of reaffirmed our engagement last night, so…We want to tell Mom and Dad and then go from there. And," Gray added with a raised eyebrow. "As for your help, *no* drag show at the reception."

He threw his head back and let a loud bark of laughter escape as he moved between them, an arm around each of their shoulders. He leaned down and left a loud, firm kiss on both women's cheeks. "Congratulations, ladies. 'Bout damn time."

※※※※

"Let me see, let me see, let me see!" Bernadette rushed over to them as they entered Gray's parents' house, her mother nearly ripping Gray's arm off as she yanked her left hand up and over to get a better look.

"Clearly, Michael called you." Gray laughed, amused as she tolerated her mother hijacking her hand.

Bernadette glanced up at her, a "busted" look in her eyes. "Don't be mad at him," she said. "He's so excited for you girls." She released Gray's hand only to grab the entire woman, crushing her daughter to her. "So happy for you," she whispered. "We were so worried."

"It's okay," Gray whispered back. "Everything's okay."

Bernadette left a noisy kiss on Gray's cheek before releasing her and grabbing Christian in an equally crushing hug. She whispered something to her as well, but Gray couldn't make it out and figured it was for Christian's ears only anyway.

One final squeeze and Bernadette let Christian go. "Okay, you two. Your dad is out back barbequing steaks for dinner, so I hope you girls are hungry." She glanced at the two of them as she turned away to lead the trio through the house. "I didn't say anything to him," she said, nodding toward the ring. "Figured you'd rather tell him yourself."

Sure enough, Dennis was in his chair on the deck in front of the special, lower barbecue grill, a large spatula in his hand. His smile was wide and instant when Gray and Christian stepped through the open back door.

"My girls!" he exclaimed, arms open for a hug.

"Hey, Dad," Gray said, leaning down and giving him a big squeeze. She stepped aside to allow Christian room to do the same before she spoke again. "So, uh, Dad," she began, glancing over at Christian and hoping she'd play along. "We wanted to tell you something." Gray's voice was quiet, serious.

She noticed out of the corner of her eye that Bernadette turned away, but not before she saw the smile beginning. Clearing her throat, she took a deep breath and continued.

"As you know, Dad, we've been together a long time, and..." She shrugged, glancing again at Christian, who nodded sagely. She looked back to Dennis, who was looking from one to the other, a great deal of concern creasing his brow. "We've decided that, after a really tough year, it's time for us to, well, to make a big decision."

"All right," he said slowly. "What, ah...What's going on?"

Another glance at Christian, then Gray struck a superhero pose, throwing out her left first as if in a punch. "Shazam!"

Dennis's eyes widened in surprise and he leaned back a bit in his chair. His mouth opened as if to say something, Gray figured to scold her, but then the glint from her ring caught his eye and he was locked on it. The wide eyes turned from startled-surprised to delighted-surprised.

"Really?" he asked, his voice quiet, almost like a little boy sounding afraid to hope.

"Really," Christian said with a winning smile.

"Yeah, she kinda asked me in front of nearly seventeen hundred people," Gray said with a smirk. "What else was I supposed to say?" She laughed when Christian smacked her. Leaning over, she gave her a quick, apologetic kiss for her teasing before turning back to her dad. "Yes, Dad. It's for real, and I've never been happier."

Dennis took her hand, leaving a lingering kiss on her knuckles. The smile he gave her as he patted her hand and released it was serene. "I'm so deeply pleased," he said softly. "You two found your way back to each other. As it should be."

❧❧❧❧

Zipping her backpack, Gray carried it to the hall and set it down next to her roller bag. Two full months of travel were ahead of her. This time, however, she was getting all her travel for her current project out of the way in one giant go, hopscotching her way across the country and into Canada.

She had a few minutes before her shuttle was to arrive to take her to the airport, so she headed toward the basement stairs. As she neared them, she smiled as she heard Freddie Mercury exclaim just how much he would rock you.

She hummed along as she trotted down the stairs to find Christian, already dressed for Erika's training in short mesh shorts and a racerback tank top. Her hair was pulled up into a ballerina's bun, feet not yet taped. She had the music blasting as her body moved to it, unable to keep still even as she cleaned the massive mirrors in the dance studio.

Gray grinned, her eyes immediately drawn to that perfect ass as it swayed in time to the music, the muscles in Christian's upper back and shoulders working under the tan skin as she used the long-handled squeegee to reach the top of the mirror to slowly remove the spray cleaner.

She sauntered over to the dancer, who caught her reflection in the mirror. She didn't stop what she was doing, didn't stop her body's movement, rather she moved with Gray once she walked up behind her and grabbed her by the hips, molding their bodies together from behind.

Gray buried her face in Christian's neck as they swayed together. She smiled when she felt Christian's hand in her hair. Leaving a kiss on the warm neck, Gray moved away enough for Christian to turn in her arms after dropping the squeegee, the two now pressed together front to front, still moving to the music.

"Leaving soon?" Christian murmured, fingers running through dark strands.

"I am," Gray said, gaze scanning the beautiful face so close to her own. Her fingers lightly trailed down Christian's spine before her hands rested on her behind.

Christian gave her a little smirk and flexed her glutes for good measure. "What am I doing to do without you here for so long?"

Gray grinned. "Celebrate? Dance naked around the house?"

"I already do that," Christian murmured, trailing a fingernail along Gray's jaw. "That's how we ended up breaking the clock in the living room."

"Right," Gray chuckled. "My hip still hurts from that one. You'll be there Saturday though, right?"

Christian nodded, her gaze falling to Gray's shirt as she picked off a Caesar hair from it. "I will definitely be there Saturday."

"Okay, good. By week's end, I'm sure I'll be ready to lose my mind." Gray looked down at herself to see what Christian had spotted. "My shuttle should be here in just a couple minutes."

"I'm so sorry I couldn't take you today, baby,"

Christian said softly.

"Don't be," Gray said with a smile. "You have a job to do. I totally understand that. It was a bummer. Mom couldn't take me, but she had to take Dad in so his doctor could get some bloodwork done for his medications or something."

"Well," Christian said, slapping Gray on the ass before leading the way toward the stairs. "I'll walk you up, at least."

They reached the entryway where Gray had left her luggage just as the shuttle was pulling up in front of the house. Christian pulled Gray into a tight hug, cupping the back of her head.

"I love you so much," she whispered into Gray's neck. "Call me when you land in Cleveland, okay?"

"I promise," Gray said, eyes closed. "I love you too, baby. With all my heart." She held her tight for a long moment before letting her go. "Take care of Mom and Dad for me, will ya?"

Christian rolled her eyes. "Kidding me?" She reached down and grabbed Gray's backpack after their hug ended. "Your mom can outrun me any day of the week and twice on Sunday."

"Yes, but you'll be busy on Sunday," Gray purred.

Christian chuckled. "*If* you're that lucky," she responded, the glance she gave her over her shoulder smoldering.

⁂

Gray drained her coffee cup, a small shiver passing through her at the strong brew. What was it with cheap, hotel coffee? Didn't matter how strong or how weak it was made, it still tasted like Mississippi mud.

She set the empty cup aside and returned her

attention to the screen on her laptop. It had been a long week filled with a ton of interviews, some pretty dry. Her first book to be written under her contract with Simon & Schuster was for a politician. He was a sophomore senator out of Ohio, and though Gray found politics interesting, it was difficult to keep her own thoughts and leanings to herself and be totally objective in her work.

Her political work at the *Times* was definitely coming in handy. She pushed her computer glasses a bit higher on her nose as she continued to organize her notes and her thoughts.

She created a new file, intending to put the added notes from that day into it when she heard a knock on her hotel room door. Glancing over, she let out an irritated sigh before pushing away from the desk.

Unlocking the door, she pulled it open to find one of the hotel employees holding a rectangular box covered in plain brown paper. She looked down at it, then up at the man standing there holding it.

"What's this?" she asked.

"This was delivered for you, Miss Rickman," he said with a nod before turning and walking away.

Gray closed the door, eyebrows drawn as she looked down at it. Curious, and a bit nervous, she brought it up to her ear to make sure it wasn't ticking. Nothing, and amused with her own theatrics, she tore open the paper, which had no markings, writing, nothing at all on it.

Walking over to the desk, she tossed the paper aside, which came off in one piece. The plain white box was about eight inches long and three inches deep. Inside she found a black satin bag, and inside that, a nicely sized, deep purple dildo.

Staring at it, Gray was utterly confused. She figured the hotel clerk had to have brought it to the wrong room, it had to belong to another guest. She was about to reach for the room phone when her personal cell rang and it was Christian.

"Crap," she muttered. After the events of the late spring, she had no idea how she'd explain this one. "Hey, baby," she said into the phone, still staring at the toy. "Well," she said in response to the question of what she was doing. "I'm actually staring at a very unexpected and very confusing delivery." She gave a nervous laugh. "I'm pretty sure it was delivered to the wrong room." She cringed. "Well. Uh. Well, it's a dildo." She waited for the gasp of shock or cackle of laughter, but neither came. "You want to see it?" she asked, surprised. "Yeah, I can take a picture if you want. I'm going to call the front desk. This was clearly not meant for me." She laughed nervously again, the entire situation feeling weird.

Gray cringed again when an image of Fatima Darmandi came to mind. That sent shivers down her spine and an instant bad taste into her mouth. She didn't have long to choke on it before there was another knock at the door.

"Okay, hang on, Christian," Gray said. "Somebody's knocking again. Crap," she growled, stuffing the toy back into the bag and into the box. "Hope the guy isn't pissed that it's unwrapped."

Gray left the phone on the desk and hurried to the door, pulling it open only to stop dead in her tracks. On the other side stood Christian, phone still held to her ear and a sexy little smirk on her face.

"I told you I wanted to see it."

Chapter Eighteen

Gray could only stare. Christian stood in the hallway just outside of her opened door dressed in a long, black cloak, the heavy material covering her entire body. It wasn't so much the cloak she wore, which was different to be sure, but the look in her eyes. She wore makeup that was dark and dangerous, her hair brushed to a shine, the golden color in deep contrast with the midnight black of the cloak.

The woman standing before Gray was the very image of lust, desire, and sensuality come to life. Gray cleared her throat from first her shock of seeing her there, then her instant and primal reaction to her. "Travel like that, did you?" she asked, her voice cracking.

Christian gave her a sexy little grin. "Oh, yeah," she said, reaching up and tugging free the tie that held the cloak closed. As if in slow motion, the black material parted to reveal the naked perfection of the vixen that stood before her, save for one little detail. "Security pat-down was a bitch."

Gray grabbed Christian's hand and tugged her inside the room, closing the door behind them. Her gaze traveled down the delicate structure of Christian's shoulders, the hollow of her throat, where her tongue wanted to be, over small, full breasts with perfectly shaped nipples, down over a flat, muscular stomach to land on something that wasn't there last time she saw her.

"Um, baby?" She stuck a finger in the little ring that the leather harness strapped to her hips left open at her crotch. She raised an eyebrow as she met Christian's gaze.

"I believe you have something of mine," Christian said, reaching down to take the box out of Gray's hand. "Thank you," she said cheerfully and walked over to the bed, shedding the cloak as she went. The heavy material sank to the ground with none of the same grace of its former wearer sauntering to her destination.

Gray stared after her, slack-jawed. Her gaze roamed over the body not fifteen feet from her, settling on her ass before, again, the black harness.

"You see," Christian began, her back to Gray, but it was clear what she was doing as she opened the box and pulled its contents onto the bed. "I knew you'd had a very stressful week, and you expected me tomorrow morning anyway," she said looking down, her voice sounding a bit distracted.

Gray could feel her heart rate picking up as she watched with expectation. Her palms were beginning to sweat, her mouth water.

"So," Christian said, turning around as she continued to adjust the purple dildo in the harness. She finished up with a little tap to the dildo, sending it doinging obscenely as it protruded from her crotch. "I got in this afternoon, rented a room just for the night, and got myself ready for my hardworking girl," Christian murmured and walked over to Gray, who wasn't sure whether to laugh at the phallus or fall to her knees and grab Christian by the ass.

Instead, Gray decided to play hard to get. "You know I have work to do, don't you?" she asked, arms crossed over her chest and shifting her weight to one hip, all attitude.

"Oh, I know you do," Christian purred, reaching her. She snaked her arms up around Gray's neck and leaned in, initiating a slow, sensuous but short kiss. "I'll just be waiting over here for when you finish," she said against Gray's lips, just before she turned and walked back over to the bed, pulling down the covers before climbing onto its surface, careful to make a nice show for Gray.

Gray wanted to whimper as she turned back to the desk and plopped down into the chair, noticeably less comfortable than when she'd initially stood up. She ran a hand through her hair, trying to focus back on her work, intending to at least get the notes and some more details down before quitting for the night, as had been her original intention.

Fingers racing across the keyboard as Gray got to work, she couldn't help but notice the mirror that hung on the wall just above and to the right of where she was working. She also couldn't help notice that the bed was perfectly reflected in it.

Just as she said, Christian was lying there quietly, minding her own business. She'd stacked up a couple pillows behind her back, one leg stretched out and one bent with her foot flat on the bottom sheet. As she reclined there, her right hand slowly, lazily stroked the phallus, playing with it.

If it had been a man doing that, Gray would have been disgusted, but somehow, Christian lying there, naked, teasing her with the simple lazy pump of her fist, made Gray burn. Groaning inside, she tried to focus on what she was doing, but it was no good.

Saving everything and slapping the laptop closed, Gray turned in her chair and locked eyes with Christian. Gray kicked her slippers off, tugged her T-shirt over her head and unclasped her bra, garments landing where they may as she moved over to the bed. Christian didn't move, other than what she'd already been doing, as she watched.

Shoving her pajama pants and panties down her legs, Gray hopped on first one foot then the other as she removed them and her socks before climbing onto the bed and over to the reclining woman. Their lips met with a fiery passion, the dildo trapped between their bodies as Gray stretched out on top of Christian, pushing her back into the pillows.

Christian was fierce as she shoved Gray onto her back and followed, holding her down by the wrists. Both were breathing heavily, Christian's breasts just barely grazing those beneath her. She looked deeply into Gray's eyes as she used a knee to urge Gray's thighs to part.

"Do you know what I've been dreaming about this past week since you've been gone?" the dancer murmured, lowering her mouth to Gray's neck as she lowered her hips between her legs, adjusting herself so the phallus was tucked nicely between the saturated folds of Gray's sex. She moved her hips slowly as the enlarged knob on the end ran slowly over Gray's engorged clit.

Gray's eyes fell closed as her head fell to the side. "What?" she asked, voice breathy as her arousal intensified with the hot mouth on her neck, soft body atop her own, and Christian's cock sliding lazily between her legs.

"I've been thinking about slowly fucking you with my little friend here," Christian whispered into Gray's ear before running her tongue all along the outside shell.

"I thought we agreed, no threesomes." Gray gasped, her hands trailing down Christian's back to cup her ass, which slowly moved between her legs.

Christian's chuckle was low in her throat and sent delicious chills through Gray. "I didn't think you'd mind," Christian murmured against Gray's lips.

"Nuh-uh. Nope. Don't mind at all."

Christian grinned. "Do you want me inside you, baby?"

Gray nodded. "Very much."

Christian said nothing but rested her weight on her forearm as she used the other hand to bring Gray's down between their bodies, stroking her fingers before moving her hand back so she could rest her weight on both arms.

Getting the idea, Gray took hold of the phallus, slippery with her own need. She spread her thighs a bit wider and guided the dildo to her entrance and slid the tip just inside, urging Christian to push in the rest of the way with a slight buck of her hips. A long, soft sigh escaped Gray's lips as she did.

She buried her fingers in Christian's hair as they kissed, Christian's hips setting a slow, lazy rhythm, much as her hand had earlier. The kisses were soft and loving, caressing of lips, small swipe of a tongue. Gray could feel her so deep inside of her, the grace and perfect motion of the dancer Christian was evident in every deep stroke.

Christian's long, blond hair fell around them like a golden curtain, blocking out the world, leaving only them. The dancer lifted her head a bit, eyes opening as they met Gray's gaze. They shared a soft smile as Christian reached back, running her nails over Gray's thigh as she urged it higher on her hip.

Gray was lost in her, lost in the sensations, the pleasure, lost in the love. Her hands roamed over the soft skin of a strong back and shoulders. She cupped Christian's breasts, lightly squeezing hard nipples between her fingers.

"Do you know what I wish?" Christian murmured as she lowered herself once more to kiss Gray.

"What?" Gray asked, wrapping her fingers around Christian's shoulders as the dancer pushed to her hands, her thrusts becoming a bit faster. "What do you wish?"

"I wish that I could cum inside you," Christian said, her eyes closing and her face registering the pleasure she was feeling as she sped up her movements in earnest. "And make a baby," she finished, breathy, a small whimper cutting off her last word.

The words hit Gray squarely in the heart—and between the legs. Her eyes closed and her head fell back into the pillow as Christian's hips set a furious rhythm. She was getting close, and from the constant little moans she heard from Christian, she knew she, too, was nearing her release.

Skin slapped against skin as Christian pounded into Gray, both breathing heavily now, far too heavy for kissing. Gray's mouth opened but nothing came out as her body exploded, her orgasm intense and all-consuming. Christian soon followed with a loud groan as she slammed into Gray one final time, grinding against her.

Finally, her hips stilled and she hugged Gray to

her. For a long moment they stayed that way, Gray trying to get her bearings back, her world to right itself. With a gentle kiss, Christian gently pulled out of Gray and rolled over to her back. They lay there in silence for a long moment.

After a minute, Christian unbuckled herself from the harness and set it on the bedside table before pulling up the sheet and cuddling into Gray, who wrapped her arm around her shoulders.

"I hope you weren't mad I just showed up like that," Christian said softly, resting her hand on Gray's stomach. "You just sounded really frustrated this week."

Gray smiled, resting her cheek against Christian's head. "No, it was a wonderful surprise, baby. Thank you for that. A lot of trouble you went to."

"Only the best for my girl," Christian said dramatically.

Caressing soft hair, Gray asked, "Did you mean what you said?"

"About what, baby?"

Gray paused for a moment, afraid maybe it had just been in the heat of the moment. "The baby."

"Yes," Christian responded. "I did."

Gray swallowed, suddenly emotion hitting her at the thought of them starting a family. "Wow," she blew out.

"Is that okay?" Christian asked, sounding unsure. She lifted her head, cradling it in her palm as she looked down into Gray's face. "Is that still what you want?"

Gray met her gaze. "Very much so. I know you said that once in New York, but…"

"I want that, Gray," Christian said with a smile.

"I think it's time. I mean, come on," she added with a raised eyebrow. "We live in the burbs now. We have a dog, a cat, two cars."

Gray grinned. "So, baby makes three?"

"Well," Christian hedged. "Five, if you ask Brutus and Caesar." She smiled, tracing Gray's jaw with her finger. "I do want to get married first, though. I want us all to have the same name."

Gray studied her for a long moment. A shared last name was something they'd never discussed, Gray figuring there was nothing *to* discuss. Christian was famous already, known the world over as Christian Scott, and Gray was just beginning to make a name for herself in her own industry.

"I'd be willing to change mine to Scott," she said.

Christian shook her head. "No," she said, voice firm. "I want to become a Rickman. Scott means nothing to me. My parents, wherever they are, don't deserve that honor for their grandchild." She gave Gray the sweetest smile, so full of love. "Your family has been part of me for so long now. I want to be a Rickman, and I want our child or children to be Rickmans too." Suddenly she looked shy. "If that's okay with you?"

Gray nodded. "It's very okay."

❧ ❧ ☙ ☙

Gray's heart was racing as Christian slid the ring on her finger. It was so final in that moment, feeling the gold upon her skin. She'd never experienced anything more solid, so real, so perfect. Even Christian with her cream-colored fitted satin dress with halter top and her hair in a chignon with white rosebuds.

Even Gray dressed in her cream-colored women's suit, escorted down the aisle by her father while her mother walked Christian down to meet her. Even their friends and family watching from their seats, some sniffling. None of that made it feel as real as the ring being slid onto her finger.

"Christian?" the officiant asked. "You have your own vows for Gray?"

Christian nodded, clearing her throat as she met Gray's eyes. "I'm not quite the wordsmith you are," she began softly. "I've been told I'm more of a dancer."

Gray smirked along with a few chuckles from those gathered. "So I've heard."

Christian gave her that small smile reserved only for Gray. She cleared her throat again and continued. "For so long I was so lost. I had no idea where I belonged, who I was, or why I was even here. Then I met you. I had no idea what to do with you—smack you, call the police on you, or kiss you."

"Pretty sure you did all three at one time or other."

Christian gave her a devilish grin. "Not yet." She ran her thumbs over the backs of Gray's hands as she held them. "No matter what you were doing, saying, or saying nothing at all," Christian said, looking at Gray with an expression that almost looked like wonder. "I knew you were always watching me, always watching *out* for me. As if, at seventeen years old, you already knew your life's mission would be to protect me." She smiled. "I loved you for that."

Gray returned the smile. *Always,* she mouthed.

"In you, Gray," Christian said softly, emotion in her eyes. "In you I found a family, my heart, my home, and my future. I've loved you since the moment I first saw you and will until the day I leave this earth and beyond." She brought Gray's left hand to her lips and left a kiss on the ring she'd just placed there.

Gray had to take a very deep breath in order not to cry, taking Christian's left hand in her own. She gently slid the ring she'd bought for her to her knuckle, then pushed a bit to slide it home, the diamond glinting at her in the afternoon sunlight.

"Gray," the officiant said. "Your vows to Christian?"

Gray nodded and blew out a breath. She took Christian's hands in her own and looked her in the eye. "I *am* the wordsmith between us, but every time I look at you, words fail me. Anyone can see you're a beautiful woman, confident, sexy." She gave her a smile. "But what they don't see is the incredible heart you have. I've never in my life met someone who's been through what you have in your life, yet for every ounce of pain you've been dealt, you give equal amounts of kindness, compassion, and deep, deep love."

Christian gently wiped away a tear as it threatened to escape her left eye. Gray smiled.

"You inspire me every day, Christian. I adore you, admire you, and I want to be just like you when I grow up." Gray smiled as a round of chuckles washed through the audience. "But mostly," she continued. "I want to know what I've done to deserve you. We're going on eight years, so I guess I must have done something right."

"Every day, baby," Christian said softly. "Every day."

"I give you my heart, my soul, my love, my trust, and I will always, always dance with you." She couldn't look away from the woman who was looking back at her, so connected in that moment.

"By the powers granted to me by the state of Colorado, I now pronounce you married! You may kiss your bride!"

Gray's smile was unstoppable as she cupped Christian's face and brought her in for a heart-stopping kiss. Their gathered company cheered and whistled at the display. She didn't care. In that moment it was just her and Christian. As the kiss broke, she rested her forehead against her wife's.

"I love you," Christian whispered.

"I love you, more."

Chapter Nineteen

Pass hung around her neck on a lanyard, Gray tried to stay out of the way. She'd never seen the behind-the-scenes madness of a competition. Coaches, competitors, security, and officials buzzed around like bees. She felt like she was stuck on the movie set of *The Cutting Edge*.

Gray turned to look out at the ice, the current skater doing her routine to a popular hip-hop song that Gray wasn't familiar with. She was doing well, formidable. Turning from her, she noticed that Yancy and Christian were still huddled together, seeming to be going over the notebook where Erika's routine was printed out, move by move. The young skater was stretching, as she was up next.

Christian turned away to call Erika over to them, catching Gray's eye in the process. In that moment, Gray saw the competitor in her wife, saw the fierceness in her eyes and rigidity in her body language that she hadn't seen since Christian had danced at her parents' theater.

Now, it almost made Gray take a step back. The fire in her eyes was sharp, focused, and deadly. No doubt that was the look from a young Christian who was about to take the ice herself twenty years ago.

The skater on the ice finished and the applause sounded as the young woman took her leave. Gray felt her stomach roil with nerves. She could only imagine how her wife and Yancy must feel, let alone Erika. She watched as the young skaters-in-training took to the ice to pick up the flowers thrown to the ice by the crowd before the skater's scores were posted by the judges. The announcer's voice echoed throughout the arena as he read the numbers.

Not knowing a lot about the sport, Gray gauged Christian and Yancy's reactions to the score. Yancy was fairly stone-faced, but Christian looked nervous, though Gray could tell she was trying to hide it. Poor Erika looked like she was going to vomit. She blew out a heavy breath when the announcer called her name as the next skater.

Gray's heart was racing as she watched Erika take the ice after an encouraging pat on the shoulder by both her coaches. Gray wanted to call "Good luck!" but remained silent, not sure how welcome her voice would be for the nervous young woman about to perform in an incredibly important competition.

The opening bars of "Gethsemane" from *Jesus Christ Superstar,* as sung by Michael Ball, began. Though she knew it was coming, Gray found herself surprised—again—by the song choice. It was a powerful piece, but Christian had said Erika was a strong skater and up to the task. It certainly had her attention.

As the young woman began her routine, Gray felt a touch and then a press against her shoulder. She glanced over to see that Christian had moved over to stand next to her. Gray smiled and leaned in a bit to give her comfort. Christian's hands were covering her mouth as she watched.

"How's she doing?" Gray murmured as they watched.

"Amazing," Christian whispered, never taking her eyes off the young skater. "Absolutely amazing."

Gray could see Christian's flair in the routine, in the skater's movements. Yancy had worked with Erika on her technical aspects, her workouts, diet, all the things to keep her strong, but it had largely fallen to Christian to choreograph the routine. She and Erika had picked the music and decided on the costume together, with Yancy's input.

Gray was captivated by the strong, intense performance, Erika hitting every mark, making every jump, landing with utter perfection. The crowd was engaged, oohing and ahhing with every incredible move the young skater made.

Finally, the two-minute routine to the abridged version of the song ended, leaving all who watched, including Gray, breathless. The arena erupted in applause, including Gray, Christian, and Yancy. Gray watched as the young woman on the ice basked in the accolades and applause, clearly very proud of herself and her performance.

"Oh, my God," Christian said, looking to Gray. "She nailed it. She absolutely nailed it!"

Gray accepted and returned the excited hug she received from an emotional Christian. "So proud of you," she murmured, not even sure if it was heard above the cacophony in the event space.

"Finally, the twins have their own rooms," Celine exclaimed, showing Gray and Christian the kids' rooms, both in disarray as the bedrooms of preteens tend to be.

"It's amazing how different they are," Gray commented, noting one bedroom had sports stuff everywhere while the other had walls plastered with posters of opera stars, musical instruments lying on the bed, and a piano keyboard print on the comforter.

"Night and day, Gray," Gray's sister-in-law agreed. "But your parents are thrilled to have them finally living close by."

"How do you feel living here?" Christian asked as the trio moved through the tour of the new house in Highlands Ranch, a suburb of Denver. "You're Canadian, so a first for you."

Celine shrugged, leading the way back downstairs. "Ivan and I made a deal when we first got married that we'd spend our careers in Canada then, once we retired from the stage, we'd head to the US."

"Are the boys happy?" Gray asked, retaking her seat at the kitchen table, her coffee waiting for her.

"I think so," Celine said, also sitting. She ran a hand through short, red hair, the newest color she'd chosen at the salon. "They miss their friends and their uncles. But," she added with a shrug. "They have dual citizenship, so we've told them if, as they get older, they decide to go to school back in Toronto or simply want to move there, we'll support them."

"I think it's wonderful," Christian said, taking her cup of coffee in hand as she resumed her seat at the table. "I know Dennis has talked a lot about taking the boys fishing next summer and of course," she added with a smile. "All of us spoiling them like crazy this Christmas."

Celine rolled her eyes. "Lordy, that's all they talk about. Presents, presents, presents." She chuckled. "I can't believe Halloween is next week. I'm just glad we're finally moved in and settled in this place."

"It's a beautiful house, Celine," Gray said. "It's so strange having my brother within minutes driving and not hours flying."

As if on cue, the front door to the house burst open and Ivan strutted inside, returning from dropping the boys off at Grandma and Grandpa's house. He grinned when he spotted the three women in the kitchen.

"Hey, sis," he said, kissing the top of Christian's head before moving on to Gray and doing the same thing. "Hey, sis."

"Hey, mister," Gray said, reaching up and squeezing the fingers on the hand that rested on her shoulder.

"Congrats on your girl, Chris," he said, reaching down and grabbing Celine's coffee cup to take a drink from it. "She was amazing. Great win."

"Thanks," Christian said, beaming. "We're so proud of her. On to Nationals, now."

"Then the Olympics, huh?" he asked, taking the fourth seat at the table.

"That's the plan."

"So," he said, bouncing up from his seat again and walking over to the fridge. "What's this I hear about you two planning to have kids?" he asked, grabbing a bottle of water from inside the fridge before rejoining them. "You're gonna have it?" he asked, nodding at Gray.

"I am," Gray said, glancing over at Christian. She looked back at him. "It's the right time for us."

"What are you looking for in a donor dad?" he asked, twisting off the cap before draining half the contents in one drink.

"Well, not a 'dad,' for one," Christian said. "We don't want the man involved at all in any sort of father capacity."

Ivan's eyebrows shot up. "Really? Don't you think a kid needs a dad?"

Gray met his gaze and her eyebrow raised. "How many single moms are out there doing it on their own, Ivan? Might surprise you, but the world doesn't revolve around men."

He stared at her for a long moment before looking down at the bottle his fingers were wrapped around. "Okay, gotcha. I'm sorry." He cleared his throat, clearly feeling uncomfortable. "Let me try again. How does that work? Having both parents be the same gender?" Contrition and genuine curiosity were in his tone.

Gray left that one to Christian, knowing she was far more diplomatic than she herself was when it came to Ivan. "We have a number of good men in our life, Ivan," the dancer explained. "We feel we have a plethora of good male role models, whether we have a boy or a girl."

Ivan sat back in his chair, stroking the goatee he was growing. "Okay. So, like, if you had a boy and he started going through puberty and all that goes with it, you'd just send him over here?"

"Or to New York for Michael and Kevin to deal with until he's twenty," Gray said with a smirk.

Celine burst into laughter. "Can I send the boys there too? And him?" she added, hitching her thumb over at her husband.

"Feeling slightly outnumbered here," Ivan muttered good-naturedly.

"You are, sweetie," Celine said, absently reaching

over and patting his leg.

"In all seriousness," he continued. "What are you looking for in your donor? Tall, broad shoulders, square jaw, six-pack abs?"

Gray snickered. "We're not looking for a Roman Centurion, Ivan."

Christian looked away, but not before Gray saw her smile. "Um," she said, pushing back from the table with her empty coffee cup in hand. "We want a donor with good health, obviously, no history of major mental or physical health problems in the family."

"Babe?" Gray said, holding up her mug. Christian reached across the table and grabbed it before heading to the coffee maker. "Intelligence," Gray added. "Honestly, we just want a healthy baby. The rest we can deal with."

"I have so much admiration for you two," Celine said, shaking her head in the negative when Christian raised her mug in offering to refresh Celine's. "I love our boys, you guys know that, but honestly, we never intended to have kids. I absolutely don't regret that we had our twins, but I definitely don't ever want more."

Ivan nodded in agreement. "I'll be a kick-ass uncle, though." He grinned. "Spoil the shit out of your kid then send him home."

Gray pretended to push back from the table and stand. "You ready to go, babe?"

Christian grinned at her.

≈≈≈

The snow fell softly outside the window, Gray's favorite time of year. She was happy; very, very happy. Lying on her side facing her wife, she smiled.

"What?" Christian asked, her own smile forming.

"You look like the cat who just ate the canary."

"Well, not entirely inaccurate," Gray said. "I'm the author who just ate the dancer."

"Oh, god, Gray," Christian said, bursting into laughter as she swiped playfully at the woman lying next to her. "True enough. So, what has you smiling like that?"

"I was looking at the bedrooms upstairs today," Gray explained. "Wondering which would end up being our child's bedroom. What would it look like as they got older? What colors? What would she or he be into?"

Christian smiled, moving her hand under the covers to rest upon Gray's hip. "I was thinking that tonight, as we were looking at our options in the packet the clinic sent to us. How do you feel about the process, though?"

"What do you mean by 'process'?"

"The impregnation in a doctor's office. Being pregnant, all of it."

Gray shrugged the shoulder that wasn't pressed to the mattress. "I'm not exactly looking forward to giving birth. Not real big on pain." She grinned. "But, worth it, I hear."

"It'll be worth it," Christian said softly. "So very worth it."

※ ※ ※ ※

Singing along to the music blasting from the speakers in the kitchen, Gray moved the first load of laundry from the washer to the dryer before starting the second load. Christian was down in Colorado Springs with Yancy so Gray was left alone to act the dancing fool as she did chores.

Sharon den Adel of the band Within Temptation was singing so loudly that Gray nearly missed the sound of her phone ringing. She hurried from the laundry room to the kitchen and turned down the volume before grabbing her phone.

"Hello?" She smiled when she heard the voice on the other end. "Hey, Dr. Calloway! We got the listings for donors—" She stood at the cooking island, eyebrows falling. "What does that mean? Okay, yeah, I can come in. When?" She leaned against the island. "Yeah. Okay. Three thirty today, I'll be there. Thanks, Doctor. Bye."

Lowering the phone from her ear, she stared off into space, the doctor's sage words bouncing around in her mind. She wasn't sure what to think, what to feel. It didn't look good, but nothing was definitive, yet, which was why she wanted her to come in.

Taking a deep, shaky breath, she lifted her phone again and tapped on the screen to get to her contacts. The line connected and began to ring. Four rings in, Christian's voice mail picked up. Gray swallowed, then spoke after the beep.

"Hey, baby. Um, Dr. Calloway called. She said there are some problems and wants to do an ultrasound. Um…" She looked down at her bare feet. "Yeah. So, I'm heading to her office in just over an hour. I'll call you when I know anything. Hope everything is going well there. I love you."

※ ※ ※ ※

The cursor blinked endlessly, a constant reminder that she hadn't typed a single word since she'd been home. Going on…Gray glanced at the clock at the bottom right of the computer screen…an hour and twenty-seven minutes. She brought her hands up and placed her fingers on the keys, but they only fell away again. The words wouldn't come, and she was desperately trying to keep tears from taking their place.

She heard Brutus jump up and begin to whimper as he ran toward the garage door, which buzzed as the motor was engaged by Christian's remote control. Gray didn't move, sitting at her desk in the home office as Christian made her way inside and greeted the excited dog.

"Gray?" she called out.

Gray said nothing, unable to speak. She knew Christian would find her, which she did moments later. The dancer said nothing, simply walked over to her and lightly nudged on her shoulder.

"Move back," she said softly.

Gray continued her silence but used her feet to roll back a bit from the desk. When there was enough clearance, Christian gingerly lowered herself to sit on Gray's lap. She gathered Gray's head and brought it forward to rest against her breasts.

Resting against the softness, smelling Christian's fragrance, feeling gentle fingers run through her hair, it finally happened. The tears hit her hard and fast, shaking her entire body as she wrapped her arms around her wife. She felt Christian's cheek rest against the top of her head, the intensity of her sobs rocking them both.

"It's okay," Christian whispered. "Everything will be okay."

"I'm sorry," Gray sobbed. "I'm so sorry."

"Sorry about what?" Christian asked gently.

"That I can't have our baby."

Chapter Twenty

"Damn it!" Gray tried to swat away the blanket of fake spiderwebs that covered her after she'd yanked on the Halloween decoration a bit too hard, sending it tumbling down on top of her.

"Okay, hold on," Bernadette said, hurrying over to her. "You're going to break it, Gray, calm down!"

Gray wanted to growl at her mother, but instead stood still while her mother carefully peeled the cobwebs off and removed the attached large fuzzy spider and skeleton. Finally, it was all gone, and she reached up to run her fingers through her hair, making sure nothing was left behind from that dastardly decoration.

Bernadette lay the spider and skeleton down into one of the many plastic tubs that sat on the stage, storage for the theater's seasonal decorations.

"You, little miss," Bernadette said, walking over to Gray after the decoration was stowed away. "Need to calm down." She looked into her daughter's eyes, making Gray feel like a lab rat. "This anger you've got going isn't going help anyone, my sweet," she said softly.

Gray glared at her. "Mom, you know I love you, but this isn't something you're qualified to comment on."

Bernadette's eyebrows shot up. "Oh? As a mother, as a daughter, as a *woman* I'm not qualified?"

she said coolly, arms crossing over her chest.

Gray dropped her gaze, never able to stand up to her mother for long when she played the "I'm your mother and I know more than you so knock it off" card. She said nothing. Her mother was right about one thing: she was angry, angry as hell, and there wasn't anyone on the planet who could change that.

"Honey," Bernadette said gently. "I think it might do you some good if you went back to talk to that therapist you girls worked with earlier this year. This isn't an easy thing you're dealing with, and she can probably help you work through this."

Gray smirked, again running a hand through her hair. "Christian already beat me to it. She's been going the last few weeks."

"Why don't you join her?" her mom asked. "Could do you both good."

"She wants to go alone," Gray said, looking down at her shoes, her toe tapping against the wood stage. "I have to respect that."

Bernadette said nothing more, simply gathered Gray into a hug and held her in a mother's embrace. Gray allowed it for a moment before she pulled away to continue striking the Halloween decorations. She felt a hand on her shoulder and turned to see her sister-in-law standing behind her. She smiled when Gray met her gaze, squeezing the muscle that connected her shoulder and her neck lightly.

"No, I think it would be better if we went the elementary school route," Gray said, her Bluetooth headset passing the message along to her editor on the other end of the line. "I managed to find a nun who is still alive from that time period and is willing to talk about her years there. What do you think?" Gray listened even as she heard Brutus's excited barks and whimpers as Christian arrived home. "Okay, yeah," she responded. "I'll give her a call and set up a time to meet with her. Great, thanks for your input."

"Dinner!" Christian called from the kitchen.

Gray glanced toward the open doorway of her office before ending the call with her editor and removing her earbuds. Pushing up from her chair, she walked out of the office and toward the kitchen, an excited Brutus meeting her halfway there. The big dog seemed to have become far more sensitive to the two women after the difficult events of earlier in the year. If he sensed there was *any* daylight between the two, he was determined to be the bridge between them.

"Hey," Gray said, walking up to the cooking island where Christian had set the large take-out bag that bore the logo of one of their favorite Italian restaurants.

"Hey, yourself," Christian said, leaning over for a kiss. "How did things go with the nun?" she asked, continuing to unpack the paper bag, setting to-go containers on the island, the gathering smells amazing.

"Well, Trish agreed with me, so I'll be doing the nun thing hopefully tomorrow." Gray eyed the growing containers. "What's all this for?" she asked, as usually a dinner like this was reserved for a special occasion. She didn't exactly think speaking to a holy woman counted. She slid the bottle of sweet red from the paper bag provided by the liquor store. Eyebrows raised, she looked to her wife for an explanation.

"I need to talk to you about something,"

Christian said, which of course cleared up nothing. "You pour, I'll dish."

"Yes, ma'am," Gray muttered, grabbing the wine glasses out of the cabinet. Less than ten minutes later, the two sat at the kitchen table with heaping plates of lasagna with all the fixings and good wine. Gray glanced up at her dinner companion, a warm bread stick in hand. "So," she prodded. "Did it go okay with Dr. Stacy today?" She was still a little sore that Christian had shared very little of her visits to the therapist. Yes, it was private, and yes, Christian had every right to get whatever help she needed, but she felt shut out as her wife.

"I didn't go see Dr. Stacy today," Christian said, glancing over at Gray as she sipped her wine.

Gray's eyebrows drew. "You said you had an appointment with the doctor today."

"I did," Christian said with a nod. "But today was Dr. Calloway."

Gray stared at her, her stomach falling as concern filled her. "Is everything okay?"

Christian met her gaze, her beautiful green eyes bright and filled with life. "Very okay," she assured. "Today was just the final visit to make sure everything was how and where it needed to be." She set her wineglass down and gave her full attention to Gray, prompting the writer to do the same, resting her bread stick back down on her plate.

"Okay."

"I know you've been upset with me because I've stayed pretty mum on what I was up to these past few weeks," Christian acknowledged. "I can understand that and I'm sorry. But, I didn't want to share with you until I had something to share, all the information that I needed to give you."

Gray nodded. It made her feel better that her wife was giving voice to exactly what Gray had been feeling and wondering for nearly a month, on top of her own personal issues after the devastating blow from Dr. Calloway.

"I went to see Dr. Stacy to deal with the things that happened to me during my skating days," Christian began softly. "To deal with some of that PTSD, what happened, the loss, everything. And," she added. "To make sure I was emotionally capable."

Gray was a bit confused but said nothing. She simply nodded acknowledgment of what had been said.

"When Dr. Stacey gave me the all-clear, I went to Dr. Calloway. My first visit was with her last week, and today was to discuss everything, test results."

Gray swallowed, her nerves beginning to make her nauseous. "Are you okay?"

Christian's smile was beautiful and bright. "In the words of Dr. Calloway, I am an extremely healthy thirty-six-year-old woman who should have absolutely no problem conceiving or carrying to term."

Gray stared at her, no clue what to say, her brain still trying to catch up. "Wait," she managed. "I thought...I thought you didn't want to go back there, get pregnant again after everything that happened with that bastard Brandon and everything."

"And I didn't," Christian said easily. "But I honestly didn't know just how much it would affect me, the knowledge that we could *not* have a family. Seeing you so utterly destroyed by what Dr. Calloway discovered with you, the PCOS and everything. Then, understanding that there would be no way in hell we could afford adoption, let alone taking in a child and falling in love with it through the foster program only to lose it." She reached across the table and took Gray's hand in her own. "I needed to see what I could do, if anything."

Gray was trying to hold back her tears, both of shock and utter joy. She laced her fingers with Christian's as she listened.

"What I've come to understand through our relationship, our beautiful, beautiful relationship, and Dr. Stacy's help," Christian added with a small smile. "Pregnancy, babies weren't the issue, not the dragon to slay. The true monster is in prison, and I put him there." Her smile was victorious. "I won. And, to have a family with you, it's an even sweeter win, for so many reasons."

"So," Gray said, feeling she was getting a grasp on all this now. "You're saying you want to go forward with having a baby, you carrying it?" She couldn't keep the hope from her voice, even as she desperately tried to.

Christian nodded. "That's exactly what I'm saying." She reached with her free hand to lift her glass of wine. "Thus why I bought this." She grinned. "Here very soon, I may not be able to have any for a while."

Gray felt every ounce of anger, tension, and anxiety that had filled her for the last few weeks seep from her. Like a deflated balloon, all of it left her. She pulled Christian to her feet and took her in a full-body hug, burying her face in a warm neck. She couldn't formulate her words of joy or gratitude or relief, so she simply let her body do it for her.

Dennis raised his glass high, along with the large gathering around the formal dining room table that had, for the first time, leaves added to it to extend its length. "I for one am a very, very happy man," he said, looking at all the faces that were looking back at him. "Our first Thanksgiving with both my children finally home, and of course, the boys," he said, indicating the twins sitting by their parents. "And, of course," he added, looking to the other end where Gray and Christian sat. "Christian, though you've been part of our family for years now, this is our first Thanksgiving with you as our legal daughter-in-law, and I could not be happier or more proud of that fact."

"Here, here!" Gray said, grinning.

"And," Dennis said with a wink to Gray, "Maybe, just maybe, we'll have another little one joining us at this very table next year."

Gray's smile grew, nearly hurting her cheeks in its breadth. She felt a hand on her thigh and turned to see Christian gazing at her, a look of contentment and peace on her beautiful face.

"Gray."

Gray turned to see Ivan leaning back in his chair to get her attention behind Celine. She raised her chin in his direction.

"I want to talk to you and Chris after we eat," he said.

Gray glanced at her wife to see her shrug before looking back to her brother. "Okay. No problem."

After the holiday meal was eaten and cleaned up, Gray and Christian joined Ivan on the front porch. It was a chilly day, the feel of snow in the air. The two women sat together on the glider while Ivan took one of the rocking chairs.

"What's up?" Gray asked. "Everything okay?"

He nodded, pulling his vape out of his pocket and taking a drag, a banana-scented cloud drifting up and disappearing into the afternoon.

"I can't believe you do that crap," Christian said.

"Hey now," he said, tucking the small device back into his pocket. "It's gotten me off the Marlboro Midnights. Progress is progress. So," he said, a seriousness taking over his tone. "It's wonderful news that you gals are back in the baby-making business."

Gray stared at him, not expecting that to come out of his mouth. "We are," she said. She reached over and placed her hand on Christian's thigh, her hand immediately covered by a soft one.

"Now," he said, looking them both in the eye. "I thought about this before, but when we thought it would be Gray, it wouldn't have worked for obvious reasons. But now that it's you doing the heavy lifting, Chris—and I have no idea where you gals are in the process, so not meaning to step on toes or anything," he was quick to add. "But I'd like to volunteer to be a donor."

Gray blinked a few times, trying to work out in her brain what he'd just said. Luckily, her wife was quicker on the draw.

"Wait, Ivan," she said. "Are you saying you want to father our baby?"

Ivan shook his head, taking another drag on the vape. "No, I am not. I had my kids," he said. "Still raising them and have no desire to have anymore. This baby would belong to the two of you. I'll sign whatever needs to be signed to make it legal. Gray is that kid's other parent, Chris, not me." He gave them a winning smile, his face handsome as ever. "I'm just supplying the family DNA."

Gray felt like the wind had been knocked out of her. She couldn't speak for a long moment, could hardly breathe. Finally, she managed, "What about Celine? She's your wife, and this would affect her too."

He met her gaze and said simply, "It was her idea."

Gray looked over at Christian, who was already looking at her. The silent communication of the truly connected commenced. Finally, Gray turned back to Ivan. "How about you and Celine come over this weekend so the four of us can talk?"

He nodded. "We can do that."

≈≈≈≈

Christmas had come and gone and New Year's was right around the corner. Discussions had been had and papers had been drawn up by an attorney and signed. Christian was going to get a special specimen cup from Dr. Calloway that afternoon on her way back from Colorado Springs and drop it off at Ivan and Celine's house for his convenience and privacy.

The previous day Gray had sent the final manuscript to edits and now had a little bit of time before the next project would be sent to her inbox. She sat in her desk chair, lazily turning it from side to side, her gaze never leaving the blank screen: a fresh, clean Word document waiting to be filled.

As she stared at the blinking cursor, something that could be her best friend or her worst enemy, she thought about her life. She thought about the woman she'd become, a woman now entering her thirties.

She thought back to who she was half a lifetime ago, though it seemed like just yesterday. Intelligent, yet didn't have a clue about anything. She'd been mouthy, yet full of manners. She'd thought she understood life, yet had not one iota of understanding of who she was as a person. Then she'd met Christian Scott. A bit older, wise beyond her years, yet rough around the edges. She'd grab your hand to stop you from falling even as she glared at you for tripping in the first place.

What if, Gray wondered. What if they'd met in the halls of a high school instead of the stage of a theater? What if they'd only been a couple years apart in age, rather than five? What if rehearsals and productions hadn't forced them to be at the same place at the same time?

"What if," Gray muttered, her fingers lifting to the keyboard.

She began to type, eventually her mind no longer telling them what to do, but instead the characters, the ideas, the visions, and the scenes. The satisfying *click-click-click* of her fingers dancing across the keys kept rhythm with the music that played softly through her computer speakers.

She didn't notice the day turn to night, never noticed the buttery light that suddenly blanketed her when the floor lamp turned on. She never consciously realized that the coffee she was sipping had magically appeared in her favorite cup, nor did she hear the gentle click of the doorjamb meeting its mate as the French doors were softly pulled closed.

All she knew was the story about a girl finding herself within the soul of another girl who, for some reason, loved her back.

Chapter Twenty-one

Gray hummed into her task, loving the flavor that only belonged to the woman she loved, a taste that she had become addicted to the very first time she had it. Christian's soft sigh and the slight lifting of her hips to meet Gray's tongue made it all the sweeter. She ran her tongue slowly down to Christian's entrance, pushing her tongue just barely inside before slowly running it back up to a hard clit.

Only wanting to get her ready, Gray lifted her head, no intention of the woman beneath her releasing that way. They had something else very, very special in mind. Pushing to her knees, Gray looked down her naked body to the phallus strapped to her hips. It wasn't just any dildo, it was one specifically constructed with ejaculation in mind, be it warm water, lube, or what hers was currently filled with: the ultimate gift from her brother.

She ran her hands down the spread thighs of the gorgeous woman who stared up at her, green eyes hooded and skin flushed. She was so sexy. Naked, wet, and wanting. She took hold of the dildo in her hands, teasing Christian's clit with the tip, watching as her eyes closed and head tilted slightly to the side.

"Ready?" Gray murmured.

Christian nodded. "Yes."

Gray watched as she carefully guided the tip down to Christian's opening, using her hips to gently push the length and girth within until her hips were nestled against Christian's. She lowered to brace on her hands, their breasts touching. Christian brought her knees closer in toward her body, allowing Gray deep penetration.

As Gray used slow, deep thrusts, she accepted Christian's kiss as the dancer's fingers wound themselves into short, dark hair, urging her to lower her head. The kiss was as slow and lazy as Gray's hip movements. She loved the feeling of Christian's tongue against her own, the taste of her mouth as the two shared the slick desire that coated Gray's lips and tongue.

Yes, making love was a huge part of their relationship, always had been as they both seemed to have an insatiable desire and passion for the other. Gray loved sex as much as anyone, but no woman had ever called to her on a primal level as Christian did.

But what they were doing in that moment was far above and beyond sharing pleasure, giving and taking pleasure. What they were doing that night was the beginning of a new chapter in their lives, attempting to start their family.

Together, they'd done the research and decided on the method, as neither wanted the sterile, impersonal environment of Dr. Calloway's office. They wanted it to be about love, about creating a life, about literally *making* love.

As she kissed Christian, felt her fingers caress her shoulders and back; as she pulled out only to push back in; as the bed softly creaked with her movements; and as Gray's own breathing increased with the pace of her hips, something magic was happening.

Though they were both breathing too hard

to continue kissing, Gray didn't leave Christian's personal space, their foreheads nearly touching as Gray pumped her hips. She tried to retain some semblance of control in her movements rather than slamming into her as her rising orgasm begged her to do.

"Baby," Christian panted. "Soon."

Gray nodded, lowering her upper body to rest on her left forearm as her right hand reached down between them to grip the hand pump. As her own pleasure was rising, it was hard to think straight, but she forced herself to stay focused on what she had to do.

Christian's eyes closed and her head arched back as her orgasm washed over her with a loud cry. Gray squeezed the pump, the contents shooting deep inside Christian as Gray thrust her hips for a final time. The physical pleasure coupled with the psychological aspect of literally cumming inside Christian hit her hard, her body releasing in a powerful wave of pleasure that was released in a guttural, primal growl.

She crushed Christian to her, wrapping her up in a desperate embrace as emotion overtook her. She had no idea where it came from, but suddenly she was crying. Christian wrapped her arms and legs around Gray, making them one as Gray was still buried deep inside her.

"I love you," Christian whispered, emotion in her own voice.

Unable to speak yet, Gray hoped all she felt came through in the kiss that she initiated. Christian immediately responded, her fingers buried in Gray's sweat-dampened hair. After a long moment, Gray pulled away. She looked down at Christian, who brushed

Gray's face with the backs of her fingers. They shared a smile before Gray was released from the prison of strong arms and legs.

Gently pulling out, Gray climbed off the bed and walked to the bathroom to remove the dildo and harness. Leaving it in the sink, she headed back to bed and pulled Christian to her as she got settled in her spot.

"How do you feel?" she asked softly, lightly playing with long, blond hair.

"As in, do I feel pregnant?" Christian asked with a smile in her voice, a smile that Gray reflected on her lips.

"Sure, why not."

Christian got settled in a bit closer, resting her hand on Gray's stomach. "No. I feel like my body is purring," she said. "Humming or vibrating." She let out a contented sigh. "Feels strange."

Gray smiled, trying to imagine what Christian was feeling. "Why do you think that is?"

"I don't know. Could be psychological, I don't know. But somehow it just feels different." They were quiet for a moment before Christian asked, "What was that like for you?"

"Intense," Gray said without thought. "Very intense." She grinned. "I can see why men have the misconception that they're in control. You do feel pretty powerful for a minute."

Christian surprised Gray by suddenly moving away and climbing atop her, straddling her hips. She rested her hands on Gray's ribs as she looked down at her. "So," she said. "What do you want more? Be honest. A girl or a boy?"

"Well," Gray said, resting her hands on Christian's

thighs. "I want it to be healthy for one. But, to your question, I don't really know. I mean, in a way I want us to have a girl because the world needs more strong women, and we'd definitely raise her to be strong. But then again," she added. "The world needs more good, amazing men, and I know we'd raise him to be an incredible young man who treats women like the queens they are—or else."

Christian grinned. "Or else, huh?" She lightly trailed her fingertips over Gray's torso. "We've never really talked names."

"I know. I've thought about that too. I've also been thinking about something else," Gray said, trailing her fingers up Christian's thighs and to her hips. "Is there anybody in your family you want to tell about this? Anyone you want involved?"

Christian studied her own hands, which were also on the move. "I wish my Nanna was still alive," she said softly. "She would have been so happy."

"How would she have taken us?" Gray asked gently. "I mean, you being in a same-sex marriage."

Christian smiled. "I think she would have been very happy that I found somebody who truly loves me. Would she have preferred I'd been straight?" She shrugged a well-defined shoulder. "Probably at heart. But, ultimately, she just wanted to see me happy." She met Gray's eyes again, a sad smile on her lips. "But, no." She shook her head. "Nobody else. There really *isn't* anybody else." She leaned down and left a lingering kiss to Gray's lips. "Just you."

⁂

"Honestly," Janice said, flipping through the

small stack of papers she had on her desk. "I think it's great." She glanced up at an anxious Gray, who sat across the cluttered desk from her. "The characters thus far are interesting, amusing, and worth emotional investment."

Gray let out a long, slow breath, relieved. Though Janice wasn't her current editor, they'd worked very well together on Richard's book and she trusted her opinion greatly. "Anything I should change?"

Janice chewed on her bottom lip for a moment as she flipped through some pages. "Oh, glad you asked," she said, coming across a portion she'd marked with red ink. "Your dialogue," she said, meeting Gray's eyes again. "Be careful, it's a little too proper and stilted." She dropped the pages and leaned back in her chair. "You've primarily worked on projects where you're writing down word for word what someone has said, no real thinking or creativity with that. Fiction dialogue is different. I suggest reading it aloud after you've written it, see how it sounds spoken."

Gray nodded. "Done. Thanks so much for the advice."

"Anytime." Janice tossed the partial manuscript across the desk to Gray. "You can look over the notes I made."

Gray nodded. "Wonderful, thanks."

"How's the wife and kid?"

Gray grinned. "The wife is fine, the kid is still in the works. No positives yet. But we're working on it."

Janice arched an eyebrow. "I've seen your wife. I'm sure you are."

A bark of laughter erupted from Gray's throat. "Interesting comment coming from a woman married to a man for ninety years."

"Twenty-seven, thank you. Oh, not a threat over here, sister," she said, indicating herself with a hand to her chest. "But Christian is a very beautiful woman."

Gray's smile was soft and filled with the adoration she had for the dancer. "She is."

"Okay, well, best of luck to ya, kiddo. Shoot me a message if you have any questions. I'll be happy to help if I can," Janice said, making it clear their short meeting was over.

"Thanks again so much, lady," Gray said, pushing to her feet. She grabbed the manuscript and gave the older woman a smile. "Door left open?" When Janice waved for her to shut it, Gray did and made her way to the elevator.

She pulled her winter jacket tighter around her as she stepped outside and into the hustle and bustle of the Manhattan streets. When she'd first moved to New York many years before, it had been shocking, the busy energy that was constantly around a person. Eventually, she'd come to like it and felt a bit privileged to be part of it. But now, having moved back to where the pace was slower, more laid back and, frankly, sane, she could never go back to the City.

She barely stopped herself from being run over by a rushing cab as she jogged across the street to the subway stairs. She wasn't in town long, just a couple days. Her publisher and current editor wanted to meet with her to finalize the book she'd just completed, a few last-minute notes given from the client, who was also the subject of the book.

Michael and Kevin had insisted she stay with them, which she was thrilled about. The two had been out for the wedding but had decided to pass the holidays in New York. So, it had been wonderful to spend some time with them.

That night, the three sat around their table enjoying an after-dinner glass of wine for Gray and bourbon for the boys. Not much for drinking alcohol these days except for special occasions, Gray nursed hers.

"How did you guys do it?" Kevin asked, leaning back in his chair, arms draped over the back of Michael's.

"Turkey baster," Michael said with a grin before sipping his drink.

"Nope," Gray said, shaking her head.

"Nah," Kevin said, looking at his husband. "They're too classy for that. Doctor's office, right?"

Gray shook her head again. "If it took, I impregnated my wife the old-fashioned way."

Michael stared at her. "Come again?"

"If I need to," she said with a lecherous grin. Bowdy laughter filled the room as Gray's phone rang from where she'd set it down in the living room. She pantomimed pulling two six-shooters out of invisible holsters and shot at both men with a wink before hurrying to grab her phone. "Hey, baby!"

She plopped down on the couch, ready to settle in for a few minutes of talk before she headed to bed. Her wife's tone told her immediately this wasn't a social call.

"What's wrong?" Her eyebrows fell as she listened to Christian's emotion-filled voice. "Why do I need to come home?" Gray asked, her own emotions rising with her fear. "Are you okay? Is everything okay?" Kevin and Michael stepped into the entryway, both looking concerned. "Oh, god," she whispered at Christian's words. "Is he…" She swallowed. "Okay.

I'll get there as soon as I can. I love you too. Bye."

She lowered the phone, looking down at her lap. Her heart was racing, her head was foggy, and her eyes were welling with tears. She felt the warmth of Michael as he sat beside her, a hand on her back.

"Dad's had a heart attack." It was like chewing nails to get the words past her teeth and lips. "He's in the Cardiac Care Unit at St. Anthony's."

"Okay," Michael said softly. "We'll get you home, honey." He glanced over to Kevin. "Sweetheart, let's get her a ticket."

⁂

The nonstop flight from New York into Denver seemed like the longest ever, especially with no way to communicate with Christian about what was going on. As soon as the plane touched down, Gray powered up her phone, relieved to see a text had come in from her mother:

Hey, honey. Your dad is still with us. Christian will pick you up outside of baggage claim and bring you to the hospital.

Eyes falling closed at the news, which was only eighteen minutes old, she made a quick call to Christian to let her know she'd landed then hurried to get off the plane. She'd spoken with a flight attendant who had made arrangements for her to get off the plane first due to a medical emergency.

She flew into Christian's arms when she spotted her standing at the curb by their car. They held each other for a long moment as the sun began to rise over the horizon.

"I'm so glad you're home," Christian murmured into the hug before leaving a lingering kiss on Gray's lips and helping her load her luggage.

"What happened?" Gray asked, climbing into the passenger seat.

"Dennis was at the park with Brutus. Apparently, it happened there. Brutus ran off and barked at a couple college kids until they finally followed him. They called 911."

Gray let out a heavy breath, feeling so scared. She was grateful for the hand that took hers and placed it on Christian's thigh, the dancer's warmth covering Gray's hand. They drove in silence in the early morning hours, the winter air heavy and cold, leaving a layer of thin ice on everything.

The hallways of the hospital were quiet, only a few people passing them, most dressed in medical attire of scrubs or lab coats. Finally, after an elevator ride, they reached the third floor and the CCU.

Visiting hours weren't for an hour, so they went to the waiting room, where Bernadette was watching a wall-mounted TV and sipping from a Styrofoam cup of coffee. When she spotted the two women, she dissolved into tears, standing with arms open.

Gray hugged her mother, who seemed so small and frail. She said nothing to her, just held her as she cried. Finally, though still softly crying, the older woman calmed a bit. Gray accepted a tissue from her wife with a smile of thanks, gently dabbing at her mother's eyes and cheeks.

"Have they said anything?" Gray asked softly, the two women sitting on the loveseat while Christian took the overstuffed chair nearest Bernadette. She held one of the older dancer's hands in both of hers.

Bernadette shook her head. "Only that we'll know more in the next twenty-four to forty-eight hours. It's awful, Gray," she said, fresh tears welling in her eyes. "They have him hooked up on every machine known to man."

Gray hugged her mother again. "We'll get through this, Mom," she murmured against blond hair. "No matter what, we'll get through this."

Chapter Twenty-two

The room was quiet, save for the soft beeps of the machines. Sure enough, wires, tubes, and electrodes were sticking out of him wherever there was room to. Gray took in everything, including the still form lying in the hospital bed. Her father had been dressed in a thin hospital gown, the tubes and such attached to him a landscape of bumps under the material.

He was resting peacefully, which was a double-edged sword. She was glad to see her father resting, but at the same time it was hard to not see that welcoming smile she was used to. It was also strange to see him not wearing his glasses. He obsessed over spots on them, constantly cleaning the lenses on his shirttail. It had become a bit of a joke in the family.

She reached down over the side rail and placed her hand on his. He was warm, if pale. She also noticed he wasn't wearing his wedding ring, though the white band on his finger told the tale of a ring worn every single day, rain or shine. It was funny, she thought, the things worn every single day that those around a person took for granted. It wasn't until a traumatic situation that it was noticed they were missing. No doubt his ring was with his glasses and wheelchair, safe with her mother.

"Been warning you about those steaks, Dad," she murmured softly, a smile reaching her lips. A small, bad joke for her own benefit as he certainly wasn't listening. On a more serious note, she said, "You can't leave us. You could have a new grandbaby soon." She smiled at the thought, though it was a weak one. She couldn't imagine her dad not being there for her child. "You're the only grandpa she or he would have, and do you *really* want Ivan to be the main male influence around here?"

She leaned down and placed a kiss on her father's forehead before letting out a heavy sigh.

"I love you, Dad," she said. "Be back later."

❧❧❧❧

Eyes closed, Gray raised her head to the warm spray, the water as hot as she could take it once they got home from the hospital that morning. She was exhausted, only catching what sleep she could on the four-hour flight. Bernadette had sent her daughters home for Gray to freshen up after her travels, then the two would return to the hospital with fast-food breakfast for the three of them. They were to talk to Dennis's doctor in a couple hours.

Opening her eyes, Gray reached for the shampoo bottle, noticing Christian walk into the master bath with an armful of folded towels. The writer smiled and returned her focus to her task. After a shower that was decidedly longer than normal, she decided to leave the soothing warmth of the water and face her day.

Gray opened the glass door and stepped out of the large shower stall. She reached for one of the two fluffy towels her wife had left on the vanity for her when she noticed something lying on a folded washcloth next to them.

She absently grabbed the top folded towel, shaking it free of its neat bonds before beginning to dry herself. Her actions froze when it hit her what she was looking at. Lying on the washcloth were three different types of pregnancy tests from three different makers, giving each one its own distinct design and look. Even so, they all indicated the same thing.

"She's pregnant," she whispered, taking all three plastic sticks in her hand as she slowly lowered herself to the closed toilet seat.

"*We're* pregnant."

Gray looked up to see Christian leaning against the doorway of the open bathroom door. She had a small smile on her face, a bit of uncertainty in her eyes. Gray could hardly breathe, her heart so full. She set the pregnancy test sticks aside on the counter and reached her hand out for Christian, not trusting her legs to stand.

Christian stepped into her personal space, one leg between Gray's spread knees as Gray wrapped her arms around the dancer's middle, her head cradled in Christian's arms. "I can't believe it," she whispered.

Christian's fingers ran through her wet hair. "I had a big night planned for us when you got home this weekend," she began softly. "To tell you then, but I think right now we need some good news."

Gray nodded, her eyes closing as she relished the closeness to the woman who could turn her on in a flash or comfort and calm her in a heartbeat. She turned her head and left a muffled kiss on a flat stomach. She lifted her head and looked up at Christian, who looked down at her, her fingers caressing Gray's jaw.

"I noticed there were too many tampons and

pads in the package last month," she said with a small smile. "I didn't want to get my hopes up."

Christian smiled, brushing wet bangs out of Gray's eyes. "I didn't want to say anything until I had definite news. I have an appointment with Dr. Calloway Tuesday at three. Can you go with me?"

Gray cupped the back of Christian's neck and guided her down until their lips nearly met. "I'll be there with bells on."

≈≈≈≈

Gray took a small step to her right, which put her almost against the back of Christian. She nodded acknowledgment to the woman and teenage girl who were walking past their little group of four in the hallway of the CCU unit. She turned her focus back to her father's doctor once the duo passed by.

"He will need surgery," Dr. Villegas was saying. "The blockage at this point isn't acute, but clearly significant." The middle-aged heart specialist looked at each woman in turn. "We'll need to go in and put in some stents to help clear some of it, allow the blood to flow and pump freely. With that and medications, I think we can get the situation under control before it leads to anything more substantial in treatment."

"When will this take place?" Gray asked.

"I'd like to get him in tomorrow morning," the surgeon said. "Okay?" His eyebrows raised above the frame of his glasses. When nobody said anything, he nodded in their general direction and walked away, lab coat breezing out behind him.

Bernadette turned to Gray and Christian. She looked tired and sad. "Well, I guess it's a little better than we thought, huh?"

"We'll help you through this, Mom," Gray said. "Whatever you need us to do."

"Absolutely," Christian agreed, briefly meeting Gray's gaze.

They'd decided not to say anything about the baby until after the magic marker of the first trimester. Dr. Calloway had assured Christian that likely her miscarriages when she was teen had been stress-induced, as well as being so young. Now, likely the pregnancy would go off without a hitch. Even so, they decided it was better to save this good news until her father was a little farther out of the woods.

The three headed back to the waiting room to get out of the hallway. Bernadette sat on the couch, her hand going to her forehead. Gray thought she looked so small in that moment, so frail. She sat next to her.

"Mom," she said softly. "We know Dad's out of danger now. Why don't you go home and get some sleep? I'll stay here tonight—"

"I'm not leaving," Bernadette snapped, giving Gray a hard look.

"Okay," Gray said, nodding. "Then how about this. You go home." She raised a hand to forestall her mother's interruption as Bernadette's eyebrows drew and her mouth opened. "Hold on. You go home now and grab a shower and change your clothes then come back with your crocheting or one of the fourteen books you're reading right now." She smiled. "We'll stay here until you get back."

"Absolutely," Christian added.

Bernadette let out a heavy sigh, glancing around the waiting room before looking back to the two women. Finally, she nodded. "All right. But," she added, a finger up for emphasis. "I won't be gone long."

※※※※※

"Okay, hold on to my shoulder, Dad," Ivan said with a grunt as he picked up the heavily bandaged man from his wheelchair and carried him over to the bed.

Gray stood on the other side of it to help get Dennis where he needed to lie comfortably. She placed a knee on the mattress and reached across the bed to tug the covers down farther so her father's legs wouldn't get set on top of them.

"Here we go," Ivan said, his powerful body and arms transporting his father to the bed. "Ready?" he muttered to Gray, sparing a glance at her.

"Yeah, go ahead," Gray said, moving out of the way.

Dennis grunted, his face contorting slightly in pain as he was lowered to the bed. Gray immediately went about straightening his legs and placing them in position for good blood flow.

"All right, old man," Ivan said, standing erect again once his father was down. "You be a good boy and stay put like the doc said to do."

Dennis glared up at him. "As opposed to?"

Ivan grinned and patted his shoulder. "I'm out," he announced, pushing the empty wheelchair to its place out of the way and left the room.

"Okay, Dad," Gray said, moving around the bed to where Ivan had been. "Let's get you comfortable."

"I'm fine!"

She looked at him, eyes wide in surprise. "I'm just trying to help you, Dad," she said softly.

"And I'm not a goddamn invalid," he barked, glaring at her. "I'm not a child," he muttered stubbornly, sounding exactly like a child.

Gray stifled a grin before it appeared as she looked down at him in the bed. Hands on hips, she let out a small sigh and nodded. "Okay. Um…" She was going to lean down and give him a kiss on the cheek but thought better of it. "Mom's making you something to eat," she said. "I'll let her know you're all settled."

He nodded then turned away, looking out the large picture window on the wall across the room.

Running her hand through her hair, Gray let out a sigh and left the bedroom, softly closing the door behind her. In the kitchen, her mother was putting the last few touches on the smoothie she'd made for him, filled with plenty of fruits and vitamins the doctor had recommended.

"How is he?"

"In a word?" Gray said, leaning back against the cabinet next to the fridge. "Grumpy." She was trying to keep the upset out of her voice. Her father had never spoken to her that way nor treated her that way. She understood these were unusual circumstances, but for a daughter who had always been close to her dad, it was hurtful.

Bernadette poured the thick, fruity drink into a plastic cup with lid and straw. Her eyebrows were drawn with lines of worry evident on her face. "I'm sorry, Gray," she said softly. "This hasn't been easy on him."

"I know," Gray said, walking over to her mother. "I need to get home to start dinner. Do you need anything else?"

"No, honey." Bernadette leaned over and placed a quick kiss on her daughter's cheek. "Go on home. Thanks for all you've done through this."

"Of course." Gray turned to head out, but stopped at her name. She glanced over her shoulder at her mother, still standing at the counter.

"She's pregnant, isn't she?" Bernadette asked softly.

Gray wanted to scream *Yes!* to the rafters, but they still had some weeks to go before they were going to share the news. So, instead she smiled. "No news to share at this time, Mom."

※ ※ ※ ※

Gray tapped out a mindless beat on her desk with her fingertips as she read over her notes. She'd gotten her new subject—a famous TV chef who was hot at the moment—and was beginning her research, which included a craptastic amount of watching cooking competition shows. One good thing to come out of that part? Christian had made them a fabulous chicken dinner a couple nights before, a dish inspired by one of said shows.

Feeling like she was being watched, Gray glanced up to see Caesar sitting regally as only a cat can in the hallway just outside the open French door. She met his green gaze before turning back to her task. It wasn't unusual for him to come around doing his supervisory duties every hour or so. Still feeling as though she were being watched, she glanced up again, surprised to see Caesar still sitting there.

A glance at the clock told her it wasn't his feeding time nor anything else important in his feline schedule. "Hey, bud," she called out to him, wondering if perhaps he just wanted a little attention. "Come here, Caesar," she prompted, patting her desk.

When Caesar didn't move, nor did Brutus come tearing into the office for equal loves, Gray felt a nervous little trickle down her spine. Pushing back from the desk, she got to her feet. Only then did Caesar stand and begin to walk toward the living room, Gray following.

She didn't see where Caesar had gone until she noticed him standing on the back stoop. It was an unseasonably warm day, so she'd left the one side of the doors open for Brutus and Caesar to come and go as they pleased.

The black-and-white cat was looking back at her, clearly waiting for her to get a clue that she needed to continue following him. Stepping out onto the stoop, her first thought was that it was getting a bit chilly to have the door open, and her second thought was, why was Brutus lying down in the middle of the lawn?

"Brutus?" she called out, getting no reaction. Walking across the back patio, she stopped at the edge. "Brutus?" Nothing. "Who wants a cookie?" she called out in a singsong voice.

When the big dog didn't even raise his head, Gray felt panicked butterflies batting at her stomach. Walking over to the bullmastiff who lay on his side, eyes closed as though he'd lay down on the grass for a little nap, she noticed he didn't seem to be breathing.

"Oh, no," she whispered, slowly squatting down beside him. "Brutus?" she said softly, placing a hand on his side. Nothing, and no, he wasn't breathing.

Head falling, tears instantly came to Gray's eyes. The ten-year-old dog had become much slower over the last couple months, sleeping more and eating less. The vet had told them that other than old age, he was a healthy boy.

"Sweet, sweet Brutus," she whispered through her tears. She watched as Caesar walked over to them, sniffing the dog and his reluctant companion before sitting just out of reach of Gray, almost as if he, too, were joining in the moment of grief.

She ran her hand along his side and back up along his velvety ears, as she'd done a million times over the years. She had no idea how she'd tell Christian. A dog she'd bought when she'd first moved to New York for protection as a woman living alone in the City, Gray had entered the picture just over a year later. He was the dancer's boy, her heart.

"We love you, big guy," Gray said, a tear running down her cheek and dripping off her chin onto his side. She wiped it away with her thumb.

Chapter Twenty-three

Gray turned off the shower and stepped out of the stall. It was early, just after five in the morning. She couldn't sleep, so had decided to get up and get to work. It had been three very difficult days since they'd lost Brutus. Hardest phone call she'd ever had to make.

Christian had initially been silent for so long that Gray worried she'd not heard her and she'd have to deliver the horrible news a second time. Soon enough, however, that notion had been dispelled by the soft whimpers heard as Christian began to cry. The dancer had arrived home soon after to say her goodbyes. Together they'd loaded the heavy dog into the car and had taken him on one last drive, which he loved so much, to the vet to make arrangements.

It had been three days now. Three days of lots of tears between them, especially Christian. Gray's eyes felt heavy and tight from her grief. Drying off, she glanced into the bedroom and saw that the bed was empty. Christian had been asleep when she'd gotten up, and she'd tried to be as quiet as she could. It also made her sad to not see Brutus lying at the end of the bed or the wrinkles in the covers from where his body had been.

She quickly looked away, as she didn't want to start crying again. Dressed in pajama pants and a bra, she headed out of the bedroom to find Christian as she combed her wet hair. She found Christian in the kitchen brewing herself a cup of honey lemon tea, which tended to help a little bit with her morning nausea. She'd been lucky thus far and hadn't actually thrown up, but instead would get hit with bad bouts of nausea day or night.

"Good morning, baby," Gray said, walking up behind the dancer and hugging her from behind. "How are you feeling?"

"Mmm," Christian said, covering Gray's hand with one of her own and squeezing lightly before releasing it to continue her task. "Little one is not happy with me this morning."

Gray left a kiss to Christian's neck before moving away to get coffee started for herself. It had been tough on Christian to give it up. But, as she put it, she was going to be a "good monkey" and do what Dr. Calloway told her to do.

"You know," Christian said softly, filling the teakettle with filtered water from the spigot on the fridge door. "When you were in the shower I was thinking about something."

"I hope I didn't wake you," Gray said from the pantry where she was picking what kind of coffee she wanted from the myriad boxes of flavored coffee K-cups.

"No," Christian assured. "Not at all."

When Gray came back out, she saw the kettle on the stovetop and Christian leaning back against the counter next to the sink. She was looking down at her feet, which were nestled in the slippers Gray had given her for Christmas.

"Lying there," Christian continued softly, still not looking at Gray, who went about making her coffee to give her wife the physical space she seemed to need. "I was thinking back to when I first got Brutus. I had just moved to New York, into the apartment. Been there maybe a month when I got him, thinking a puppy would make me feel safer." A surprising laugh burst from her lips. "I had no idea just how big that little puppy would get." She smiled and met Gray's eyes.

Gray chuckled, nodding. "Always look at their feet, my love," she said, amused.

"Hey, we never had animals when I was a kid, so I had no idea what on earth I was doing. Anyway, so I got him and learned along the way how to be a pet mom. Then, just over a year later, you came back into my life." Her grin turned into a smile, beaming. "He was there for all those changes, Gray. You moving in, Caesar adopting us, career changes for us both—"

"Moving to Colorado," Gray added.

Christian nodded. "Coming back home. And," she added softly, hands going to her stomach, which had yet to change much. "This little one."

"I'm pretty sure he was hiding under the bed during that one." Gray smirked.

Christian smiled with a nod. "No doubt. But, what came to me, he was there for all of that, all of the first part of us, Now, here we go on a whole new adventure," she added, rubbing her stomach. "Maybe he knew it was his time to go home and let the next puppy take over, grow up with our baby."

"His job was finished," Gray added softly.

"Exactly."

"So," Gray hedged. "Are you saying you want to get another one?"

"Not yet," Christian said, shaking her head. "But

I think when it's time, the right little one will fall into our laps."

※ ※ ※ ※

Early June was upon them and it was a gorgeous day out with robin's-egg-blue skies, not a cloud to be seen. Gray stood at the barbecue grilling up burgers and hot dogs for the gathered family.

"Caleb, Colby," she called out to her twin nephews who were tossing the football back and forth in the yard. "These are almost done. Go tell Aunt Christian and find out what everyone wants to drink."

"Okay," Colby, the more vocal of the two, said, tossing the ball to the grass as he and his brother hurried inside.

The rectangular, glass-top table was already set for lunch, a special little bundle tied together with purple ribbon strategically placed at specific place settings.

"What can I do?" Bernadette asked, stepping out from the house.

"You can take this in," Gray said, handing her the plate with cooked burgers on it. "The cheese is inside."

"I can do that," Bernadette said with a wide smile as she accepted the plate.

"When is Dad getting here?" Gray asked, antsy, as today was a very special day.

Immediately, Bernadette's expression darkened as she looked away. "He should be here soon," she said quietly. "His new medicines can give him bathroom problems."

Gray nodded. "Okay."

Everyone was seated where they'd been told to sit, though they'd done it with a lot of confused expressions. Everyone, except for Dennis.

"So," Ivan said, pushing his empty plate away, three burgers and two hotdogs long gone, and raised the package that had been at his place setting. "What's all this about?"

Gray glanced at Christian, already looking at her. Gray nodded. "Well," Christian announced to those gathered. "We had hoped Dennis would be here, too, but that's okay. Go ahead and open those."

The boys tore into their first, purple ribbons flying. They unfolded their specially made T-shirts that read *Cousin*. Next came Celine's: *Aunt*. A keening sound of excitement left her lips as her hand came up to cover her mouth. There was *Uncle* for Ivan, and finally, *Grandma* for Bernadette.

"Oh, my god!" Bernadette gasped, wide eyes turning to Gray and Christian. "So, it's true? You're pregnant?"

Christian grinned, nodding. "We just entered the second trimester on Friday."

That was it. The family erupted in excitement with cries of surprise and joy, and hugs abounded. Ivan grabbed Gray in a tight, almost painful, hug. When he released her, he regarded her with a look of pride in his eyes. The ironic thing, Gray mused, was it didn't seem like he was proud of himself and what he'd done for them. He was proud of *her*, almost like one father to another.

Gray wasn't entirely sure how she felt about that, but took it for the positive from her brother that it was. Later on, he helped her clear the table, the boys deciding to set up croquet in the backyard while the grown-ups cleaned.

"You know," he said, stacking plates after scraping any remaining food onto the top plate. "Dad's not sick today."

She glanced up at him. "What?"

"He was sitting on his ass watching golf when we picked up Mom," he explained, meeting her gaze.

"Golf? Since when does he like golf?"

Ivan shrugged. "No clue. I wasn't going to say anything because, honestly? I figured he'd ruin a fun family barbecue. Let him act like an asshole all by himself. I mean," he added with a snort. "I seriously think Mom is about to boot his ass."

"I've noticed almost every time I've called her that she's been at the theater," Gray said, collecting all the napkins and silverware. She stared down at her gathered assortment for a moment. "You know," she said quietly. "I feel bad." She glanced over at him. "For a minute there I was really beginning to wonder if she was seeing somebody."

"No," he said, shaking his head. "For one, it's not in her to do that, and for two, Celine and the boys have been with her a lot since they've been out of school. It's like he's fallen into some sort of depression or something. Or, maybe his new meds are messing with him?"

"Oh, hell, Ivan," she said. "He's on blood thinners and cholesterol medication, blood pressure stuff."

He shrugged. "Well, something's wrong."

As soon as he said that, something inside Gray told her to go talk to him. Now. She grabbed his shirt, still bundled in ribbon, and stormed into the house.

"Gray?" Christian called out from where she and

the other two women were cleaning up the kitchen. "Where are you going?"

"To kick some Dad ass," Gray muttered, grabbing her keys off the miniature coat rack that hung by the garage door.

※ ※ ※ ※

Gray pulled up to her parents' house, which was quiet, the wooden front door closed. Her father's modified van was parked out front as always when he was home. She grabbed his T-shirt before climbing out of the car, slamming the door.

She was angry, but she had a feeling of anxiousness building inside her that she couldn't quite explain. She walked up the path that split the front lawn into two rectangular sides. Standing on the front porch, she raised her hand to knock, but that same something told her to go in. She pulled open the glass storm door, and when she realized the big wooden door was unlocked, she let herself inside.

The TV was on, and sure enough, tuned to golf. Her father wasn't in the living room, nor was his wheelchair. She walked farther in, ducking her head into the kitchen to find it, too, was empty. The bathroom was empty as was the master bedroom. She knew there was no way he could get himself up the stairs to her or Ivan's old bedroom. That left either the backyard or the office.

The office door was open and still no Dennis, but something she saw in her parents' bedroom caught Gray's memory. Heading back inside, she noticed that her father's nightstand drawer had been left open. Walking over to it, she saw some balled pairs of socks that clearly had once been in the drawer were now set on top of the nightstand. In their stead, perhaps once hidden by them, was an empty gun holster.

"Dad!"

Panic filling her, Gray raced through the house to the backyard, nearly crashing through the sliding glass door. She struggled with it and finally got it open. When she did, she threw herself through it and to the back patio. Nearly hyperventilating, she saw her father sitting in his wheelchair in the middle of the yard. His head was down, like he was looking at his lap.

Tears instantly sprang to her eyes as she ran over to him, terrified of what she may see. To her eternal relief, he was alive, lifting his head to look up at her. His eyes looked tired, profoundly so.

"Give it to me," she said, holding out her hand, her words not much more than a whisper. "Give it to me," she said again, voice stronger.

Dennis said nothing, simply raised his hand that held the pistol and gently rested it in the palm of her hand.

With the heft of the gun in her hand, Gray nearly fell to her knees in relief. "Jesus Christ," she whispered, eyes squeezing shut as she took a step back to balance herself. "My God, Dad. What were you thinking?"

He said nothing, his head just fell again. Gray quickly unloaded the pistol, rendering it harmless, and stuffed the parts in the pockets of her cargo shorts. Her emotions were running through her in a frenzied kaleidoscope that made her feel dizzy. Finally, she settled on anger.

"What were you thinking, Dad?" she asked

again.

"I'm sorry," he murmured, head still bowed.

"What is happening with you?" She was trying desperately to keep calm but was failing miserably. "The father I know would *never* do something like this! Ever!" She moved to stand in front of him, looking down at him. "You have a woman that you've been with for more than forty years who is so goddamn confused and hurt by you. She's lying for you, Dad. Fucking *lying* for you about why you didn't show up today. Do you want to know what today was about?"

He spared a glance up at her before looking away, shaking his head.

"This!" Gray threw the bundled T-shirt into his lap. "Open it." When he didn't make a move to do anything, she nearly growled at him. "Open it!"

Dennis took the bundle in his hands, tugging the ribbon free. He lifted the shirt, which unfolded with the help of gravity. When he saw the word *Grandpa* unveiled in big, block letters, he lost his composure and began to cry, the shirt slipping from trembling fingers.

Gray fell to her knees in front of him. "Dad," she said, emotion in her own voice. "Dad, you are so loved. My God, you are so loved and so needed." She waited until he looked at her, a broken man. "I can't do this without you," she whispered.

He reached for her, sobbing like she'd never seen him cry before. She held him, rocking him as he cried, wondering what could have driven him to this. Maybe he'd been carrying too much after the accident that had robbed him of his legs, his livelihood, and his very identity. Maybe he'd never really dealt with it in order to stay strong for his family. And maybe the heart attack and subsequent surgery had left him just helpless enough that it took him back to a very dark place.

"What can I do?" she asked.

It took him a long moment to get himself under control enough to respond. "I feel so useless," he whispered. "Like I'm no good to anyone."

She went to grab the grandpa T-shirt to wipe his face, but he pushed her hands away. "No! Not that."

He tugged his own T-shirt off over his head and used it to wipe his eyes and his cheeks, removing his glasses. She took them from him and washed them on her own shirt. Holding them up to the sky to make sure they were clean, she handed them back to her as he pulled his shirt back on, little wet spots all over it.

"I can tell you a thousand times how needed you are in this family, how loved you are. I can tell you a thousand times that I can't fix crap in my own house and have to call you every other week because I'm a shitty lesbian and can't use power tools."

He smiled at that as he put his glasses back on. "This is true," he muttered.

"But," she said softly. "It doesn't matter how many times I say it or how many examples I give you of just how *not* useless you are. Only you can know that and feel that."

He nodded, looking down at his lap where he held the grandpa shirt, stroking the soft cotton material almost reverently with his thumb.

"You know," Gray continued. "Christian and I were so lost, Dad. I mean, we were on the verge of calling it total quits."

He looked up and met her gaze, surprise in his eyes. "I knew things were difficult for a time, but I had no idea it was that bad."

"It was. I almost lost everything that meant anything to me," she admitted.

"Why didn't you say anything to me?" he asked, a hand reaching up and gently touching her cheek, as he always did when he was worried about her.

"I was embarrassed," she said simply. "I didn't know how to fix my own relationship. Didn't know what was wrong." She eyed him. "Guessing kinda like you right now. Right?"

He nodded, looking down, shame on his face. "What did you guys do?" he murmured. "How did it get fixed?"

"We went to therapy." Gray waited until he met her gaze again. "I'm not one to tell anybody what they should do when it comes to that sort of thing, and it doesn't work for everyone, but Dr. Stacy worked miracles for us." She smiled encouragement at him. "Maybe you should give it a try, Dad. Work out some of this stuff that you've been pushing down for a long, long time."

He nodded. "Okay." Clearing his throat, he nodded toward her bulging pockets. "Don't tell your mother."

"I have to, Dad," she said gently. "Mom needs to know what's going on. You've got to be honest with her."

He took a long, shaky breath. "Okay. You're right." He smiled at her, again his hand touching her face. "Thank you, Gray," he whispered.

Chapter Twenty-four

"This place is seriously cool," Gray murmured, looking around the diner they sat in, eating the best waffles she'd had in her entire life. And, who would have thought to put homemade peach jelly on the thick, fluffy waffles rather than syrup?

"I want to find out how to make this," Christian said, mouth full of a large bite of waffle. She held up the mini mason jar they'd been given full of the sweet, peachy gooiness. "Amazing. It's too thin to be a jelly yet too thick to be a syrup. Peach perfection."

Gray grinned, sitting back in her seat. "Peach perfection? When did you become the poet?"

Christian gave her a side-glance. "Don't talk smack to a woman who's five months pregnant."

Gray's grin grew. "You're adorable."

"Mm-hmm," Christian hedged, giving her another side-glance.

The two—well, technically three—were in a tiny mountain town called Wynter, which was about an hour and some change outside of Denver. Gray had never heard of it, but it was beautiful, in a little valley surrounded by foothills and of course, the Rockies. Very picturesque, looking like it belonged more in a movie or a book than real life.

They were eating at a local joint called Pop's, which was essentially an old-school diner that had been slightly modernized.

"How y'all doin'?"

Gray glanced up to see an attractive woman who looked to be in her late thirties or early forties with her shoulder-length red hair pulled back by a rolled bandana. Her turquoise eyes were bright and her smile was friendly. Her nametag read *Wyatt*.

"What sort of ransom would it take to get the recipe for this?" Gray asked, holding up the jar.

"Oh, come on, now!" The woman laughed, waving her hand at Gray. "If'n I tell y'all that, I go outta business."

Gray smiled, enjoying the woman's smooth, easy Southern accent and friendly nature. "What if we don't tell anybody else?"

"Now, now," Wyatt said, eyeing them both. "That is a recipe passed down from my granny's granny."

"Secret's in the sauce?" Christian asked.

Wyatt grinned. "Yes, ma'am. Can I get y'all anythin' else?"

Gray looked at Christian's plate, noticing her sausage was already long gone. Knowing it had become one of her favorite foods in recent months, she said, "Our little mama-to-be will take some more of those amazing sausage patties, please."

Wyatt's eyes widened. "Butter me an' call me a biscuit! You're pregnant, darlin'?"

Christian smiled, hand on her belly, which was still mostly flat. "I am."

"When is the littlin' due?" she asked, hand resting on the back of Christian's chair.

"November, could be Thanksgiving."

Wyatt leaned in and gave her a quick but warm hug. "Us mamas gotta stick together," she said, giving Gray a hug too. "On the house, ladies," she said, walking away, only to return with their ticket. She clicked a pen to life and wrote *OTH* across it with her initials. "Y'all part of the filmin'?" she asked, sliding the ticket over to Gray on the table. "Just give that ta Jessica at the register."

"Thank you," Gray said, sliding the ticket closer to her plate. "My wife is the choreographer. I'm so excited you guys have a movie filming here!"

"I'll tell ya what," Wyatt said, hand on hip. "Faith, our Mayor"—she leaned forward as if revealing a big secret—"and my wife, fought and fought for that production ta come here. Figured," she added, standing up again and indicating the town around them. "If the outskirts of Wynter can't pass as an Old West minin' town, nuthin' can."

"Didn't this start out as one?" Christian asked. "Back in the eighteenth century."

"Sure did." Wyatt stepped aside as a waitress hurried over with a side of the sausage patties. "Thanks, Jess," she said with a kind smile before turning her attention back to the ladies. "If y'all have time today, check out the museum we set up in Mr. Billy's old barn."

"I saw that in my research of the town's history," Gray said, excited. "Mr. Billy was William Wynter, right? Last living relative here of Jerimiah Wynter. Founder, right?"

Wyatt gave her a side-glance. "Well, look at you! Yes, ma'am. We lost Mr. Billy a few years back," she explained. "He was more than a hundred years old, if you can believe that. Wonderful man. In his will he left the money for his place to be transformed into a never-forget."

"Wonderful," Gray said with a wide smile. "I've

got time to kill today, so I know where I'll be. Do you guys have a coffee shop or anything around here?" She'd brought her laptop to get some work done while Christian did her thing, but the diner would be too noisy, if it remained how it was at the moment.

"Of course." Wyatt pointed toward the front of the eatery. "Just across the street and down a few paces you'll find Bessie's. A big ol' ice cream cone is out front, but that's just downstairs. Upstairs is the coffee shop."

"Wonderful. Thank you," Gray said, excited to check out the place. She loved local shops and eateries, period.

The door to the diner opened and an impressive woman in full police dress blues walked in. She was very attractive with short, dark hair and Hispanic features. Intense dark eyes scanned the diner, not as though she were looking for someone, but more so out of habit.

"Why, Chief!" Wyatt looked at the newcomer, hands on hips. "Don't you just look dashin' in full uniform."

The cop grinned as she walked over to the three of them, tipping her uniform cap at Gray and Christian. "Mornin', ladies. Yes," she said to Wyatt. "I'm here on official business."

Wyatt sighed dramatically and turned around, hands behind her back as though waiting to be cuffed.

The chief burst into laughter, playfully pushing Wyatt away. "Don't tempt me, Mrs. Fitzgerald. I'll tell your wife."

Wyatt laughed. "She'll help you book me."

"I've been asked to escort any crew to the filming site," the police chief said. "I figured they'd be here."

"Why," Wyatt said, indicating Christian. "We have one of 'em right here."

The uniformed woman turned to the ladies sitting at the table. "Well, that was handy. Hey there. I'm Chief Montez, though please call me Grace, and I'm here to personally deliver you safely to the set." She pulled out her phone from a pocket, tapping and swiping until she got to what she wanted. "What's your name, ma'am?"

"Christian Scott." She'd kept her professional name as Scott but had taken Rickman in her personal life, which always made Gray smile.

Grace nodded. "Yes, ma'am, Miss Scott. You are on the list." She gave her a winning smile. "Anyone else in here, Wyatt?"

"That fella over there," she said, pointing to a man sitting by himself eating near the jukebox. "That's it."

"Excellent." Grace turned to Christian. "I'll be right back, ma'am. If you want to finish up here."

"Thank you, Grace," Christian responded with a nod.

"You're Christian, then," Wyatt said, then turned to Gray, a questioning eyebrow raised.

"Gray," Gray said, holding out a hand in proper greeting.

"Gray, Christian, I'm Wyatt, and it is mighty nice to meet you ladies." She pointed at Gray. "Go get yourself a Wynter in July at the coffee shop," she directed, turning away as a large party of guests entered the diner. "Ya won't be sorry!"

Gray watched the friendly woman walk away before turning back to her wife, who looked equally amused. "Okay, now *this* is why we left New York, baby," she said with a laugh.

※ ※ ※ ※

The coffee shop above the ice cream parlor was amazing. It spoke to the town's pioneer founding, replete with miniature swinging saloon doors at the top of the narrow staircase and a rugged motif inside. Rough-hewn tables were scattered around as well as a few comfy chairs tucked into corners.

Soft music was piped in, though not loud and obnoxious like the big coffee shops where a person broke the bank for a latte then froze and went deaf while trying to enjoy it. The place was nearly empty, save for the woman with short, blond hair behind what looked to be a genuine bar top. Her back was to the customer area of the shop as she leaned over the counter there, seeming to be reading or writing something.

Stepping up to the bar at the register, her laptop bag slung over her shoulder, Gray said, "Hey there."

The woman turned around. "Hi! Give me one sec and I'll be with you."

"Sure, take your time. You guys have Wi-Fi?"

"Sure do." The woman reached across the space from the back counter to hand Gray a small piece of paper with the Wi-Fi information on it. "Get yourself all set up and I'll be done here."

Gray found herself a table out of the way and pulled her computer from its padded bag. As she waited for it to boot up, she saw Chief Montez, sans uniform jacket and hat, walk in with a little girl on her hip. The girl had curly dark hair and was no doubt the biological daughter of the chief.

"See Mommy?" Grace said, bending down and setting the girl, who looked to be no more than three or maybe four, on her little feet. She pointed at the blonde behind the bar. "Go get her."

"Mommy!" the little girl crowed when she saw her, running as fast as her little legs would carry her, disappearing behind the bar.

"Hey, baby girl!" the blonde exclaimed, bending down to scoop her up and give her a big hug before setting her on the bar top. "How was lunch with Grandma and Grandpa?"

Gray was utterly charmed as she watched the little family. Grace walked over to the customer side of the bar, leaning over to get a kiss from the woman behind. She felt like she was intruding but couldn't take her eyes off the three.

Her mind went to Christian and the baby she carried. The only indication she was pregnant was that her stomach wasn't as muscled as it usually was, but it hadn't grown much. Her doctor said that a woman in the tremendous shape that Christian was in from decades of dancing likely wouldn't show as quickly as the average woman. But, Gray knew it was coming.

She watched the little girl interacting with her moms, and it was so beautiful. She smiled as "Mommy" and the little girl, apparently named Isabella, waged a name-calling war against each other, based on types of nuts: *You're a peanut. No, you're a walnut! No, you're an almond! No, you're an acorn! What's an acorn?*

A small chuckle fell from her lips at that one. There was so much love among those three, evident in every word, every absent little touch of affection, every look of adoration between the women.

That, Gray thought, that was what she craved.

That was her future.

❦❦❦❦

Later that night, Gray spared a glance at Christian as the two folded laundry in the bedroom, the laundry basket of washed and dried clothing dumped out over the expanse of their bed.

"What am I going to do without you for a whole week?"

Christian met her gaze, a small smile on her lips. "Celebrate?"

Gray raised an eyebrow and tossed a rolled pair of socks at her.

"I'm really excited to work with Rick again, though," Christians said, her eyes aglow with excitement. "He was such an amazing director on *Angel*. I have to admit, I'm not sure who thought a musical and the Old West were a match made in heaven, but it's a fun movie."

"I think it's awesome, baby," Gray said, truly happy for and proud of her wife.

"Oh!" Christian dropped the shirt she was folding and hurried from the room, returning in quick order with her wallet. She fished out a business card and handed it to Gray. "Before I forget. I was telling Rick all about you and your books, and wouldn't you know it, he and Richard are close friends."

"Really?" Gray said, taking the card and looking at it. "Very cool."

"Yes, and he loved the book," Christian added. "He said to have your people call his assistant. That's whose number is on the card."

Gray wiggled the small stiff card in her fingers.

"Um," she mumbled. "I don't have any 'people.' Do I?"

Christian grinned. "He means your agent, love," she said softly, amusement in her voice.

"Oh," Gray said, her stomach dropping. It took her a minute to be able to say anything else. "Um, why?"

"I think he's interested in working with you, Gray," Christian explained, picking up the abandoned shirt and folding.

Gray stared at her, shocked. "He wants a book?"

Christian held her gaze, slowly shaking her head from side to side. "A movie."

Gray felt like she was going to throw up. "I don't know anything about movies, Christian," she said, panic in her voice. "Other than what I like to eat while watching them."

Christian's smile was broad. "Yes, and you didn't know anything about books other than reading them either." She raised an eyebrow. "Until you tried it."

"Holy shit," Gray whispered, again looking down at the business card. "Okay," she said with a deep intake of air and a slow release. "I'll call Natalie this week while you're in Wynter on set."

"See?" Christian said, head tilted and grinning. "And here you thought you'd have nothing to do."

Gray smiled, setting the card on her bedside table before continuing her task. "Mom said Dad is doing really good with Dr. Stein and the antidepressant meds. Even though the doc says it's situational depression, it's still important."

"I think that's really wonderful," Christian said softly, rolling a pair of socks. "Your dad is such an amazing guy. Between my own father and Brandon,

I've not had a ton of luck with father figures in my life. Your dad changed a lot of that for me." She tossed the socks onto the growing pile that belonged to Gray. "When are you going to give him his gun back?" she asked gently, meeting Gray's eyes. "I know how uncomfortable it makes you having that thing in the house."

Gray nodded. Though her father had kept a gun for self-defense as far back as she could remember, she herself was strongly anti-gun. "I know Dad will ask for it back when he feels he's in a good place for good. He was pretty horrified that I walked in on him like that." She let out a sad sigh. She and her father hadn't talked about it since it happened, but she knew eventually it would come up. "I think he's really ashamed."

"Well, he should be more proud that he was willing to get some help. Far too many people think it's weak to talk to somebody or ask for help."

"Hell, look at us." Gray said. "When things started to go sideways."

"I'll always be grateful for Dr. Stacy, and I'm so glad your dad has Dr. Stein." Christian was quiet for a long moment before she said, "You know, we need to decide if we're going to do it or not."

Gray knew by her tone what she was talking about. She nodded. "I know. We haven't really talked about it." She tossed the shirt she'd just folded onto Christian's pile. "I guess the question is, do we want to know?" she said simply. "Do you?"

"Yes. No. Maybe." She smiled. "Not helpful, right?"

"Yeah, no." Gray grinned.

"Do you?" Christian asked.

Gray shrugged, sitting down on the bed and

running her hand along the soft fur of Caesar, who was supervising. "I don't know. I'm not big on surprises and that's one hell of a surprise, but still…"

Christian nodded. "I understand. Look," she suggested. "I leave in the morning and will be back by Thursday or Friday, depending on how quickly the cast gets the routines. Let's both think on it this week, then make a decision when I get back. Okay?"

Gray nodded. "Sounds reasonable. I concur."

Chapter Twenty-five

"Okay, Christian," Dr. Calloway said softly as the three women huddled in the small room. "This will be a little bit cold, sorry about that." Dr. Calloway sat on a rolling stool next to the table Christian lay on. Her shirt had been removed and was held by Gray, who sat on a second stool next to her wife. "But this will help our little magic wand move over your belly better so we can see the baby."

Christian nodded before letting out a long, slow breath. She held Gray's hand a little tighter. Gray could feel the nervousness coming off the mother-to-be in waves. Christian was now at twenty-six weeks and was beginning to get a baby bump finally. On the precipice of the third trimester, they knew she'd begin to really start growing soon, as it was the time for the baby to gain weight.

"How big is the baby now?" Gray asked.

"Well," the doctor said, spreading the goo. "Your little one should be in the thirteen-, fourteen-inch range." She glanced over at Gray. "Weighing about a pound and a half or better."

"Wow," Gray said softly. She was nervous now as the doctor finished with the gel and seemed to be ready to get down to business.

The screen came to life to show whatever the ultrasound was picking up. At the moment, it looked like a collection of undefinable blobs in black, grey, and white. Gray rested her elbows on the side of the padded table next to Christian's hip, leaning forward to get a better view.

"All right," the doctor said. "The black is fluid, the white is bones, and the grey is tissue, like organs and such," she explained. "All the good stuff."

"There's the head." Dr. Calloway smiled over at Christian. "This little one is active like its Mama."

Christian grinned. "Tell me about it! I feel it moving right now."

"Okay, so this is an arm," Dr. Calloway continued, using her finger to point out the long blob. "See, it's doing this." She demonstrated with her own arm bent so her hand was tucked up against her shoulder. "And, look at this." She pointed to a quickly moving little blip on the screen. Her smile was wide as she looked at Gray and Christian. "That's your baby's heartbeat."

Gray looked from the doctor to the screen and stared. Tears gathered in her eyes, as that was such a fierce sign of life, and a fierce little heartbeat. She felt Christian's fingers tighten around her again, to which she responded with a little squeeze of her own.

"Oh, here we are, Mamas," the doctor said. "Right here." She circled the area with her finger. "You have a little girl."

Gray sucked in a breath, her heart swelling so much in her chest that she thought she'd start to sob. Somehow, knowing the sex made their child all the more real. Knowing they would raise a daughter left her speechless.

Gray smiled then leaned down and left a kiss on Christian's lips. They were going to be parents.

Gray stared at the wall of paint cards, a veritable rainbow of choices, and every choice in fifty different shades. She blew out a breath and ran a hand through her hair. "Okay, so we've decided on some semblance of yellow for the base color, right?"

Christian nodded, stepping up to the intimidating wall and pulling a few cards with the colorful squares on them. She stepped back to stand next to Gray. "What do you think of any of these?"

Gray grimaced. "Not that one," she said, tapping one of the cards. "Baby-poop yellow. We'll have enough of that to deal with without having it on the walls of the nursery."

Christian smirked and nodded. "Duly noted." She replaced it back in its slot on the wall. "Are we still wanting to go with our favorite colors for accents?" she asked, glancing over her shoulder at Gray while still standing next to the color cards.

"Yes, ma'am," Gray said, stepping up a bit farther down. "You're the purple girl, so why don't you grab what colors of purple strike you and I'll hit the reds over here."

"Done."

After they had gathered a few sample paints to take home, Gray glanced over at Christian as she maneuvered them through traffic. The dancer had been quiet since leaving the home improvement store, almost as though something in her had shifted. Gray wasn't sure what was wrong.

Moodiness certainly became part of their life when Christian had become pregnant, and certainly unexpected emotions, but this seemed deeper than mere hormonal changes. Carrying the things they'd purchased into the house, Christian immediately went to the fridge and retrieved her ever-present bag of baby carrots. It had been one of the bigger cravings she'd had for the past six months. That and prunes dipped in cream cheese.

Gray set the sample cans on the cooking island and glanced up at the quiet dancer. "What's wrong, baby?" she asked, keeping her voice soft and gentle. She'd learned over the months that to come at Christian while pregnant in *any* sort of tone that could be misinterpreted as irritated or confrontational could end up in Puddle d'Christian.

Christian didn't answer for a moment as she munched on a carrot. Finally, she turned to look at Gray, leaning back against the counter. "It hit me today. If I hadn't made the decision I did about the second pregnancy, that baby," she said softly. "Would have been an older sister or brother to this one." She placed her hand on her slightly protruding belly. "Quite a bit older, but older, nonetheless." She crossed her arms over her swollen breasts. "The first pregnancy ended in a miscarriage. I'm okay with that," she said, nodding. "I've always seen that as God or whoever is trying to protect that baby and even me from such a bad situation. But the second one…"

"Christian," Gray said softly, moving closer to her but not touching her. "Both those babies were conceived in a crime, a crime against you, a child at the time." She brushed back some of Christian's hair, tucking it behind an ear. "You were given few, if any, choices back then. I remember you saying your parents would have stepped in and taken that baby from you. You were still a minor. What could you have done?"

Christian met her gaze for a long moment then nodded, letting out a long, slow breath. "That's basically what Dr. Stacy said too." She crunched another carrot. "If I'd had a teenager when we met in New York, would you still have wanted to be with me?"

Gray smiled. "Baby, you had *worse* than a teenager. You had a Brutus that slimed me the first time I met him."

To Gray's delight, Christian chuckled at that. "True."

Seeing it as her window of opportunity, Gray took Christian in a warm embrace, stroking her hair. "Baby," she said into the hug. "You've been given a second chance." She left a kiss on the side of her head before pulling away so she could look into her face. "You're a grown woman now, free to make your own choices, and you made the choice to bring a child into this world." She smiled, brushing her thumb across Christian's cheek to wipe a tear away. "And, you'll do everything in your power to make sure this little girl is safe because you've been there, you've seen the monster under the bed."

Christian nodded. "I have. And you're right," she added, voice hardening. "I'd kill anything or anyone who tried to hurt this baby."

"I know you would." Gray's smile widened. "That's why I knew you'd be a badass to have a child with."

Christian said nothing, simply took Gray in another hug, the kind that lasts many minutes and is the connection and bonding of one soul to another.

Gray lowered her arm, tiling her head this way and that before taking in the entirety of the ceiling. "What do you think?" she asked, looking down at Christian, who sat on her butt on the opposite side of the room with paintbrush in hand. She was working on the detailed work of fixing missing spots near the baseboards when the walls were painted their cheery yellow.

Christian, humming along softly along with Renée Fleming over the house speakers, looked up. Her eyes widened as her mouth fell open. "Oh, my goodness," she murmured.

Nervous now, Gray set her paintbrush into the tray atop the ladder and stepped down to the floor. Her steps crunched on the plastic that protected the floor beneath. They'd chosen a sunny yellow for the walls, but Gray decided to take it one step further. Since their favorite colors were purple and red, she added some orange and pink in there and made what could be a perpetual sunrise or sunset across the ceiling. She'd used the yellow from the walls to create a sun in the corner of the ceiling for the other colors to sprout from.

"This is incredible," Christian said, setting her own brush aside in her own paint tray and pushing to her feet with a little grunt of exertion. Hand on her back for support, she stepped over to Gray. "Absolutely beautiful."

"Can you tell what it is?" Gray asked. As the artist, clearly she knew what it was supposed to be, but that didn't mean everyone else could see her vision.

"Of course," Christian said, looking at her like she was crazy. "The sun is rising."

"Or setting."

"Or setting," Christian agreed with a nod. "This is amazing. Really, really cool," she said with a little laugh of wonder. "You know what we should do?"

Gray shook her head. "No, what?"

"We should get one of those little projector things that shine on the ceiling—"

"That makes the night sky!" Gray finished, excited at the idea.

Caught in the moment of music, her eyes slipped closed as the tragic opening notes of the aria "Amami, Alfredo" from the opera *La Traviata* began. She and Christian rode out the powerful song in mutual silence, both absorbing the moment. Gray's heart felt like it would burst with the immensity of the human instrument when wielded by masters such as Renée Fleming.

"My word," she said after the song was over. "Sorry. Can I put in a request to come back as Maria Callas or Sarah Brightman or Renée Fleming when I die?" she said with a laugh. "Anyway, brief intermission over."

Christian grinned. "Favorite aria ever. But yes, like a night sky." She looked at Gray for a long moment, so long it was beginning to make Gray wonder if she'd accidentally painted her entire face. "Do you know what my first clue was that you were the love of my life?"

"How amazing I am in bed?" Gray asked, teasing in her voice.

Christian cleared her throat dramatically. "Do you know what the second clue was that you were the love of my life?"

Gray grinned. "No, what?"

"The fact that you love opera as much as I do, that you get it." Christian smiled, turning to Gray and placing her hands on her hips. "Opera isn't for everyone."

Gray smirked. "Neither am I, so I guess it makes sense that we were made for each other, huh?"

Christian slapped Gray's ass playfully. "Isn't that the truth. What sort of crimes did I commit in a past life for you to be the burden I must bear in this one?"

"With opera as your soundtrack," Gray added.

Christian burst into laughter. "Indeed. Get back to work, you pest," she said, leaving a kiss on Gray's lips before moving away from her.

Amused, Gray walked back toward the ladder to do a few touchups on her ceiling masterpiece. Hands on the sides of the ladder, she noticed her father's van pulling up to the curb. He parked, then a moment later Gray's phone rang with his ringtone.

"Hey, Dad. Yeah, we're both home. Everything okay?" She glanced over at Christian. "No, just finishing up painting in the baby's room. We'll be down in two shakes, 'kay?" She grinned and nodded. "Sounds good. See you in a sec." Ending the call, she said, "Well, Dad has something for us apparently and said he hopes we won't kill him."

"Oh, boy," Christian muttered. "Tell me it's not more green chili. I can't handle that stuff when I'm *not* pregnant."

Abandoning their chore for the moment, the two stopped to wash their hands in the upstairs hall bathroom before heading down to the main floor. The large wood door was open, so through the glass storm door they could see Dennis wheeling himself up the path, fingerless leather gloves on and a white cardboard box on his lap.

"That box is big enough to contain a craptastic amount of green chili," Gray muttered.

"God help me," Christian responded as the two walked over to the door, Gray pushing it outward so it wouldn't hit Dennis's chair. "Hey, Dennis!"

"Hey, gals," he said, wheeling himself past Gray.

"What's going on?" she asked.

"Well," he said, wheeling his way to the wide-open space of the living room. "I sure hope you two don't get mad at me and your mom for this, but…" He glanced at both of them as they joined him. "We felt he was perfect." He sat the box down on the floor. "If you two don't agree, don't worry," he assured. "We have a Plan B."

Oh, boy, Gray thought. "Okay."

"Christian, will you open that flap right there, please?" he asked.

"Of course," the dancer said, squatting down to the white box that had a few little holes punched into it. Opening the flap, she waited, along with Gray squatting next to her. Nothing happened.

Gray got to her hands and knees and leaned over, looking inside. Looking back at her with sleepy eyes and bedhead was a little puppy, white and about the size of a potato.

"Oh, my god," she murmured. "Hey, little fella," she said softly. Her heart melted when big brown eyes closed as its little mouth opened, a pink tongue sticking out as it yawned with a little puppy squeak. Reaching in, she gently grabbed the warm, pudgy body and pulled it out, cradling it in her arms.

"This little guy is Trevor," Dennis explained.

"Now, you can rename if you want, he's still little enough. But I named him that for a reason."

Gray glanced up at her father, curious. "Why?"

"Well, little Trevor here was the runt of nine and has a bum leg," Dennis said, smiling at the little pup. "Vet says he can live a totally normal life, just might slow him down a bit."

"But," Christian said softly, moving over to Gray, running her thumb along the top of the little guy's head. "Why Trevor?"

"Back when the accident happened, when I first found out I was going to have to use this for the rest of my life," he said, patting the tires of the wheelchair. "There was a man, a nurse in the hospital who helped take care of me while I was there. He'd lost one of his legs in Vietnam and had a fake one. He really helped me to see that I could still have a full life." He smiled. "His name was Trevor."

Gray stared at him for a long moment. "I never heard that story," she said softly.

Dennis nodded. "Yup. Used to hear from him a few times a year until he died six or seven years ago."

Gray held the puppy up so she was eye-to-eye with him. "Trevor it is," she said, leaving a little kiss on his head before looking over at Christian, who had tears in her eyes. *Can we keep him?* she asked with her eyes.

"Definitely," Christian said.

"He's part Old English Sheepdog and part terrier," Dennis explained. "My buddy, where I got him, said if he's like the other litters they've had, he'll take on more of the terrier and, from his size now, probably the smaller size as well."

"He is so precious, Dennis," Christian said, taking him in her arms as Gray gently set him there.

"Well, I know how hard losing Brutus hit you gals," he said. "I figured it would be amazing to have my granddaughter raised with a dog from the get-go, you know?" He watched Christian for a moment, a soft smile on his lips. "And, since you have a few months before she's born, you guys can work with Trevor. Which," he added. "Gray, would you mind grabbing the stuff out of the back of the van? Wasn't about to bring you a little life to take care of without any supplies."

"Of course!" Gray grabbed his keys and hurried outside.

When Gray came back in, carrying a dog crate that would be used to train the puppy as well as become his den for sleeping, she saw Caesar sitting in the hallway. The feline's thoughts were clear: *What. The hell. Have you done?*

"What was Plan B?" Christian asked as Gray set the crate down.

"Well," Dennis said with a chuckle. "Me on the couch with a new canine friend."

Chapter Twenty-six

Gray's fingers danced across the keyboard as she made some last-minute additions to the chapter she was working on in her newest contracted project, the chef. She had her laptop resting on her lap as she reclined on the bed next to a sleeping Christian.

They'd come into the bedroom to discuss rearranging it a bit, as it was large enough to accommodate a little baby corner for the crib and a rocking chair for Christian to nurse, as well as a changing station.

In the middle of the discussion, Christian had picked up Trevor and was playing with him on the bed. Next thing Gray knew, she was talking to herself and both dancer and dog were sound asleep. Hands on hips, she'd contemplated just getting to work on her own but decided that would wake them up.

At eight months along, Christian's belly seemed to double in size by the day, and she was exhausted all the time. When she wasn't sleeping, she was eating. When she wasn't eating, she was yawning. So, Gray had decided to join her family and at least get some work done.

She typed a few last sentences and was nearly done when she saw the screen on her phone light up, the ringer on silent. Grabbing it, she saw she had a text from her father.

Dennis: Coffee break?

Gray: Definitely! I'll get a pot started.

Setting her phone aside, Gray made sure Christian was still asleep then eased herself and her computer off the bed. She set the laptop aside on the bedside table before grabbing Trevor, who was beginning to wake up with the movement.

"Come on, baby boy," she whispered, cuddling the sleepy puppy against her chest and kissing his head. "Time to go potty."

Trevor out back, Gray got the coffee started. She texted him and told him to just come in rather than ring the bell, as she didn't want to wake Christian. Two mugs set up at the kitchen table and one of the chairs removed for her father's chair to take its place, everything either of them could need on the table and within reach for him, she was glad when he arrived.

When she'd been in high school, her dad would show up and pick her up for a "dentist" appointment and the two would get lunch and sit and talk. During college it was a bit more planned but achieved the same result.

Gray loved her mom and was close to her, but she'd always had a very special relationship with her father. Somehow, she'd always felt she could say things to him that she couldn't to Bernadette, as her mother could be quicker to judge or get upset.

She put a finger to her lips before pantomiming a large belly and then palmed hands to her face as though sleeping when Dennis entered the house. He nodded and waited to guide the storm door to close softly before wheeling his way down the wide entryway hallway and to the kitchen.

"Hey," he said, accepting a kiss to his cheek.

"Your mom used to sleep half the day when she was pregnant."

"Dr. Calloway said it was normal, but it's so strange for her," Gray said, grabbing the carafe filled with freshly brewed coffee after making sure her dad was settled okay and not caught on the rug beneath the table. "That woman has more energy than you and me put together normally." She poured them both a cup.

"Your mom too. Christian reminds me of Bernie in a lot of ways," he said, preparing his cup the way he liked it with the provided creamer and sugar.

"Want something to eat?" Gray asked, replacing the carafe on the coffee maker's hot plate.

"No, just had lunch with your mom. Speaking of," he added with a grin. "She's at the theater now so that company we use can take the proscenium curtains down and do the yearly steam cleaning."

"And," Gray said, taking a seat. "Mom must supervise."

"Exactly."

Gray grinned, grabbing the flavored creamer to add to her coffee. "How are things going?"

Dennis gave his coffee an experimental sip before setting the cup down and adding a bit more sugar to satiate his sweet tooth. "Really, really good." He was quiet for a long moment, then finally met her gaze. "Gray, I'm so sorry about what happened. As Dr. Stein says, I really lost my way, and that was not something that a child should have to see. Ever."

Gray was quiet for a long moment, deciding how to respond. They hadn't outright talked about that day, but she'd known it was coming. "I'm not going to lie," she began carefully. "It was a horrible day, but

I'm so glad it was me and not Mom." She held his gaze for a long time, wanting him to understand the impact of what he'd done. "She lives there and would have had that memory forever."

He nodded, looking down into his mug. "Crazy thing is," he finally said. "I was in the backyard because I thought it would be..." He shrugged. "Easier isn't the right word, but maybe, less bad?" He shook his head. "I don't know." He gave her a loving smile and reached over to cover one of her hands with his own much larger one. "I wasn't in my right mind, clearly. And I'm so sorry. I thank you, though. You saved my life, Gray. You truly did."

"You're welcome." She smiled.

"So, how's the baby doing?"

Gray's entire soul lit up at the mention of her little girl. "Really good. I see your snazzy T-shirt there."

Dennis grinned and pulled the shirt taught. *Grandpa's princess is on the way!* "Well," he chuckled, releasing the shirt. "You inspired me with the first shirt, so I had this one made. Bernie put her foot down at one for grandma too."

Gray's laughter was out of her mouth before she could stop it.

"Hey, I even offered to have little sparklies and stuff added to it, but no go."

It was then that Gray heard an anxious Trevor at the back door. She pushed back from the table and managed to grab the squirming little pup before he charged into the house. "Grandpa's here," she cooed to him, his little body a wiggle worm of excitement in her hands.

"Hey, little fella!" Dennis accepted the excited

puppy who whimpered as he climbed Dennis's body to get a better lick at any part of his face that he could. "How's training going?" Dennis asked as he tried to avoid being French kissed by the pup.

"Really good, actually. Since your friend had already begun crate training him, we just continued it. Accidents here and there, but I think he'll get it." Gray watched, thoroughly amused until finally Trevor calmed down. "He's a good boy. A real sweetheart."

"I'm so glad." Dennis put the puppy down on the floor, and both father and daughter watched as he tried to scramble away, little nails sliding on the hardwood floor before he finally got traction and shot off like a rocket. "So, what's my granddaughter's name?"

"Now, now, Dennis, you know better than that."

Gray glanced over to see a sleepy Christian waddling their way. She smiled and quickly got to her feet, racing around to pull a chair out for her. They shared a quick kiss before the very pregnant dancer lowered herself onto the chair.

"Okay?" Gray asked softly. When she got a nod, she hugged Christian's head to her breasts and kissed the top of her head. "Can I get you anything, baby?"

"Hot tea?" Christian asked hopefully.

"You got it." One more kiss, then Gray headed into the kitchen to fill the order while her wife and her father chatted, Trevor whimpering at Christian's feet for her attention. She set the teakettle down before racing over to pick Trevor up and put him in Christian's lap, her wife in no way able to get over her belly to grab him, then raced back to continue making hot tea.

Dennis chuckled. "Get used to it, Gray," he said.

"This will be your life for a while."

※ ※ ※ ※

"As we raise our glasses," Michael exclaimed. "I salute Christian's virgin daiquiri, the only virgin at the table."

Gray burst into laughter, as did Christian and Kevin, their three glasses also raised. "Here, here."

"And, likely the very last time this lady will be out eating at such a fine establishment before she pops," he added.

"Who you tellin'?" Christian laughed.

"You're due in what, about six minutes?" Michael asked, glancing at his watch for dramatic effect.

"Ha ha," Christian said. "Five days, thank you."

Glasses clinked together, the group sipped from their respective drinks. Gray set her wineglass down and looked across the table at her two best friends and the most trusted person outside of her blood family. A quick glance to Christian, then she asked the question the two women had discussed on and off for months, though the decision had been easy.

"So, we know you guys live clear across the country," she began. "But we'd like to ask you for a very important favor."

"Uh-oh," Kevin said. "Sounds serious."

"We'd like you guys to be our daughter's godparents," Christian said, reaching for Gray's hand.

Kevin and Michael looked at each other, emotion flitting through Michael's extremely expressive eyes. "Wow," he said softly.

"If you guys need to talk about it, we understand…" Gray began.

"Absolutely," Michael said, his voice cracking a bit. He cleared his throat, exchanging another look with Kevin before saying again, "Absolutely. We'd be honored." Kevin nodded in agreement.

"What exactly do godparents do?" Kevin asked.

"Get my kid amazing shit for her birthday," Gray said, relaxing back in her chair like she was queen of queens.

"What Guido here means is," Christian said, patting Gray's leg under the table. "Yes, being amazing uncles would be spectacular, but we trust you two that, if something went wrong, if something happened to us," she said, indicating herself and Gray. "Our daughter would be okay."

Michael was quiet for a long moment, swallowing a few times before he nodded. "Truly an honor," he said, his voice deeper than usual with emotion. "And yes," he added. "We will be fabulous uncles."

"Speaking of fabulous uncles," Kevin said. "While we're in town we're looking at some property here in the mountains."

"What?" Gray said, eyes wide. "Why?"

"We're tired of giving all our money away to that greedy bastard Uncle Sam, so we're going to start investing in property, as well as get ourselves a lovely vacation home in the mountains," Michael said with a grin.

Thrilled, Gray said, "That's wonderful! Oh, my god, I'd love to see you guys more than once or twice a year."

"We miss you guys too," Kevin said. "And, we're both putting in seventy-, eighty-hour weeks, so we really just need somewhere to go to get away from all of it."

"Speaking of investing," Christian said. "I wanted your opinion on something, Michael, with all your financial finesse."

Gray glanced over at her, confused.

"Sure. What's up, sweets?"

"Bernadette told me that they're talking about selling the theater and school," Christian said conversationally. "Would that be something viable to invest in?"

Gray felt a knife to the heart at those words. Why was this the first she was hearing about this?

"I think Bernadette and Dennis have made a pretty good run of it over the years, so if you can get me the numbers, I can definitely give you my opinion," he said.

"Wonderful. Thanks, Michael."

༺༺༻༻

Gray was quiet as they got back to the house. For her, dinner had ended the moment it had come out that her mom wanted to relinquish control of the theater that she'd run for so many years—decades, really. It felt like her entire childhood was being ripped away, let alone the betrayal that her mother hadn't seen fit to talk to her about it, to tell *her*.

She walked through the kitchen to the bedroom where Trevor whined, excited they were home but also excited to be taken from his crate to go potty.

"Are you going to tell me what I did wrong?" Christian asked, following her.

"Why would you think something was wrong?" Gray asked, bending down to unlatch the crate, barely catching the little fuzzy explosion from inside. "Hey, bud. Let's get you outside."

"Maybe because nearly every single bone in your body is tense," Christian called after her as Gray hurried to get to the back door before the tiny bladder let go.

The puppy outside, Gray shrugged out of her heavy winter jacket and tossed it to the couch so she could get dinner for both Caesar and Trevor while he did his business.

"Perhaps it's because you made me look like a complete ass tonight," Gray called out, opening the pantry door to grab a scoop of puppy food for Trevor's bowl.

"I think you're doing that all by yourself with your tantrum," Christian said, her jacket also now removed and her hands placed on her massive belly. She grabbed one of the cans of Caesar's wet food and popped it open. "Can you please stop being passive-aggressive and just tell me what's wrong? I'm tired, I don't feel well, and I really don't have patience for bullshit tonight."

Gray stared at her, shocked by her tone and the anger in her eyes. "All right, fine," she said. "What the hell is all this business about Mom not only selling the theater and school but about you wanting to buy it? Did it not occur to you to talk to *me* about that before Michael?"

Christian looked at Gray like she'd lost her mind. "What are you talking about? You knew about this."

"No, Christian, I didn't." Gray closed the pantry door and set Trevor's food down on his rubber mat. "I had not one clue until you said something tonight."

"Bernadette said your dad told you," Christian

said, eyebrows drawn as she scooped the nasty-smelling mush into Caesar's bowl, the black-and-white cat meowing and brushing against Christian's legs in anticipation.

"Well, she was wrong," Gray said, getting more upset at the situation. "Why the hell would she sell it?" she exploded. "Why wouldn't she tell me?" Tears were streaming down her face now as it began to set in.

"Come on, Caesar," Christian said, patting the cabinet. They didn't normally allow the cat on the counters, but Trevor not only ate his food, but went after Caesar's as well.

The cat hopped up on the cooking island and began to eat.

"I can't tell if you're pissed at me or if you're pissed at your mom," the dancer said, taking the aluminum can to the sink to rinse before tossing it into the recycle bin.

"Yes," Gray responded stubbornly, heading to the back door to let in a very cold-looking little puppy. The November night was freezing and more snow had fallen earlier in the day.

Without so much as a hello, Trevor tore through the door as soon as it was opened and to his food bowl, nearly sliding past it in his haste. Ordinarily Gray would have found it adorable or would have filmed the inevitable with her phone, but she was in no mood.

"Yes, well—" Christian, who had been standing at the island petting Caesar while he ate, something the former stray always loved, froze. A look of pain washed over her face for a brief moment before she took a deep breath and continued stroking the soft fur. "I was hurt you hadn't said anything to me, so I think we're even."

"This isn't a pissing contest, Christian," Gray retorted, angry at the laissez-faire attitude. "I grew up in that theater."

Christian's expression hardened as she stared at Gray with intense green eyes. "We *met* in that theater, Gray," she exclaimed. "Don't stand there and act like it means nothing to me. Why do you think I was—" Her hand left Caesar and joined the other on her bulging belly as she cried out, her face screwing up in pain.

Seeing her wife in pain made Gray forget everything else. She quickly moved to her side. "Are you okay?"

"Fuck," Christian growled between clenched teeth.

Gray looked over at the clock on the stove to note the time. "What do you want me to do?" she asked, her hand on the dancer's lower back.

Seemingly breathless, Christian shook her head, her eyes closed. She took a deep, shaky breath after a long moment. "Maybe we should call Dr. Calloway," she finally said.

Chapter Twenty-seven

"Okay, Mom," Dr. Calloway said, sitting up straight on the stool at the foot of the birthing chair. "We're at seven centimeters now." She gave Christian an understanding smile before replacing the birthing gown. "Things should start to move quickly now, ladies. I know it's been a very long night and morning, but we're getting there." She stood and walked over to the sink. "You ladies need anything?" She met Gray's tired gaze. "Mama Two, can I get you some coffee?"

"That would be heaven," Gray said.

"Okay. Christian, more ice, hon?" the doctor asked. At Christian's nod, she left the labor room.

"How are you, baby?" Gray asked unnecessarily. Dr. Calloway had declared that labor had officially started at 9:27 the previous night, and now as it marched on to noon, both Christian and Gray were exhausted and anxious.

"I want her out," Christian gasped as another contraction began to grip her. She squeezed Gray's fingers so tightly Gray was certain for the sixteenth time that her fingers were broken.

"Breathe, baby," Gray said. "Breathe."

Christian whimpered as it seemed to let up, her breasts heaving with the effort. "In the immortal words of Kirstie Alley," she gasped, eyes still closed. "'Fuck my breathing.'"

Gray smiled at the *Look Who's Talking* reference. "I know, baby," she murmured, brushing sweaty hair off Christian's forehead.

She grabbed a washcloth she'd wet beneath the faucet in the bathroom some time ago, dipping it in the cool water that was left from the little cup of ice chips Christian had been chewing on. She stood and leaned slightly over her wife to gently wipe the sweat off Christian's face and try to cool her down.

"We're almost home, sweetheart," she whispered. "Almost home."

The door opened again and the doctor returned with a Styrofoam cup in one hand and a plastic cup of chipped ice in the other. "All right, ladies," she said, handing Gray the steaming cup. "Gray, she was almost at eight centimeters when I checked her. Once she hits that, we're looking at anywhere from a half hour to two hours, so if you need to step out and call anyone, now would be the time to do it."

Gray looked to Christian with a question in her eyes. At Christian's nod, she leaned down and left a kiss to her forehead before hurrying from the room to find the elevators and the way out of the building.

It was bitterly cold outside, a week and a half before Thanksgiving. Shivering slightly, Gray walked over to a bench and pulled her phone out of her pocket. She was amused when her mother picked up the phone almost before it even started ringing.

"No," she said with a smile. "Not yet. But Dr. Calloway told me we're on the final stretch, so you guys should get down here." As she listened to her mother's nervous, mile-a-minute words, she noticed a man step out that she'd seen upstairs in the maternity ward. He was a large man with a bald head and full beard. He leaned against a brick wall and lit a cigarette. "She's okay," Gray responded to the litany of questions. "She's exhausted, we both are. No, she's just almost at eight but the doctor said it should go fast from here." She nodded. "Okay. Love you too. Bye."

Ending the call, Gray tucked the phone back into her pocket and stood, stretching her hands high overhead and leaning to both sides, then forward and backward, with a louder-than-meant groan. She grinned at the man, who looked over at her at the sound.

"Sorry. Long night," she said.

"I hear ya." He smiled stubbing out his cigarette butt on the brick before lighting up a second. Gray understood. If she were a smoker, she'd be doing the same thing. "I seen you upstairs. You with your sister or somethin'?" he asked conversationally.

"No, my wife," Gray said proudly.

"Ah, man, that's cool," he said with a grin. "First?"

"Wife and baby," Gray said, garnering a chuckle from deep in the man's throat.

"Second for me and my girl," he said. "Man, it never gets easier."

"Pretty sure this is our only, so if we can get through today…" Gray smiled at him as she turned to go.

"Hey, good luck," he said, holding out his fist.

Gray bumped hers against it. "You too."

"Maybe our kids will be in school together or somethin'." He chuckled before taking another drag.

Gray smiled, liking the idea, then headed back inside.

It was as breathtaking as it was heartbreaking to see Christian in so much pain. Her hair was plastered to her head as her face scrunched up again in her exertion to do as asked: "Push!" The cry/growl that ripped from Christian's throat was terrifying as she squeezed the blood right out of Gray's hand.

Gray gasped as the shrill cry of a baby rent the air—a very unhappy baby. "Oh, my god," Gray whispered, realizing that very unhappy baby was *their* baby.

"Your little girl!" Dr. Calloway pulled the baby free of her mother, covered in birth juices. "Gray, want the honors?"

Looking at the surgical scissors held out to her, Gray took a deep breath and took them. "This won't hurt her?" she asked, pretty terrified to do the task.

"Not at all," the doctor said softly and showed Gray where she needed to snip.

Gritting her teeth for that uncomfortable moment, she cut the umbilical cord and the baby was immediately taken to do the things that the medical staff needed to do with a newborn.

Gray returned to Christian's side, cradling her head and kissing her lips. "You did it," she murmured.

"She's a healthy baby girl," the nurse said, bringing the cleaned baby over to them and setting her on Christian's stomach. "She's a healthy seven pounds, nine ounces and twenty inches long. Nice work, Mom."

Christian smiled, and the look on her face was one Gray had never seen before. It was a look of utter amazement, utter love, and utter joy. Gray looked at the tiny bundle of pink skin and a head full of dark hair.

"Look at her little face," Gray said. "All squishy."

Christian smiled, meeting her gaze. "She's perfect." She carefully touched each and every finger and toe, all ten accounted for. "So perfect."

"She's beautiful," Gray agreed. She reached her hand out and, hesitant for a moment, finally touched a fat little arm. "So soft," she whispered in awe. She looked at Christian and left a lingering kiss on her lips. "I love you."

"I love you too," Christian whispered in return.

༺༻

Christian and the baby were settled on the bed in the private room they would occupy for the next twenty-four hours. A nurse had come in to help Christian breastfeed for the first time, Gray standing by with mixed emotions about the whole thing.

"What does that feel like?" she asked once the nurse left and the three of them were alone. She sat on the bed with her wife and child, gently touching the baby's crazily soft hair.

"Umm," Christian murmured softly, watching their baby nurse. "I can tell you that it's a bit of a pressure release," she said with a smile, meeting Gray's gaze. "My boobs felt like they were about to explode. It's kind of tingly, warm inside. I don't know," she said, shaking her head as she looked back to the baby. "It's a very strange feeling."

In all their reading over the months of pregnancy, one thing that came up time and time again was the bonding time between mother and child during feeding times. Christian had decided it was unfair that she be the only one to be able to do that, so had suggested she pump mostly. That way, the baby could still benefit from mother's milk, but they could both share the duties of feeding time and the bonding time with their daughter.

Now, sitting with her wife and child, Gray was so grateful for Christian's incredibly generous attitude as, strangely, her own breasts ached as she watched her daughter nurse. No doubt a psychological response, much like a person who felt an amputated limb, but certainly real.

"She's the beginning of our second act," Christian said softly, meeting Gray's gaze again.

Gray studied Christian for a moment before looking at the baby. Finally, she said, "Well, technically third," she said with a grin. "Act one is when we met. Act two was when we met again."

Christian smiled. "And I was smart enough to not let you get away again."

"Indeed," Gray agreed. "So, act three in this very, very long opera, is our little one here."

"You know," Christian said, her voice soft as she stroked their daughter's cheek. "I know we had our name picked out for her, but somehow it doesn't fit."

"I've been thinking the same thing," Gray said.

"I have a crazy idea," Christian said, meeting Gray's eyes. "Aria. That's what she is for us, our new song, the next act in our lives."

Gray held that beautiful gaze for a long time before she smiled and nodded. "I absolutely love it." Her smile felt like it would break her face, she was so happy with their decision and their new little bundle.

"Hello, baby Aria," she whispered. "Welcome to the world." In that moment, a squinty little eye opened and looked right at her. "Should I go get the troops? Introduce them to the newest little soldier?"

"Absolutely," Christian said. "I think she's about done here, so let me get ready for my close-up, Mr. DeMille."

Gray chuckled, leaving a kiss on the top of Christian's head and then Aria's before climbing off the bed.

Walking down the hospital corridor to the waiting room at the end, Gray felt such a mixture of things. She felt like she was walking on air, floating even, filled with more love than she'd ever thought possible. Though, at the same time, there was a heaviness on her shoulders that kept her feet on the ground. It was the heaviness of responsibility, the understanding that she and Christian were solely responsible for keeping that itty-bitty bundle of life alive and safe, catering to her every need and want and to help her grow and learn. It was daunting, and they hadn't even gotten her home yet.

The waiting room came into view and she was happy to see everyone was there. Immediately, Bernadette stood when she saw Gray enter the room.

"Hey, guys," Gray said, offering a tired wave. "How's it going?" When she was met with a wall of expectant silence, she continued. "Christian is fine. Exhausted, but she did great. The baby weighed a hefty seven pounds, nine ounces and is twenty inches long."

"What's her name?" Dennis asked, wheeling his chair up to her.

"Aria Christine."

The smile that slowly spread across his face was like sunlight piercing the clouds. "Beautiful," he whispered. "Can…Can we see her?"

"Of course." Gray waved everyone on. "Follow me."

Gray wasn't sure if they'd get in trouble for having so many people at once, but as she entered room 315, she didn't care. Sure enough, in the minutes that Gray was gone, Christian had gotten her nursing gown resituated and her breast tucked away. A swaddled Aria was in her arms as the Rickman family entered the room.

"Baby, you know everyone," Gray said with a smirk. "Everyone, baby Aria."

Standing aside to allow her family to meet the newest tiny member, Gray felt very strange and powerful emotions wash over her. Even though she had not one reason to worry about any person in that room doing anything to hurt Aria, she felt the lioness in her come to full wakefulness, ready to pounce on anyone who dare harm her daughter.

On the other side of that very dizzying coin was the sense of pride she felt. Her chest was so filled with pride and love that her heart literally hurt. In her more than thirty years on the planet she'd accomplished a lot of things, things she never thought she'd do, see, or be part of. But in that moment, watching her mother cradle her baby, she knew this: that child was her greatest accomplishment, the biggest thing she'd ever do, no matter what life had yet to offer.

Now, if she could get through it without screwing it up.

Gray pushed at the fire with the poker, a few sparks flying. Satisfied that the fire would hold and build, she set the poker aside and closed the glass door. Walking to the kitchen, Trevor following behind, she filled the kettle with water and got it situated on the stove. Her smile was instant when she felt the hug from behind.

"She finally go down?"

"Yeah," Christian said, head resting on Gray's shoulder. "Took some coaxing, though."

"Just wait until she's six," Gray said, covering Christian's clasped hands at her stomach with one of her own while using the other to turn on the burner.

"Uh-huh," Christian muttered, making Gray smile.

"Got a fire going," Gray said, turning in Christian's arms and taking her into a warm embrace. "Cold night."

"Can't believe Christmas is just a few days away," Christian murmured against Gray's neck.

"Santa came early," Gray said with a smile on her lips, which grew at Christian's snort.

"Best stocking stuffer ever." She left a kiss on Gray's neck before pulling out of the hug. "Are you having some?" she asked, pulling a mug from a nearby cabinet.

"Sure." Gray went to the pantry to grab a couple of tea bags. She knew Christian was counting the months until she could start drinking coffee again. Since she'd not taken any real amounts of caffeine during the pregnancy, she didn't want to while breastfeeding, either.

Tea made, the two moved to the couch and sat

down. Gray had no sooner set her mug on the end table when, to her surprise, she ended up with a lapful of Christian.

"Hi there," she said, hands going to Christian's hips.

The dancer smiled, brushing dark bangs out of Gray's eyes. "Hello. I hope this is okay."

"Of course." They had both been exhausted all the time from lack of sleep, Gray doing all she could to pick up the slack around the house while still working to allow Christian to heal after giving birth. It had been a trying month. But, she admitted, so worth it.

"I wanted to thank you," Christian said softly.

"For what?" Gray asked, rubbing small circles over Christian's back atop the material of the long-sleeved T-shirt she wore. Her hands slipped up underneath the hem of the shirt, not attempting any sort of sexual gesture—no matter how much she'd like to, as she was leaving that to Christian to decide what her body was ready for—but she needed to touch her, feel her warm skin on her fingertips.

"All that you've done since we brought Aria home," Christian said. "I know it's been hard, and I know you're trying to juggle taking care of us and your job." She smiled, caressing the side of Gray's face. "Just want you to know how much I appreciate it."

"Of course," Gray said again. "You did the hard part, so it's the least I can do."

Christian smiled then lowered her head, brushing Gray's lips with her own. "I'm still really sore," she murmured against Gray's lips. "But I need…"

Gray nodded. "I understand."

Gray sighed as her wife came back for another

pass, softness brushing against softness, testing, exploring. She sighed again at the first touch of Christian's tongue against her own. She responded, enjoying the feel of fingers in her hair as the kiss deepened. It had been so long since Gray had been touched in any sort of sexual way by Christian. She had no choice but to be understanding, but that didn't mean it was easy.

Christian's kiss was growing more passionate, her hand slipping beneath Gray's shirt to cup one of her breasts. It was killing Gray, as all she wanted to do was throw Christian down on the couch and grind against her.

"Will you let me love you?" Christian murmured against Gray's lips.

Yes, please! Gray wanted to beg, but just couldn't do it. "No, baby," she said, voice breathy as her body was burning just from a simple few minutes of making out. "Not until you're ready."

Christian tugged Gray's shirt up over her head before taking her mouth in an almost possessive kiss. "Let me love you," she begged. "Please."

Gray nodded, her body not allowing her to give any other response. Together they worked to get Gray's flannel pajama pants and panties pulled off as Christian knelt on the floor in front of her. She looked up the length of Gray's body, the sheer hunger in her eyes sending a shiver of anticipation throughout Gray.

The long neglect of her body was about to come to an end, and when Christian wrapped her arms underneath Gray's spread thighs as she aggressively tugged until Gray was positioned at the edge of the couch where she needed her to be, she nearly came.

Gray's eyes closed and her head fell back against

the cushion at the first touch of a deft tongue against her clit. Her hips moved with the rhythm Christian's mouth was setting. She knew in the back of her mind they didn't have a lot of time, but she also knew it wouldn't *take* a lot of time.

Burying her fingers in soft, blond hair, Gray tried to keep her moans quiet as she was licked and sucked. Her breasts heaved as her breathing and pleasure increased. Finally, she squeezed her eyes tightly shut as her mouth fell open in a silent scream of release.

Christian hummed as she sucked harder on Gray's clit while batting at it with her tongue, sending a second orgasm crashing through Gray. Her hips jerked involuntarily as her entire body followed suit, shuddering from the intensity of her bottled up need.

As her body crashed back into the couch and back to earth, Christian let up, leaving a soft kiss in the volcanic wetness before leaning up. Gray met her for a quick, warm kiss as she tried to get her breathing back under control.

"I needed that," she managed with a soft chuckle.

"I'm sorry," Christian said, running her fingers through Gray's hair and leaving another kiss on her lips. She pulled Gray to her feet so she could get redressed, but not before pulling her into a tight, full-body hug.

Gray reveled in the closeness, her body humming with relief. "Don't be," she murmured. "It's all been worth it."

"As you said," Christian said with a contented sigh. "Tell me that when she's six and doesn't want to go to bed."

Chapter Twenty-eight

"No, I fully agree with what you did on page sixty-seven," Gray said, her voice picked up by her Bluetooth earbuds. "I think that was a much better turn of phrase, so I'm fine with it. It wasn't a direct quote from him anyway, so it works."

Gray typed a few things into the dialogue box she and her editor were currently using together. Edits for the chef's bio were complete, save these last few hairs that they needed to trim or tame. She read what was being typed and cocked her head to the side to consider if she liked it or not, one hand going instinctively to the little bundle that was pressed up against her chest in the carrier she had strapped to her front.

"Okay…you know what, how about this?" she said, fingers going back to the keyboard and making a couple changes to what had just been typed by the woman in New York. "What do you think?" She smiled. "Excellent! Yeah, I'm good with everything. All right, great work, lady." She smiled and left a kiss to the top of the baby's head, careful to avoid the soft spot. "Kiss delivered for you. Have a great day, bye."

Gray removed her earbuds and tucked them back into their charging case before pushing to her feet. She grabbed her phone and slid it into her pocket before leaving the office to head to the kitchen.

"Time to make Mama coffee" she said, though

softly. She and Christian had made the decision to maintain some semblance of everyday sounds while Aria was asleep so she'd learn to get used to noise, be it them talking, the animals doing their animal things, or other basic sounds of life.

She was grabbing a mug from the cabinet when she saw her mother's SUV pull into the driveway. She smiled. Christian had gone off with Bernadette to buy groceries, her first time of any length away from the baby. It had taken some coaxing, but finally Christian had agreed to leave Aria behind.

The two ladies, loaded down with grocery bags, walked up to the front door, which Gray pulled open for them. Christian caught the storm door with her elbow so it wouldn't close on Bernadette.

"Hello, my ladies," Christian said, entering the house. She gave Gray a quick kiss on the lips as she hurried to the kitchen.

"How's my girl?" Bernadette asked, stopping to give Aria a kiss on the head before heading deeper inside.

Easing the door closed so the slam didn't scare the hell out of the baby, Gray followed the women inside. She walked over to Christian and presented her back to her as she held on to the baby. The dancer got the carrier unbuckled, then carefully pulled the sleeping six-week-old out of it.

"Mommy missed you," she cooed, cradling her daughter. She rained kisses down on her face and head. "Oh, Bernie, come here."

Gray, who was standing a bit behind Christian, saw the smile, which Aria had just started doing a few days before. Like any good modern mother, Gray pulled out her phone and hit record.

Bernadette gasped, her own smile wide and beaming. "Look at her!"

As the two women began to baby talk to Aria, Gray worried about any perishables still left in the car. "I'll just go grab the rest of the groceries," she said, backing away from the two as she put her phone away. At the non-response, Gray turned and shook her head, amused as she headed outside.

As it was very cold and she didn't have a jacket on, she loaded herself down with as many bags as she could in one go, leaving herself only a twenty-four-pack of soda and bottle of orange juice for her next trip, along with the mail.

Dumping her last load onto the cooking island, she saw that Bernadette had taken Aria and was in the living room with her while Christian began to put groceries away.

"Thanks, baby," Christian said with an apologetic smile.

"Of course." She tossed the mail to the island top and began to unpack bags. "How'd it go?"

"Well," Christian said, eyeing Gray shyly. "I managed to only have two emotional breakdowns, one in the ice cream aisle and one in produce."

Gray smirked. "I'm proud of you."

"How'd it go here?" Christian asked, unloading bags of veggies into the crisper.

"Really, really well." Gray glanced over at her daughter who she knew would end up royally spoiled by Bernadette. "We had a bottle, we had a changing, we had a nap." She met Christian's amused gaze. "We got to be part of our first editing session…"

Christian laughed. "Our very own poet laureate."

"I hope so," Gray said, heading into the pantry

with an armful of boxed and canned goods.

"Baby, what's this?" Christian asked. "From your publisher."

Gray poked her head out from the small room. "Really?"

"Yeah," Christian said, holding up a piece of mail that had been in the small stack Gray had brought in.

Gray finished her task then closed the pantry door, making sure Trevor didn't get stuck in there—again. She took the envelope and carefully slid it open with her thumbnail.

Bernadette made her way into the kitchen, a sleeping Aria in her arms as the proud grandmother gently swayed with the baby.

"What's that?" Bernadette asked.

Gray didn't respond as she unfolded the letter within. Setting the empty envelope to the cooking island, she began to read aloud, words quiet, not much more than muttered. "'Dear Miss Rickman…response to your agent-submitted novel…pleased to inform you…'" Gray gasped, eyes wide as a hand went to her open mouth. She could hardly breathe as the letter shook in her trembling hand.

"What is it?" Bernadette asked again, concern in her voice as she continued to sway in place with Aria held against her.

Gray met her mother's gaze before looking down at the letter again, reading it silently again to make sure she'd read it right. "They've accepted *Just Me*."

"Is that another bio?" Bernadette asked.

"No, Bernie," Christian said softly, emotion in her voice. "That's Gray's novel."

Bernadette looked at Gray. Her own eyes, the same color as her daughter's, widened. "Oh, honey," she whispered before taking Gray in a one-armed hug. "I'm so proud of you."

"I can't believe they reviewed it so quickly," Christian said, reading over the letter. "I thought it would take up to nine months?"

Gray nodded, stunned and a little scared. What if it was a bomb? What if nobody wanted to read it? What if nobody liked it who did read it? "Oh, boy," she whispered.

"They already know she's a money maker," Bernadette said, releasing Gray from the hug and turning her attention back to Aria. "Hell, that first book you did for Richard Cox was a *New York Times* bestseller. They know what they've got."

※※※※

"It amazes me how much of your features she has," Christian murmured. She and Gray lay in bed facing each other, Aria asleep on her back between them. She was in a diaper, her little legs bowed out with her arms up over her head, champion style.

"It helps that she looks so much like Mom," Gray said, lightly rubbing the Buddha belly of her daughter. "And," she added with a smile. "So do I."

Christian met her gaze. "She's got so much of us both. Looks like she'll end up with my eyes, but your dark hair."

"Which I got from Grandpa Fletcher."

"She's so beautiful." Christian ran her fingers over a chubby little cheek that, when she smiled, would dimple. "I never thought I could love somebody so much. You know?"

"I do." She smiled. "I definitely do." She looked

at her wife. "I'd take a bullet for you, but I'd tear somebody apart with my bare hands for her."

Christian grinned. "If I don't do it first." They were quiet for a moment before she spoke again. "Gray, I've been thinking about something a lot lately. Your mom dropped it after Aria was born, but I can't stop thinking about it."

Gray studied the beautiful face of the woman who held her heart, Christian's gaze set on their baby. "God, you're beautiful," she whispered, surprised she's spoken the words out loud.

Christian's gaze flicked up to meet hers, a soft smile on her lips. "Thank you," she mouthed. "I want to take over the school and theater when Bernie retires."

Gray wasn't entirely surprised by what she said. Her mom hadn't talked to her yet about it, but seeing her with Aria, she knew her mother was ready to spend time with her grandchildren, to slow down. And, from what she'd seen of her parents together after all that had happened around his heart attack, they needed to spend more time together as well. "Okay," she said, urging Christian to continue.

"That place means so much to the people of Denver, Gray," Christian said. "Your parents have touched the lives of so many. It means everything to me," she said, placing her hand on her own chest. "For so many reasons, that theater changes my life." She reached across their sleeping daughter and took Gray's hand. "Plus, I can keep Aria with me there and continue to work with Yancy's skaters."

Gray nodded, unsure what she thought. "True."

"Which," Christian added. "Would mean we'd no longer have a need to have the studio in our home.

We've talked about selling this place to get a house with the bedrooms on the same floor."

"I'd love to look in Wash Park," Gray said. Washington Park was an older neighborhood in Denver proper known for its beautiful old homes, which Gray had always admired.

"Oh, yes," Christian said with a large smile. "I love those old homes there."

Gray nodded, but still wasn't sold. "Can I have some time to think about it?"

"Of course." Christian caressed her face. "I'm only in if you are."

※ ※ ※ ※

Lightly tapping her ring of keys against her leg, Gray stepped into the quiet, dark theater. She was standing in the lobby, no need to turn the lights on. She knew every square inch of that space, knew where the velvet ropes were, knew where the doors were to enter the auditorium, knew where the concession was, and knew where the hallway was that led to the bathrooms and the stairs for the second floor.

Standing there, she could easily see a thousand days and evenings in that lobby, dodging patrons running errands for her mom on show night, or directing them like cattle once she was a little older. She smiled, thinking of that damn tux that she hated wearing once she was old enough to become an usher and then manage the whole affair.

She walked to the first set of open doors and into the auditorium beyond. She flicked on a set of house lights so she wouldn't kill herself on the stairs. No matter how well she knew the theater, breaking her neck on those was entirely possible.

She walked down the slanted aisle to the stage, empty and dark. With the baby due in November, Bernadette and Dennis had decided to not do a holiday show, so the theater had been empty for weeks. The new year of classes would begin in a couple weeks.

Her booted feet thudded dully on the wood. She walked to center stage then turned and looked out into the house, all the empty seats before her. The auditorium held so many memories for her, not only shows and classes.

She'd watched with so much pride as Ivan had gotten his first starring role on that stage. So many of her birthdays had been celebrated there. Anniversary parties for her parents. Her graduation party, Ivan's graduation party. She turned to the spot that would be burned into her memory forever—the spot where Christian had been standing that moment when their eyes had met for the first time.

She smiled, remembering that night and the attitude that Christian had shot her way. Such a confusing time, falling in love with Christian Scott. Almost fifteen years later, she was still falling in love with her daily.

Tucking her hands into her pockets, Gray let out a long, heavy sigh. Could she watch this place go to strangers? Could she share her memories with those who would paint over them and create new ones? Was it time, perhaps, to let it all go?

She had all that she could have ever dreamed now: a wife she adored, a baby she could eat alive she loved her so much, and now a book deal. It was no longer about telling other people's stories, but finally telling her own.

She heard the front door to the theater open and waited. A moment later, a dark figure appeared in silhouette at the door at the back of the auditorium, a figure darker than the darkness in the lobby.

Smiling, she waited as the figure began to move, slowly coming into view of the house lights. She raised her hand in greeting, getting a little wave of fingers in return. "Hey sexy," she called out.

"Hey, yourself," Christian called out from the fourth row back as she headed to the stage. "Sorry I'm late. Our little angel decided it was the absolute perfect time to have a blowout as I was about to leave Grandma and Grandpa's house."

Gray chuckled. "Of course she did." She waited for Christian to join her on stage. "She's like her Mommy and has your dancer timing."

Christian smirked. "Or, she's like her Mama and knows when to leave her mark."

A bark of laughter escaped Gray's throat. "That's gross."

Christian's smirk was just this side of sexy as she made her way across the stage to Gray. She was so beautiful, her hair grown longer than Gray had ever seen it, down to her mid-back. She'd lost most of the baby weight, though Gray didn't care about that. To her, she was the most stunning woman on the planet, no matter her jeans size.

"Here we are, huh?" Christian said, bringing up her arms, clasping her hands behind Gray's neck. "Why did you want me to meet you here?"

"I wanted to talk about this," Gray said, resting her hands on Christian's hips.

Christian left a lingering kiss on her lips before moving away from her. "Okay." She walked a few feet away, looking at things as she tucked her hands into the back pockets of her well-fitted jeans. "What are you thinking?"

"You know I won't have a lot of time to dedicate to this place," Gray said honestly. "The whole adage, publish or perish."

"I know that, sweetheart," Christian said softly. "I'd never take on a business and try and strong-arm you into making my dream work."

"It's not just your dream, though." Gray looked out over the auditorium again. She honestly had no idea why those words had popped out of her mouth, but as they had, she knew they were true. "I just worry you'll be overwhelmed."

Christian gave her a sweet smile. "No, Bernie still wants to stick around part time, she said. Plus, she has some wonderful dancers working here now that have helped take the brunt over the last few years."

Gray nodded. "Do you think we can really make this a go? I mean, Mom and Dad have been incredibly successful, but…"

"Baby," the dancer said, walking back over to her. "Your parents did some amazing things here, but it's a whole new generation now. Some of my closest friends are the biggest names in this business. They'd come in a heartbeat to do a class, a show, autograph session, whatever. And," she added. "I really want to do something that Dennis always wanted to do but just never did."

"What's that?" Gray asked, curious.

"Have special classes just for kids. They had them for teens, but never the little ones." Christian's smile was wistful, as was her voice. "I want to introduce the three- and four-year-olds to dance, to direct all that energy into something positive. Something that our daughter can be part of in a few years."

"Well," Gray said with a small smile. "Unless she got my total lack of coordination."

Christian smiled, walking over to her again, snaking her arms up around Gray's neck. "I can teach anyone to dance, even if it's just to do the Chicken Dance."

Gray was amused and began to hum the telltale music to the wedding reception favorite. "God help me," she murmured. "Aria will be singing that until she's twelve."

"No, by then I'll have moved her on to the Macarena."

"Okay, no, no." Gray pretended to move away, but was held tight. She looked deeply into Christian's eyes, all teasing aside. "You really want this?"

"Absolutely," Christian said. "I can make this a huge success for us, Gray. I promise you."

Gray brushed Christian's jaw with the backs of her fingers as she nodded. "Okay. Let's do it."

"Really? You mean it?" Christian asked, hope shining in her eyes.

"Yeah. Yeah, I do."

Christian pulled her into a painfully tight hug, Gray's eyes falling shut as she relished the connection, the decision they'd just made about their future.

"You know," Christian murmured into the hug. "We're standing where we first met."

"Mmmm, no," Gray said, pulling out of the hug just a bit and gently pushing Christian to the left three steps. "Now we are. This was where I got my first glare from you."

Christian's laugh was beautiful. "First of many."

"Don't I know," Gray muttered with a grin.

"First time for everything," Christian said softly, burying her fingers in Gray's hair. "Time for our first kiss here on stage."

Gray's eyes closed at the feel of soft lips against her own. After a long, breathless moment, she rested her forehead against Christian's. "We've come full circle, I guess."

Christian nodded, her hand sliding down to cup Gray's jaw. "Yes. I knew I loved you the first time I saw you here. What I didn't know was, I'd love you even more the next time we'd meet here."

"I'm kind of amazing that way," Gray said, smiling when Christian playfully smacked her behind. "I love you," she whispered. "Aria is with Grandma and Grandpa tonight for her first overnight. Wanna go home and practice making babies?"

"I definitely think I can get behind that," Christian purred.

"Oh, kinky."

"Lead the way," Christian said. "There is that big ol' couch in the office upstairs…"

Without another word, Gray grabbed Christian by the hand and tugged her toward the stairs on the stage. She had a destination in mind on the second floor.

About the Author

Kim has spent her life in Colorado and can't imagine living anywhere else. She's been writing since she was 9 and stumbled into her first book being published in her mid-20s. She's worked in the film industry as a writer, director and producer, but now enjoys the quiet, happy life of a professional author. She can be reached on Facebook and on her website at, www.kimpritekel.com

IF YOU LIKED THIS BOOK...

Share a review with your friends or post a review on your favorite site like Amazon, Goodreads, Barnes and Noble, or anywhere you purchased the book. Or perhaps share a posting on your social media sites and help spread the word.

Join the Sapphire Newsletter and keep up with all your favorite authors.

Did we mention you get a free book for joining our team?

sign-up at - www.sapphirebooks.com

Check out Kim's other books.

Curtain Call - ISBN - 978-1-952270-42-0

What do you do when you come from a long line of dancers that spans the globe and generations, yet you can't tell your right foot from your left? You fall in love with a dancer, of course!

Gray Rickman is an awkward seventeen-year-old when she first sets eyes on Christian Scott at the dance studio/theater Gray's parents own and run in Denver, Colorado.

Though only a handful of years older than Gray, Christian carries herself with poise and wisdom far beyond her years. A woman of few words, she speaks volumes with her body.

Before Gray even really knows what her type is, Christian stars in endless daydreams and even fulfills a couple of her fantasies before vanishing out of thin air, leaving Gray in an empty bed with nothing but bittersweet memories and broken dreams.

With no choice but to move on, Gray attempts love, even moving with her college girlfriend to New York City to pursue a career in journalism. But her standard has been set, the bar way too high for any other woman to reach or clear. It's an unexpected encounter in an obvious place when Gray sets eyes on her dancer again. Will the bright lights of Broadway illuminate the way back to the woman of her dreams? Or will they blind her to any other possibility of happiness?

Break a leg, Gray. The Great White Way calls.

Finding Faith - ISBN - 978-1-952270-16-1

Faith Fitzgerald thought that if she got an education and became a high-powered attorney in Manhattan, maybe—just maybe—she'd gain the attention and respect of her absentee father. Considering he was the only parent she had left after her mother's suicide when Faith was just a child, she thought that's what it would take.

She was wrong.

What she dreamed would be glamorous and satisfying turned out to be grueling and thankless. Since she wasn't willing to play the game between the sheets, she was forced to stay in the cubicle jungle doing all the heavy lifting while the men got the credit and the rewards.

Deciding she is done, Faith packs up and, with the flip of the bird to the rearview mirror, leaves New York and heads home to Colorado. She has nothing there: no job, nowhere to live, no relationship with her father. Truth is, she barely has a relationship with herself.

On the drive home, she finds herself in Wynter, a tiny mountain town at the foot of the Rockies. Looking more like it belongs in a made-for-TV Christmas movie than on the map, Faith is utterly enchanted. When she tries her luck and buys a raffle ticket at Pop's, Wynter's charming café, her prize is far more than meets the eye—or the heart.

Enter Wyatt, a feisty, sexy southerner and waitress at Pop's, who just happens to be married to a local sheriff's deputy. All is not as it appears with the All-American boy and his Georgia peach.

A colorful cast of unforgettable and charming characters will teach the jaded attorney that sometimes to find yourself all you have to do is go back to the basics…and have a little Faith.

Taking Liberty - ISBN- 978-1-952270-24-6

A victim of a massive corporate downsize, Liberty Faulkner suddenly finds herself without a job, without a home, and without a plan. Though certainly not part of her vision, Libby decides that the familiar is the safest path back to her life goals. In this case, the devil she knows is home: the tiny mountain town of Wynter, Colorado, a close-knit place where everybody knows everybody and everybody's business. Seems like the perfect place for the twenty-five-year-old to start over and figure out who she is without being noticed…not.

Sergeant Grace Montez escaped her dead-end job and toxic relationship in New Mexico and moved to Wynter to help build their police department from scratch. Now an established figurehead in the community, she's got her professional life dialed in and even mentors new recruits on the force. After a challenging childhood and lifetime of abandonment and disappointment, Grace hasn't been interested in another relationship—especially because no one has caught her eye since a certain quirky college student who used to make her caramel macchiato at the local coffee shop moved away three years ago.

Now that quirky college student has returned as the beautiful, mature woman Libby has become. Can Grace keep her distance, or will she finally take liberties with what is being offered?

Justice Won - ISBN - 978-1-952270-36-9

In 1890, seventeen-year-old Justice Kilkoyne and her mother, Ninny, are one bad decision away from living on the streets of Azrael, Pennsylvania. Ninny's propensity for the bottle has left Justice to play the adult, her androgynous good looks helping her pass as a young man to gain employment and keep them—if just barely—above water.

Determined to find a better life for them, Justice saves every penny to get them on a train headed west to the sunshine of California. Before they can leave, the bigotry of one shopkeeper sends Justice on the run, chased by the police for a crime she didn't commit and straight into the unwitting arms of a stunning young prostitute, who, after an unexpected connection, becomes Justice's Angel.

The day arrives to leave Pennsylvania for good. As Justice and Ninny get settled, they're surprised by the appearance of Angel, also wanting to start anew. When the trip is violently interrupted in Colorado, Angel just may be lost to Justice forever.

Can Justice find a new life when she makes her way to the fledgling mining town of Wynter, Colorado? Can her heart ever be whole again?

Zero Ward - ISBN - 978-1-943353-19-4

Danny Felts grew up in the heart of the Midwest on a dairy farm, expected to follow in her mother's footsteps and marry a farmer and become a mother. Danny had other ideas. As World War II heats up, she makes a decision that will change her life forever as she becomes a lie, serving with the Seabees in the Navy as Daniel Felts.

Kate Adams is about to graduate high school in her prestigious and elite San Diego neighborhood when she's dragged to the USO for a dance with friends and servicemen. There, she meets the person that will catch her eye and her heart, only for jealousy and vengeance to tear her apart.

Are Danny and Kate strong enough to win the battle within and fight for their love?

Connection - ISBN - 978-1-939062-24-6

Julie Wilson lives a charmed life as a beloved teacher and aunt in the small town of Woodland. Close to her brother and guardian of two adorable Yorkies, she loves her life, the only negative being ex-boyfriend, Ray who can't seem to understand the phrase, "We're done." Believing that's her only problem, Julie has no idea what hell awaits her during a normal summer afternoon.

Remmy Foster is the quirky, friendly drifter who has never found roots after a difficult childhood, as well as the difficulties her very special gift brings into her life. Though she may call it exploring, the truth is she's running from ghosts that haunt her every step.

After a chance meeting with Julie while hitchhiking, Remmy will be thrown head first into darkness she could never have foreseen, regardless of her abilities. As the clock ticks, life and death is on her shoulders to make the right connection.

Warning - Some scenes may be too intense for some readers.

1049 Club - ISBN - 978-1-939062-97-0

Almost two hundred souls, one plane, six survivors, endless heartbreak.

When flight 1049, headed from Buffalo, NY to Italy falls from the sky, a firestorm of drama, pain, angst and sorrow ensues. Can an author, a business owner, a teenager, good ol' boy, veterinarian and ruthless lawyer survive? Better yet, can those left behind?

1049 Club is a story of survival, love, deep regret and miracles. Can the living make peace with the presumed dead? Can the presumed dead make peace with the lives and loves they thought they had before?

Blinded – ISBN – 978-1-943353-53-8

After a horrible explosion sends local television news reporter, Burton Blinde reeling both physically and emotionally, she walks away from her life and the dream job she was about to start at a major news network.

For six long years she hides out in a small mountain town, working at the local library, though is haunted by the life she had, including mysterious messages and gifts she was receiving before her life was turned upside down, a veritable bread crumb trail leading to the unknown.

Unable to resist, Burton begins to follow the clues, which will lead her into the darkest places of human nature that she may not be able to return from.

Damaged - ISBN - 978-1-939062-45-1

Family. A group of people you are related to by blood or love.

Nora Schaeffer has come home to her family after twenty years working around the world as a photographer for National Geographic. She's welcomed into the open arms of her father and siblings.

Family. A group of people who support you, lift you up when you fall.

Shannon, the youngest of the four Schaeffer siblings, has vanished, leaving her five-year-old daughter, Bella, terrified and alone. To help find Shannon, Nora has no choice but to turn to the dark-haired specter who has haunted her for twenty years. Along the way, she finds her own long-dead heart and uncovers chilling family secrets beyond imagination.

Family. A group of people who will stick together to hide the rotten soul at its core at any cost.

Who will live? Who will die? Who will be the most damaged? And who will learn to love again?

The Gift - ISBN - 978-1-948232-47-0

The dead do speak. You just have to listen. Homicide Detective Catania "Nia" d'Giovanni is the only daughter in a large Italian family of six children. The backbone—a position not applied for nor wanted—she continues to create new glue to hold the dysfunctional group together. For Nia, family time feels more like herding cats than spending time with her brothers and feisty, aging parents.

Her heart has always been in her career with the Pueblo Police Department, especially since it will never be okay with her very Catholic mother to openly give her heart to any woman, until she meets a secretive waitress who has her at, Can I take your order?

And then it begins…

Three murders that are so gruesome, so horrible, they rock the small town to its core. Nia and her partner Oscar are left to piece together a deadly puzzle to find the key to unlock the monster they hunt.

Or, are they the hunted?

As they dissect the murder scenes where not one shred of evidence is left behind, more bodies begin to show up, each cleaner than the last, the shadowy specter that is the killer vanishing without a trace, making the woman Nia loves disappear right along with it.

When there is no evidence to follow, Nia must trust her instincts…or, is she being guided?

The Plan – ISBN – 978-1-948232-43-2

As the dark days of the Dust Bowl came to an end, the midsection of the United States tried to rebuild and revitalize. In the small, dusty farming town of, Brooke View, Colorado, teenager, Eleanor Landry and her mother were dealing with her father, a self-appointment fire and brimstone preacher to his congregation of two. A plan to survive.

As the dark era of the robber baron comes to an end, giants of industry and innovation emerged with fabulous fortunes manifested in the mansions that dotted the landscape across the country. Lysette Landon, the teen daughter of the wealthiest family in Brooke View, was everything a good, proper girl of privilege should be. Only problem was, she wasn't dreaming of finding a young man to raise a family with. A plan to be free.

One look, one touch, all plans are off.

Secrets deeper and darker than the grave would bring

Eleanor and Lysette together, their families connected by a web of lies and broken promises. A plan to escape.

Be careful because, life has other plans...

The Traveler Book One: The Hunted - ISBN - 978-1-948232-91-3

A story so epic one book can't contain it.BOOK ONE:

1977: In the era between flower power and the yuppie, Sonia Lucas is a young wife and mother, just starting out in life. Without warning, a strange presence and dark force enters her life, clouds building...

1917: ...and a storm brewing as the world reeled from the horrific events of World War I just before it was ravaged by a Spanish flu epidemic that would kill millions. Sephora Lloyd is a 16 year old girl lost in the responsibilities of an adult world helping to support herself and her mother. A beautiful young nun-in-training enters her life, bringing love and hope with her. That is, until a force bigger than either of them threatens everything Sephora holds dear.

Four women - three deaths - two words - one house
THE HUNTED

The Traveler Book Two: The Hunter - ISBN - 978-1-948232-93-7

A story so epic one book can't contain it. BOOK TWO:

1890: In the dying days of the Old West, Sally Little runs

her booming brothel with the passion and tenacity the business of sex requires. Savvy and indulgent, there's one itch Sally can't let herself scratch. Afraid of hurting the woman she loves, she instead unleashes...

Present Day: ...her renovation crew and fixer upper TV show on a dilapidated mansion that has known nothing but death since a murder there in 1977. Samantha Leyton sees ratings gold in bringing the sagging old house to life, but instead she discovers only she has the power to unlock the mystery that hunted four women across time, leaving death and destruction in its wake. Can she release her sisters who came before her and finally be granted the gift of love that is stronger than any evil?

Four women - Three deaths - two words - one house
THE HUNTER

Other books from Sapphire Authors

Talk to Me – ISBN – 978-1-952270-20-8

Claire takes a turn for the wild side when she chances into a job at San Diego's KZSD radio to work with Marly, the sharp-tongued lesbian shock jock of Gayline. Under Marly's close tutelage, Claire feels the sparks fly as she learns to screen calls and handle board operations. It's enough that her formerly quiet life has been upended after separating from her husband, and at first, she keeps her feelings hidden. Even as bomb threats force the radio station employees to clear out, Claire's attraction to Marly's charisma, wit, and atypical beauty keeps her coming back. Meanwhile, she struggles to maintain a relationship with her teen daughter while her soon-to-be ex makes it clear he wants to try again. Its two steps forward, one step back as Marly and Claire grow closer and admit their feelings.

Will Marly's outrageous "anything goes" attitude be too much? As their on-air shenanigans and romance heat up, Marly's crazed plan to boost ratings threatens their relationship, and ultimately, their lives.

Keeping Secrets – ISBN – 978-1-952270-04-8

What would you do if, after finally finding the woman of your dreams, she suddenly leaves to fight in the Civil War?

It's 1863, and Elizabeth Hepscott has resigned herself to a life of monotonous boredom far from the battlefields as the wife of a Missouri rancher. Her fate changes when she travels with her brother to Kentucky to help him join the Union Army. On a whim, she poses as his little brother and is bullied into enlisting, as well. Reluctantly pulled into a new destiny, a lark decision quickly cascades into mortal danger.

While Elizabeth's life has made a drastic U-turn, Charlie Schweicher, heiress to a glass-making fortune, is still searching for the only thing money can't buy.

A chance encounter drastically changes everything for both of them. Will Charlie find the love she's longed for, or will the war take it all away?

Broken, not Shattered – ISBN – 978-1-952270-22-2

Even when it seems hopeless, there can always be a better tomorrow.

Jill Bishop has one goal in life – to survive. Jill is trapped in an abusive marriage, while raising two young girls. Her husband has isolated her from the world and filled her days with fear. The last thing on her mind is love, but she sure could use a friend.

Alex McCoy is enjoying a comfortable life, with great friends and a prosperous business. She has given up on love, after picking the wrong woman one too many times. Little does she know, a simple act of kindness might change her life forever.

When Alex lends a helping hand to Jill at the local grocery store, they are surprised by their immediate connection and an unlikely friendship develops. As their friendship deepens, so too do their fears.

In order to protect herself and the girls, Jill can't let her husband know about her friendship with Alex, and Alex can't discover what goes on behind closed doors. What would Alex do if she finds out the truth? At the same time, Alex must fight her attraction and be the friend she suspects Jill needs. Besides, Alex knows what every lesbian knows – don't fall for a straight woman, especially one that's married…but will her heart listen?

Diva – ISBN – 978-1-952270-10-9

What if…you were offered a part-time job as the personal assistant to someone you have idolized for years? Meg Ellis has just completed the school year as a nurse in the Santa Fe school system. It isn't her first choice of profession, but a medical problem derailed her musical career years ago. The breakup of a bad relationship is still painful. The loving support from her close-knit family and good friends has buoyed her spirits, but longing still lurks below the surface. She can't forget the intoxicating allure of the beautiful diva who haunts her dreams.

Nicole Bernard is a rising star in the world of opera, adored by fans around the globe. When Meg learns that Nicole is headlining a new production at the renowned New Mexico outdoor pavilion—and then is asked to accept a job offer to be her personal assistant—she is beside herself. After a short time learning the routine and reining in her hormones, Meg discovers that Nicole's family will be visiting for the opening. Her responsibility to the charismatic singer immediately becomes more difficult when Nicole's young husband Mario shows up and threatens the comfortable rapport between Meg and the prima donna.

The two women brace for a roller-coaster interlude composed by fate. Will the warm days and cool nights, the breathtaking scenery, and the romance of the music create summer love? A heartbreaking game? Or something very special?

The Dragonfly House: An Erotic Romance - ISBN- 978-1-952270-14-7

On the outskirts of a small, picturesque Midwestern town, sits a large, lovely old Victorian house with many occupants. This residence, known simply as The Dragonfly House, is home to Ma'am, the proprietor, along with several young women in her employ. One such woman, Jame, is very popular among the female clientele. One such client, Sarah, fresh from a divorce and looking for a little adventure, as well as some gentle handling, becomes one of Jame's repeat clients. Once Sarah enters the picture, Jame and Ma'am, as well as the brothel, will be forever changed.